So Far from Heaven

by RICHARD BRADFORD

J. B. LIPPINCOTT COMPANY
Philadelphia and New York

A condensation of this novel
has appeared in *Redbook*.

U.S. Library of Congress Cataloging in Publication Data

Bradford, Richard, birth date
  So far from heaven.

  I. Title.
PZ4.B7987So [PS3552.R22]   813'.5'4   73–7885
ISBN–0–397–00853–8

Poor New Mexico! So far from Heaven;
so close to Texas.

—Manuel Armijo
  Governor of the Department of New Mexico
  1827–29, 1837–44, 1845–46

So Far
from
Heaven

Chapter 1

THE MEN CARRIED deer rifles, .30-caliber carbines mainly, and they approached the Park Service Museum building as if it were a deer, ready to spook.

They had parked their pickup trucks along a dusty road in the adjoining canyon, climbed the sandstone cliffs, crossed the narrow tableland on their bellies—though no one was looking for them, or would have cared had they seen them—and scrambled down into Cumbre Canyon, onto Federal land.

Carlos Tafoya was with them. He was a lawyer from Santa Fe, no outdoorsman, and he was uncomfortable in his Levi's and boots and checked shirt and wool-lined jacket. He puffed from the exertion and altitude, wheezed from too many cigarettes and too many bourbon-and-waters. One of his brothers was the Governor of the state. Of the forty men, he alone carried no weapon. He thought Primo should have been there, too, but Primo was addressing the Junior Chamber of Commerce in Roswell.

Cumbre National Monument was a twelve-mile ribbon of land along both sides of a mountain stream in Cumbre Canyon, one of a hundred streams that drained the Floridita Mountains. Two Park Service Rangers and their families lived there, as well as a permanent population of mule deer. In the summer, a concessionaire sold souvenirs and soft drinks, but she closed her shop at night and went home. Until the snows fell, there were always forty or fifty families of overnight campers strung out along the creek bed, burning frankfurters and getting woodsmoke in their eyes, a privilege for which they paid the National Park Service a dollar a night.

The Cumbre National Monument was not so gaudy an attraction as the Grand Canyon, nor so bear-ridden as Yellowstone. It sheltered a tiny, fortresslike Indian village —abandoned since the twelfth century—and some cliff dwellings carved into the soft sandstone canyon walls, where the Indians had holed up during raids. When the inhabitants moved out, they left behind a few pitiful reminders of their stay: broken pottery, flint hammers, some ears of petrified corn, the mummified skeletons of thin children. These artifacts, said to be of ethnological significance, were protected in a small museum, admittance free.

The Ranger on duty that evening, a tall knobby young man named Fletcher Arbuckle, was adding a column of depressing figures in his little office behind the museum's display cases. His wife, Betty, was pregnant. She was also, he feared, getting solitude-happy, the occupational disease of Rangers' wives. She had begun talking to herself, with considerable vivacity, and she had begun not to talk to Fletcher. Sometimes she talked to the unborn baby.

Fletcher's figures kept coming up $5,300 before taxes. Forty-eight hundred of it was his salary. Betty's income, from a trust fund, was $500. That was the addition. The subtraction was the gloomy part, including as it did the forthcoming baby, another year of graduate school for

Fletcher, some dental repair for Betty, and reweaving a pair of Fletcher's uniform trousers, which he had torn while rescuing a terrified tourist from a seven-hundred-year-old grain-storage cubicle in the cliffside. Unless Fletcher did without fripperies like food, the subtractions amounted to $5,760.

Earlier that evening, a camper had knocked on the museum door to tell Fletcher that a bear had raided his grocery box. Fletcher walked back to the camping area with the man, shined his lantern about the scene of the robbery, explained that bears seldom left porcupine tracks, and returned to his office. The tourist was still nervous when Fletcher left him; he had heard that porcupines shot quills at people.

The missing $460 was beginning to get Fletcher down when he heard another knock on the museum door. He expected it was his tourist, this time with a million porcupine quills in the seat of his trousers. He threw his figuring paper in the basket, walked past the display case labeled "Primitive Agricultural Techniques of the Cumbre People," and opened the door.

The small forest clearing was full of men, Spanish-American men, dressed for hunting. A short, plump man, looking uncomfortable in his rough clothes, blinked in the light as the door opened.

"Are you a Federally empowered officer of the U. S. Forest Service?" the man asked him in a monotonous sing-song, as though he were reading the words from a treaty.

"No, sir," Fletcher said. "I'm Park Service. Can I help you?" He looked at the other men and saw they carried rifles. "Are you lost? Hunting? You can't hunt here, you know. It's all game reserve. You really can't even bring rifles."

"I demand to know," the short man said, "if you are a Federally empowered officer of the U. S. Forest Service." He seemed agitated and was sweating.

"Mister," Fletcher said, "it's Park Service. Do you want to use the phone? What are you? A posse?" He chuckled when he said "posse." He heard a rifle bolt click in the darkness.

"Not Forest Service?" the little man said. "This isn't Federal land?"

"Sure it is. Listen, mister, if you'll tell me what I can do I'll be happy to help you."

The little man put his hand on Fletcher's shoulder. "You're under arrest," he said. "I arrest you in behalf of the Compañía de Tierra y Libertad."

"What?" Fletcher said.

Two of the armed men moved quickly toward the door. One of them put the barrel of his rifle against Fletcher's forehead. The other stepped behind him, grasped his wrists, and tied them with leather thongs. Fletcher was too stunned to offer resistance.

"Will you please tell me what the hell is going on. You just can't walk in here . . ."

The little man seemed to have recovered some of his poise. "This land belongs to the people," he said. "You are here illegally."

The man behind Fletcher pushed him into the clearing. Fletcher's eyes were becoming accustomed to the darkness, and he looked more carefully at the men. None of them was smiling. Fletcher saw headlights as a pickup truck drove through the Monument entrance and stopped. The headlights stayed on. In the light, Fletcher saw his bear-scared tourist, now wearing woolly slippers, maroon

12

slacks, and a pajama shirt. The tourist was carrying a roll of toilet paper and seemed angry.

"Mr. Ranger," the tourist said. "I am telling you there is a bear out there. I could hear him snuffling around the toilet area. My wife is scared to death. She . . ." The tourist was flourishing his roll of toilet paper. "She . . ." He peered about him through thick, rimless glasses, saw the rifles and the headlights and the Ranger's bound arms.

"You'd better go back to your camp, mister," Fletcher said. "We've got a little trouble here."

The tourist stood in the headlights, clutching his roll of paper, his mouth opening and closing in ragged tempo, looking outlandish in his red pants. "Guns," he said, finally. "You have guns. Will one of you please go with me and kill that bear? This Ranger . . ." He looked at Fletcher. "What did you *do?*" he asked. "Why are you tied up?" He turned back to the men. "This Ranger won't do anything about that damned bear, and my wife is terrified. She's terrified. She's not used to the country. She's from Omaha. Omaha, Nebraska. They don't have bears there." He glanced quickly around him, saw nothing but stern faces and rifles. "*Will somebody tell me what's the matter! Harriet! Harriet!*"

Carlos said: "What's your name?"

It came out in a rush. "Everett Van Swearingen Council Bluffs Iowa Insurance. I'm going. I'm going." He began to walk, backward, toward the path to the camping area and the stream. After a dozen steps he turned and ran clumsily in his slippers. The man behind Fletcher pointed his rifle barrel at the sky and fired once, a startling, loud crack. The tourist stopped running and froze into a posture of stony rigidity.

13

From the camping area, Fletcher heard a few muffled cries. "What is it?" "Hey, knock that off."

"Put him in the truck," Carlos said. He pointed to the immobile tourist. "Him too. He's trespassing too." The man behind Fletcher pushed him toward the truck. Three other men went to the tourist, turned him around by hand —he seemed to have lost the use of his voluntary muscles —and half carried him to the truck.

"You are making one hell of a mistake," Fletcher said to the man behind him.

The tourist was crying. "I didn't do anything," he said. "You don't have to shoot the bear if you don't want to."

As the men lifted him into the bed of the pickup truck, Fletcher looked toward the cliffside, toward the cabin he shared with Betty. While he looked, the porch light went on, and Betty opened the front door.

"Fletcher," she called out. "Fletcher. I thought I heard a noise. Fletcher?" She looked down at her belly. "Where do you suppose Daddykins went off to, Babykins?"

Chapter 2

HE HAD STARTED in the early evening, driving west from Houston, pushing himself and his car hard. He believed that if he drove fast and steadily enough through the black, gray-floored tunnel of the highway, he would break through the cloud of ink and mush that surrounded him into a brilliance to match the rising sun.

He remembered reading somewhere that all the systems of the human body, those systems which can be described by anatomists, reach their lowest ebb at five in the morning: the temperature sinks to 97 or so; the metabolism, which may have been chattering and ticking during the day, slows to a dim thyroid thump; the libido takes its mind off thighs and thinks of green fields and tranquil pools; the hands and feet get cold, no matter what the weather. The breakthrough he expected would be more mental, or perhaps spiritual, than physical, and he knew it would come at five, when the deep centers of the brain took over from the sleepy cerebrum and showed it a thing or two.

The night traffic on Texas highways thins out earlier than in other states. Nobody is driving to or from night spots because there are no night spots. Everyone in central

Texas is at home after eight or nine, digesting a chicken-fried steak and a Coke and worrying because the spirit of ecumenism is edging sideways into the Southern Baptist Convention. There is another reason for the empty highways, he thought. At night, it is difficult for the few people afoot to tell whether you are driving a this year's or a last year's Cadillac or, if you're raggedy-assed enough to be making do with a Pontiac or even, God almighty, a Ford, to tell whether or not it's air-conditioned. You'd be wasting all those dollars on owls and jackrabbits and Hereford steers.

He stopped at ten and at midnight. At both places he had a hamburger and a lake of thin, sour coffee. The two roadside restaurants were identical. They even had the same customers and the same waitresses, and the same degree of brilliant, bone-chilling air conditioning. In the first one, the doughy woman, whom he named Waitress A, had sweat stains under her arms and a smear of French's mustard on her apron. In the next restaurant, two hours later and, he hoped, a hundred and fifty miles further west, he gave the doughy woman the name Waitress A-prime. If she had differed even minutely from the first one, he'd have called her Waitress B. She had sweat stains under her arms and a smear of French's mustard on her apron. He wondered why she was sweating. He marveled that she could sweat at all, in the air conditioning, even after fifteen minutes of sit-ups. The fat from his hamburger had congealed on his plate before she set it down. "Is the kitchen air-conditioned too?" he asked her.

She shook a profound, moronic lethargy from somewhere behind her eyes and said yes, it was. It was colder if anything than in here. She passed her hands roughly over her apron and disguised the mustard with Del Monte catsup. "You want a warm-up?" she asked. A bright, lewd picture flashed in his mind: a long, shivering queue of male customers, the freezing conditioned air biting through their Lee Riders and Levi's and thin cotton shirts, crowding the little restaurant. As each approached the counter, Waitress A-prime said, "You want a warm-up?" Each nodded, his lips blue, and followed her through the kitchen, to a back stairway, up to a hot, close bedroom. There, on a standard Hollywood bed, covered with a J. C. Penney $5.95 lime-green chenille spread, she gave the customer his warm-up. On the little table beside the bed there would be a jar of French's mustard, a bottle of Del Monte catsup, and a copy of *Alpaca*, by H. L. Hunt. As she hoisted the white uniform skirt, she said, "You want it with catsup or mustard?"

The picture—it was more of a short newsreel—faded, and he saw that A-prime had refilled his cup. As he drank it he thought he heard Mary Agnes's voice behind him again, demanding and whiny, asking somebody for a Fresca. He almost turned to stare, but checked himself. It sounded like Mary Agnes, but she would never ask for a Fresca in a public place. She would ask for a brandy Alexander on the rocks made with Kahlua, a green chartreuse and ginger beer, or a wall-banger.

The chill didn't leave him for miles. He bored on through the tunnel, paused at a Humble station to drain off some of the coffee, stopped along the road afterward— this time at a place not identical to the first two, a little clapboard joint with its own private and separate personality, roach-ridden, baking, un-air-conditioned, under a bank of green lights which attracted locusts from as far

17

away as Manitoba, the scent of a chemical toilet out back mingling with the Lysol, the shake-on precrumbed breading for the chicken-fries and the . . . what was that? Ah, yes. The coffee. That, at least, was identical all over Texas.

There was a town somewhere in north-central Texas. Was it Dentan? Waco? Abilene? Wichita Falls? Here, skilled artificers made coffee for the whole state. It was like Navy coffee. There was a plant full of 500-gallon, slightly greasy copper caldrons, into which the *Kaffeebraumeister* let trickle alkali water until the great vat was nearly full. He turned on gas jets beneath it and heated the water to a point barely past lukewarm. Then—off with the gas, into the pot with a 150-pound muslin sack of burned acorns. Poke the bag around in the vat with a long stick until the water turned brown. Outside the plant, great trucks, their tanks just recently drained of crude oil, waited for the liquid to fill their reservoirs. When the panting trucks were pumped full of coffee, they roared off toward the points of the compass, to Dallas, Houston, San Antone, Van Horn, Lubbock, delivering their cargo to the waiting urns.

He had several more cups and continued westward. It was nearly three, northwest of San Angelo, when the idea of the breakthrough struck him. To keep himself awake, for there is very little caffeine in burned acorn, he had been singing to himself, his voice loud and relatively tuneless in the car, but with the rush of wind from the open window blurring the worst spots. The songs were of a stirring religious or military nature: "Onward, Christian Soldiers," "Battle Hymn of the Republic," "Die Wacht am Rhein," and, dredged from the murk of his childhood, "Remember Pearl Harbor."

"Anyone would think I was nuts," he said to himself, "if they saw me speeding by at three in the morning, alone, singing to myself." He stopped the singing, but he feared he might lose the feeling of impending break-through in the silence, and so began again. When he had sung "Dixie" through four times, he began to get hoarse and switched to poetry. To his dismay, he found that he knew very little poetry by heart—scraps of Service, a dis-hearteningly small number of Mother Goose rhymes, some stirring speeches from Shakespeare with large, confusing gaps in them, old bits of the martial poetry Churchill had disguised as speeches. Somehow the disconnected frag-ments became unified in his mind and rounded themselves into a perfect whole, brilliant with insight and the solution of ancient problems concerning man and the universe. By reciting the poems and orations, by singing the heart-quickening songs, he had straightened everything out. It was fitting, he believed, to have everything straightened out before breaking through.

He closed the car windows, and the sound of the wind rushing past was muted to a whisper. The whisper had meaning, too. He turned on the dashboard radio and quickly found an all-night station from Dallas or Okla-homa City that broadcast music to an almost-unlistening air. He recognized the music as Bach. (Years later, he would hear it again and remember the night clearly. It was the Fifth Brandenburg Concerto.) The beauty of the music, which he felt deeply, and the mathematics which he knew was present but understood only superficially, added precise arcs to the circle his mind was creating. The hour for the breakthrough was at hand. The many cups of coffee were wearing off; the metabolism was slumping down to its nadir; his cigarettes, which had been tasting more and more like straw, began to seem smooth and potent as hashish. The sky was at that inkiest point just preceding the false dawn. He could nearly see the stars wheeling about Polaris out the right window; circularity and unity were all about him. The words he had sung and spoken, the music, the sound of the wind, the flavor of the tobacco, the identical waitresses he had noted hours ago —all combined with intricate perfection.

Suddenly, intruding upon the perfection, a stringy jackrabbit with unbelievably mulish ears sprang into his vision from the right. He swerved, missed the rabbit, went into one of those rubbery garbage-scow skids which is usually possible only in a product of Detroit, and thought briefly, "This isn't the sort of breakthrough I had in mind." The car trundled sideways with a flatulent squeal, straightened, went down a gentle grassy embankment and up another, plunged effortlessly through three strands of barbed wire, avoiding two cedar posts, and finally, as a sort of physical afterthought, turned slowly on its right side and lay still, the two upper tires spinning, like Michelin X roulette wheels. A Hereford steer which had been quietly asleep near the fence arose in some pique and ambled away in the faint light, seeking a more placid spot for repose before its trip to Omaha.

The driver of the car, having rapped his head smartly against a door handle, lay huddled and unconscious on what was now the floor, while dew condensed on his automobile and evaporated when the sun finally rose. An ambitious turkey buzzard, sensing the possibility of a meal, swooped low over the car, noted the presence of life, and flapped away toward the northeast, where the day before it had seen an ailing and—it hoped—moribund prairie dog.

The man awoke briefly, the exquisite vision of the breakthrough receding. His head ached, but not seriously. He felt himself for broken bones or the pain of ruptured organs, and felt none. He could not smell gasoline. He was terribly, terribly sleepy, he decided finally, and his position, nestled against the downward door, wasn't too uncomfortable. Just before he went back to sleep, he recalled the story of the footpad and the Jew and thought, "So it shouldn't be a total loss, I guess I'll take a nap." He slept deeply, and dreamed he was walking through the Labyrinth, armed with nothing but a book entitled *How to Tame Minotaurs*. As the West Texas sun rose he began to sweat in his sleep.

It was difficult to read and to walk the dark, descending Labyrinth simultaneously; he kept tripping and bumping into the clammy walls. The Minotaur's roars became louder and more threatening, and through the furry bellows he could make out the words "four million six." He turned the last corner in the maze and saw, against a far wall that dripped with moss, the Minotaur, standing flank-deep in manure. He glanced for reassurance at his book. "Fix the Minotaur's eye with a masterful glance," it read. "Show it that you are in control." The half man–half bull waded through the ordure toward him, paying no attention to his masterful glance, its face suffused with brilliant purple, two gleaming steel-colored horns branching from the temples, a long, thick cigar clamped between the yellow teeth. It was the face of C. C. Cotton, Sr. "Four million six," the Minotaur roared. "Four million six, you son of a bitch, and all you can say is you're 'sorry.' 'Sorry.' That's goddamn near a million dollars a letter." The

Minotaur reached him and picked him up by the shoulders, lifting him high off the floor of the cave. His head ached brutally, and he was dizzy. "If you got a broken back," the Minotaur said, "the doctor's gonna be sore as hell at me."

The face of the Minotaur dissolved, and a different one took its place, brown, homely, full of concern, a tall and dirty rancher's hat above it.

"Can you move your feet? Got any feeling below the waist?"

"Yes. Yes. Put me down." He hadn't been handled with such authority since he was a baby. The brown stranger had him under the arms, and he knew his feet were off the ground. He was free of the car.

"I couldn't smell gas," the stranger went on, "but you never can tell. You want to get down? Sure, I'll put you down. Just lie quiet. What's your name?"

"Look, mister, there isn't anything the matter with me. I'm fine. When the car turned over, there wasn't anything I could do, so I just took a little nap. Don't you ever take a little nap?"

"What's your name?"

"David A. Reed."

"Well, David A. Reed, you got a big cut on the right side of your head, you got blood all over your face and your shirt and your coat, and you got one pupil the size of a dime and another the size of a pencil point. Now, I admit to you that I'm not a neurologist, and maybe you always had pupils like that, but just because I'm a mean son of a bitch I'm going to lay you down and sit on you if you give me an argument. If you want to sue me later, my name is Cruz Tafoya, and I bet I got a better lawyer than you."

David Reed sat in the long brown grass beside the overturned car, his head aching, and knew that it would probably never be possible to recapture the exciting spirit of the near-breakthrough that had driven him, just a few hours before, so close to the Answer, or the Pattern, or whatever it was. Then, smelling the dry wind and the soft odor of livestock, feeling the throb in his head, he realized that last night was as close to genuine, lock-him-up crazy as he'd ever been. He had lost the aftertaste of all the wild joy; he was just a man sitting on a drying cowdab with blood on his shirt. He turned to Cruz Tafoya, the ex-Minotaur who had reached through the upper window and plucked David Reed's 180 pounds out of the way of danger as easily as pulling a dandelion.

"Where am I, Mr. Tafoya?"

Cruz looked at him with deep suspicion. "Oh, Jesus!" he said. "I read about it but I never thought I'd see it. You got traumatic amnesia, and the state's going to have to feed you hot soup for the rest of your life."

David shook his head abruptly, causing the pain to sharpen and lodge behind his eyes. "No, I don't mean that. I know it's somewhere in West Texas. I just mean the exact spot. I wasn't paying much attention to where I was last night."

"We're about twenty miles northwest of Lamesa. What the hell happened? I don't smell any liquor on you, and you didn't have a blowout. Your tires are still hard. It looks like you and your car decided to roll over and go to sleep. Hey, you know you're looking kind of blue. You want to lie down for a little while? My boy'll be back with an ambulance pretty soon."

"No, really, I'm perfectly all right."

"Just lie down. And don't worry about you have to

keep me entertained or anything like that. I got something to read."

David lay back gently in the shade of the automobile, and found that it relieved the throbbing.

"You got insurance against damage to personal property?" Cruz asked him. "I hope so, because you took out three strands of Billy Joe Shields's barbed wire and then ran over and crushed some of his grass. He'll probably claim you scared some of his stock, too. He's the tightest bastard in Dawson County, Texas."

David was beginning to feel sick and dizzy as he lay in the shade of the automobile. Cruz took a paperback book from his hip pocket and, sitting down beside David, began to read, his back to the sun, his hat making a shady place for the pages.

"What are you reading?" David asked.

"I told you, you don't have to make conversation with me. You got a concussion, maybe a skull fracture. Lie still and think about dairy farms in Wisconsin or something. Luis'll be here with the truck pretty soon, and the ambulance will come, and you and I can pretend we never saw each other. Of course, if you like, I can talk to Billy Joe Shields and tell him you didn't bust his fence deliberately. He probably won't believe me. He'll think you and I are in some kind of cahoots to raise his maintenance costs. That's just the kind of word old Billy Joe would use, too. 'Cahoots.' He's been watching too much television."

"What did you say you were reading?" David asked.

"I didn't say. It's *The Passionate State of Mind* by Eric Hoffer. He's hell on us Catholics, but I think he mainly means the converts. To tell the truth, the converts give me kind of a pain in the ass myself." Cruz straightened and turned his head. "Here comes your ambulance," he said. "You hear it? The way that boy's got his siren going, you'd think there was an eight-car smashup."

The wail of the siren faded as the ambulance turned off the highway and into the gap David's car had made in the fence. Two muscular young men wearing spotless white jackets climbed out and walked to the overturned automobile.

"Mercedes Five-sixty-GR," one of them said. "Brand-new, too. Even if he didn't screw up the engine that right side's gonna cost like hell."

"These foreign jobs," the other ventured, "they got some kind of a guarantee on 'em. Send a mechanic over from Germany or some place, fix it up, it don't cost you a thing. I don't smell no gas, but I bet there's sure as hell some oil leakin' around in there. Have to open that door with a maul."

The first ambulance attendant was kneeling down, examining the undercarriage. "Look how they got this chassis protected," he said. "Man, they really put this stud together. Six, seven thousand these things cost. Every nut hand-tightened by a Dutchman."

"You'd think for that much money they'd do something about that paint job. Gray don't show me a thing," the other said. "Maybe a coral-and-beige two-tone, like on my Merc."

"I don't know about the color," the first attendant said. "All I know is it just rips my guts to see a sweet old heap like this layin' on its side all crinkled up. Just makes me want to cry. Man, if I had this car for just ten minutes down in Alpine, I could line up enough poon to last me two semesters." He ran his hand lovingly over the left front fender. "Must be twenty, thirty coats on there. Smooth as a baby's ass."

Cruz stood up and walked over to the fender connoisseur. "That man on the ground, with the blood on him. That's the patient. He's got a concussion, a possible skull fracture, and he's in light shock. Maybe if you take him to the hospital he'll survive, and then he'll be able to tell his grandchildren about the time two jocks from Sul Ross University almost let him bleed to death."

"You don't look like no doctor to me," the coral-and-beige two-tone fancier said. "You look like a wetback, Pops. Whyn't you tend to your tortillas, and me and Buzzy will tend to healing the wounded."

Buzzy was now crouching over David, regarding his face with a mixture of sympathy and revulsion. "Maybe he's right, Wayne," he said. "This guy's kinda pale, and he's breathin' funny."

"Well, they told us he was dead," Wayne said. "They said go out twenty miles on State One-thirty-seven and pick up a stiff. It ain't *my* fault he's alive."

"Perhaps if you hit him with a tire iron, you can make the facts fit your information," Cruz told him. "Now, goddamnit, pick him up gently and put him in the ambulance and take him back to Lamesa. What's the hospital paying you clowns for?"

"You better watch who you're talkin' to, greaseball," Wayne said. "There's nothin' I like better than stompin' on chilibellies."

A Highway Patrol car, its red light flashing, pulled onto the shoulder and disgorged a giant specimen in the full field uniform of the West Texas *Wehrmacht*. He strode through the gap in the fence, bent swiftly over

David, and thumbed back one of his eyelids. "This man isn't dead," he said. "Why isn't he in the ambulance?"

"Because this Mex has been giving me a line of crap, that's why," Wayne said. "And he's impersonating a doctor. That's a crime, isn't it?"

"What you do is," the patrolman said, "you and this other birdbrain, you pick up this man real easy and lay him on your stretcher. Then you take some of those little sandbags in your ambulance and you brace his head so it doesn't roll and bounce around when you're going back to Lamesa." He turned to Cruz. "It's Mr. Tafoya, isn't it?"

"That's right, officer."

"Did you notice whether he looks like he's got his back broken?"

"No, he was walking around a little bit until I made him lie down. Says his name's David A. Reed."

The patrolman turned back to the two ambulance attendants, who were standing in an indecisive manner, spitting for distance to build up confidence. "MOVE!" They nearly stumbled getting to the stretcher in the back of the ambulance.

"Drunk?" the officer asked.

"I don't think so. Probably fell asleep. I didn't see it, but he was all by himself." Cruz took off his hat, and wiped his head with a red bandanna. "You didn't see my boy Luis in Lamesa, did you?"

"Yeah, he dropped by the station and told us, and we called the ambulance. He ought to be along pretty soon. That Nash pickup he's driving isn't exactly a Ferrari."

The boys had David on the stretcher and were tiptoeing back to the ambulance with him. "You jiggle that man once," the patrolman said, "and I will personally testify I caught you committing sodomy in the activities room of the First Baptist Church. Anybody says nature abhors a vacuum ought to take a look at you two."

As the attendants lifted the stretcher, David opened his eyes. "Where am I going?" he asked.

The patrolman walked over to him. "To a hospital in Lamesa, Mr. Reed," he said. "Do you want us to notify anybody?"

"No, thank you," David said. "There's no one to notify." He went back to his nap as the ambulance doors closed. The attendants climbed into the front seat and the vehicle backed up. The patrolman put his head into the front window, and it stopped.

"You drive back to town between thirty-five and fifty miles an hour. Flash your light, and don't turn your siren on; your passenger has a big enough headache as it is. And next year, as a special favor to me, why don't you comedians get a summer job doing something beside driving an ambulance? There's enough misery in West Texas already."

Looking very sober and responsible, Wayne backed the ambulance around and headed through the gap and onto the highway. He hit the siren once, remembered, and turned it off. Cruz and the patrolman watched it disappear toward the southeast. "That's what happens when ten generations of first cousins marry each other," the patrolman said. "About two out of every three calls I get, it's Wayne and Buzzy, or somebody that looks just like 'em. Wayne and Buzzy stuck up a drugstore; Wayne and Buzzy ran a Ford into a concrete abutment; Wayne and Buzzy got likkered up and climbed naked up a telephone pole; Wayne and Buzzy threw up in the Busy Bee Café in

Brownfield. Man, do I get sick of Wayne and Buzzy." He slapped his visored cap against his leg. "Well, so long, Mr. Tafoya. You going into Big Spring as usual?"

"As usual, officer," Cruz said.

"I still don't see why you drive so far to do your shopping, but if you want to spend your money in Texas that's great with me. Like the Chamber of Commerce always says, that new out-of-state money gets circulated around and everybody benefits. Hell, maybe some day so much of it'll get to circulating that they'll raise my salary and give me a uniform allowance. You and Luis take it easy in that old clunker. *Hasta la vista.*"

"*Hasta lueguito, cuate,*" Cruz said. The patrolman drove away, confident of seeing at least a dozen Waynes and Buzzies before his shift was up.

Cruz read for a while, his back propped against the underside of David's Mercedes. When he heard the familiar engine noise of the Nash, he stood and brushed off the seat of his faded jeans, wiped his neck and face with the bandanna, and walked through the fence to meet Luis.

Cruz had always been disappointed in his son, though he tried as well as he could never to show it. A stringy, sallow man of thirty, Luis seemed to pass jerkily through life just missing whatever unambitious target he aimed for. When he sheared sheep, he always nicked skin and the wool turned sticky with blood. He set traps for coyotes and wolves and caught his own herd dogs. The fenders of the Nash pickup were dented, creased, and scratched as the result of Luis's inadequate depth perception. He had tried growing a mustache, hoping to produce a bushy RAF whisk broom, and when the thin black hairs finally emerged, he looked like a Bulgarian pimp. He cut himself

29

seriously when he shaved it off. When he was still in high school, he tried showing off to a girl by jumping a barbed-wire fence. Employing the scissors kick, he misjudged the height by a mere two inches and nearly gelded himself. Cruz had to drive him into Albuquerque for surgical repair.

Luis wasn't handsome, but as his father's son he had a certain importance in the region, and Marta Romero, a pretty, apparently good-natured girl, accepted quickly when Luis proposed to her. She was two months pregnant with a disturbingly blond son on her wedding day. When Luis pointed out that the baby, officially two months premature, weighed nearly eight pounds at birth, Marta demonstrated some examples of the violent temper which quickly replaced her premarital cheerfulness. "Well, how come he's blond?" Luis asked her.

"Your grandmother was an Anglo, wasn't she? That's why he's blond, stupid."

Luis thought that over a long time. It didn't seem to add up, but he finally accepted it, although his Anglo grandmother's hair had been coal black.

Cruz got into the cab of the pickup, and Luis, grinding the gears noisily, turned back onto the highway headed toward Big Spring.

"Luis," Cruz said in Spanish, "that man wasn't dead after all. He was just knocked out." Cruz usually spoke Spanish with Luis; for some reason, English was a language his son never got his tongue around properly, although it was spoken half the time in the house when he was growing up. He had gone through high school with the label of "linguistically handicapped" attached to him. It was fortunate that he had the label; his poor English had obscured his basic dullness.

"Well, I didn't know," Luis said. "I don't know why you stopped anyway when you saw the car. We have to get into Big Spring. You slowed us up."

"The man was in trouble," Cruz explained patiently. "You have to help a man in trouble. Of all the sins, the worst is to see a man in trouble and not help him."

"What if he doesn't want help?"

"Then we come to the second worst sin, helping somebody who doesn't want to be helped. That's why I never give money to those goddamn foreign missions."

"I sure wish Father Serex could hear you talking like that," Luis said. "He'd really lay some penance on you."

"Father Serex isn't going to lay anything on me, Luis. When the Archbishop transfers that horse's ass and brings in a new priest, a priest I like, then maybe I'll go to confession again and take my medicine."

"I shouldn't listen to that kind of talk," Luis said. He clenched his weak jaw and gripped the steering wheel more tightly, the knuckles showing white through his light tan skin. "Why don't you sell this old *cabrón* of a pickup and get something decent? It's almost twenty years old."

"I like this old *cabrón* of a pickup," Cruz said. "This old *cabrón* of a pickup has a hundred and twenty thousand miles on it, and each year it gets more dignified. Also it's got steel on it like a battleship. The way you bump into things, we need something tough around the ranch. What do you think would have happened if you'd rammed one of those brand-new tissue-paper pickups into the watering tank last week? We'd be carrying the alfalfa on our backs."

"There are going to be some changes around that ranch when you retire," Luis said. "And the first thing that goes is this old *chingadero* of a Nash." This constituted the only threat that Luis ever made against his father, the only weapon in his arsenal. Youth, he felt, always had the advantage over age, and if Luis had nothing else, he had his youth. Years stretched out before him like a four-lane, freshly marked highway, unencumbered by speed limits and patrol cars. He was going to take it at 90 miles per hour and bump into water tanks whenever he felt like it.

"You mean when I die, Luisito," Cruz said. "You got a hell of a long wait."

Chapter 3

FROM the Albuquerque *Standard:*

SANTA FE—State Police are still investigatnig the aparent kidnapping which took palce at Cumbre the apparent kidnapping which took place at Bumbre National Monument last week.

A National Park Service Ranger, Fletcher Arbuthnot, and an Oklahoma tourist, Everett von Sorenson, were forcibly taken from the Monument campground by Spanish-speaking men in a turck and returned unharmed the follownig mroning.

State Police Chief Steve Lemann told The Standard's Santa Fe reporter, "I have no comment whatever to make at this time. This kidnapping was obviously the wrok of dedicated, probably communistic outside agitators financed from Moscow and stirking at every value held dear by Americans, but I would prefer to withhold commnet until more three cups of sugar in a heavy saucepan and melt over fcats are etaoinshrdluxxxxx
facts are available."

Chapter 4

THEY WERE VERY KIND to David in the hospital at Lamesa. It was true, he reflected as he lay in the private room, his head wedged tightly between two sandbags, that the business office made the initial examination and released him to the doctor only when he had established his solvency, but this happened in all hospitals. When Wayne and Buzzy wheeled him into the emergency ward, he extracted his billfold, having to raise his butt painfully to get at it, and removed from it eighteen hundred-dollar bills which he clutched with a corner showing. A sweet lady in a gray suit came in and asked the ritual question: "Do you have hospitalization?"

"That's what I'm here for."

"What?" She had bright, clear, Iowa-cornflower-blue eyes, which could recognize a deadbeat through several feet of radiation shielding.

"I am here for hospitalization," he said. "I require hospitalization. That is why I'm lying on my back on this stretcher. I'll put it to you as a formal request: Please hospitalize me, before my head falls off."

The nice lady turned to Buzzy, who had put a dime into

a large red machine and was now seeing if he could drink a Coca-Cola in one long swallow. "Is this man in shock? He isn't making any sense."

"Christ, I don't know," Buzzy said.

She put her hand on David's shoulder and rocked him from side to side. "Are you in shock? What's your name?"

"My name is David A. Reed. If I'm not in shock now, I will be if you keep moving me around."

"Do you have hospitalization? Medical insurance?"

"No, but I have something almost as good. Will you please take your hand off my shoulder before I bleed on you."

She jumped back and regarded him again with her clear blue eyes. "There isn't anything as good as hospitalization," she said. "It's my job to ask about it. If you don't have it, we'll have to make other arrangements."

David held up the hand in which he clutched the money. "I have this," he said. "Does your hospital accept it?" He thrust his hand toward her, and she jumped back again with what appeared to be terror. "Oh, I can't accept money," she said. "Not cash. I don't deal in money. It's my job to ask about hospitalization, and if you don't have it . . ."

"I don't," David said.

"And if you don't have it, to say that we have to make other arrangements."

David closed his eyes and listened for a few seconds to the throbbing in his head. "All right," he said. "Here's your other arrangement. You take this money and put it in your stocking, or down the front of your dress." Buzzy giggled near the Coke machine. "Or put it in a shoebox or the office safe. When I've had a hundred dollars' worth of services here, take one of the bills and give it to the cashier and say, 'Credit this to the account of David A. Reed.' How does that sound to you?"

The nice lady began to wring her hands. David had never seen anyone actually wring her hands before; he thought it was a literary expression indicating distraction or grief. "It isn't my job to handle money," she said, while her hands wrung themselves. "What I do is, I ask about the hospitalization, and if people have it, then that's *good*. And if they don't, why then we have to make . . ."

"My head hurts," David said. "May I see a doctor, please?"

A nurse came to the side of David's stretcher and picked up his wrist. "How are we today?" she asked. "I see we received a nasty cut on our head. Hmmm, our pulse is regular, but not strong. What's our name?"

"We call ourselves David A. Reed," David said. "We would like to see a doctor."

She dropped his wrist. "Would we now? My, we are peppery today, aren't we."

"We're sorry we got rude," David apologized. "Listen, Miss, couldn't we . . . couldn't I see a doctor? I may have a concussion or a skull fracture. I have a terrible headache."

"I don't believe we should diagnose ourselves," she said. "Unless, of course, we're a doctor. Are we?"

"No. No, we're not. Can't we just go to bed and wait for the doctor there?"

"Well! Snappy. Very snappy. There's a GU on duty, an OB-GYN, and an ENT. Which would we prefer?" As she spoke, David noticed that she was separating into two equal halves, like an amoeba. He closed one eye, but she remained divided. Her voice had developed a hollow, echoing sound, which went up and down in volume in time with the pulse in his head. David tried to raise his head, but it was stuck firmly between the sandbags. Like an echo in the Grand Canyon, the word "prefer" kept coming back. Prefer, prefer, prefer. Hum hum hum.

"We're going to throw up," David said.

He awoke in a cheerful, pale yellow room, with a handsome Frederic Remington print on the wall. An Indian, a Sioux, probably, was hanging on to his galloping horse with one hand and rescuing a wounded warrior with the other. The Sioux was not asking, "Do you have hospitalization?"

David's left arm was stretched out uncomfortably, taped to a plywood board. A bottle of something or other hung upside down above it and fed liquid through a rubber tube into his arm. With his right hand he gingerly touched his head. It was wrapped in a bandage. He pressed a button attached to an electric cord which lay on his bed, and a nurse, a different one, appeared in the door.

"How do you feel?"

"Would you say that again, please?" David asked.

"All right. How do you feel?"

"Not 'How do *we* feel?'"

She came in and laid her hand on as much of his forehead as the bandage allowed. "I know how I feel," she said. "I feel okay, except my feet hurt and my girdle's too tight. But otherwise, I feel just fine. Now, how do *you* feel?"

"Thank you. I feel much, much better. My head doesn't hurt as much. And there's only one of you. There were two of the other one."

"That's right. That's diplopia. Double vision. It's very common after a blow on the head."

"There were two of her even when I closed one eye."

"Really? That's diplopia monophthalmica. It's not nearly so common. You're to be congratulated. May I take your pulse, please?" She didn't reach for his wrist until he gave permission, a superb example of nice manners, he thought. Her fingers were cool and dry on his wrist.

"Nice work," she said. "A steady seventy. We're not supposed to tell patients their pulse rate, their blood pressure, or their temperature, but I think that's silly. You're not paying just for care, but for information, too. Right?"

"That's right," David said. "Oh, did you see eighteen hundred dollars of mine lying around? It isn't important; just all the money I have in the world."

"Dr. Cave found it in your hand, in what you might call a death grip. We thought we were going to have to use a wrecking bar to get it away from you. It's in your wallet. Your wallet's in your pants, and your pants are hanging up over there in the closet. They have blood on them." She walked to the foot of the bed, and studied the chart. "Type A, Rh-positive. Not a very interesting blood type, I'm afraid, but a lot cheaper than AB, Rh-negative. Type A positive is only seven fifty a pint." She pointed to the bottle. "There goes the third one. It comes to twenty-two fifty, so far. Here, hold this under your tongue. The doctor will be here in a few minutes. You'll like him. He's a very good concussion man." She patted David's knee and left the room.

With the thermometer in his mouth, David relaxed and tried to recapture the sense of fullness and wonder he had experienced the night before. The memory it cast was much like a dream, in which the dreamer has found the solution to every problem in the world, one brief, potent flash of insight. Often the dreamer wakes and writes the answer, the formula for perfection and salvation, on a pad of paper near his bed. The next morning, eagerly, he reaches for the paper and reads—if the writing is legible at all—"Man is to woman born, and woman borne to man," or, "Jill and Jack went up the track to fetch a Double Gloucester."

The whole of the night before was dreamlike to David, from the first cup of bitter coffee after sunset through the wild, savage, solitary drive, the gentle automobile accident, the Minotaur fantasy, the conversation with Cruz and the painful trip in an ambulance, when he overheard snippets of the attendants' conversation in which football and brisk sexual adventure were blended.

But it had been no dream, and he knew it. In an increasing state of befuddlement and misty drunkenness, he had driven a car at dangerously high speeds, howling and singing to himself while waiting for the night's darkness to part like a blackout curtain and admit a stream of pure white light, down which God would come sliding to pat him on the shoulder and say, "Here's the answer, David, old buddy, and welcome to it." It would have been a decent thing for God to do, and he regretted that he hadn't kept his car on the road long enough for the confrontation. With the answer—whatever it was—he would never again find himself walking fearfully into the Labyrinth, where C. C. Cotton, Sr., dressed in his Minotaur suit, waited to shake him, curse him, and bring up as crass a subject as money.

The nurse came back and read the thermometer. "Ninety-eight point six," she said. "The same as mine."

"It's a small world," David told her. She gave him an

exaggerated look of disgust. "Do you think I could be going crazy?" he asked. "I mean, does my behavior seem normal to you? You're so honest about my temperature, I think you'll give me a straight answer."

She shook her head. "I'm just a poor old registered nurse. If they catch me diagnosing people, they'll take away my cap. To me, you're just a nice man with stitches in his head and eighteen hundred dollars in his pants. I do think it's a little crazy to go around with that much cash in your pockets. Those two teenyboppers who handle the ambulance would have rolled you for it if they'd known it was there."

"That isn't what I mean," David said. "Do I sound crazy? Did I babble and rave when they brought me in?"

"You gave Miss Fleming a *very* hard time. She was almost in tears. I wish you'd put a boot up her . . . well, nobody likes her very much. She's the nurse who says 'we' to all the patients."

"But not crazy?"

"No crazier than anybody else in West Texas. You'll be all right in a couple of days. Just lie quiet and eat some nice, nourishing food. Incidentally, do you want some? I don't recommend it, but it'll keep you alive. Dr. Cave put you on the 'regular diet,' and today it's chicken-fried steak and corn muffins made out of Lone-Star Corn Bread Mix. You might be happier with a glucose drip."

Like a little soldier, David Reed ate his chicken-fried steak and slept, and awoke to meet Dr. Cave, who examined the sutures and seemed as proud of his stitchery as a ninth grade home economics student. He asked about the headache and the double vision. "No trouble? You can probably go home day after tomorrow, Mr. Reed. Bet you'll like that, eh?"

David nodded. When the doctor had gone, he stared at the ceiling and wondered, "Home. Home. Now, where do you suppose that might be?" He rang for the nurse, and when she arrived he asked her.

"Don't *you* know where home is? Your driver's license may have it. People do forget things after a skull injury."

"I don't mean that," David said. "I know where it was; it was in Houston. It's just that home isn't there any more. Poor little orphan child. No mamma, no papa, no whiskey soda. Old China service joke. I was never there, personally. Maybe it was an Indian Army joke. Doesn't matter. What I mean is, I don't live in Houston any more, I have eighteen hundred dollars, less whatever this is going to cost, less the repair on my car, which I may sell instead, and I have no place particular to go. Can you suggest something? Where are *you* from, for instance? You're a pleasant young woman, although no beauty. And what's your name?"

She closed one eye and examined him critically with the other. "I'm Miss Kovacks. You keep raving on in that fashion, Mr. Reed, and I may change my diagnosis. We have a very primitive psychiatric ward on the fourth floor that smells like paraldehyde. You wouldn't like it; they make you eat your chicken-fried steak with a rubber spoon." She placed her hand on his forehead again. "I'm from Matador, Texas," she said. "I grit my teeth once a year and go back there to see Mother. It's the garden spot of the world, if you happen to be a horned toad. And, what do you mean, I'm no beauty? You're supposed to fall in love with your nurse around here. Another crack like that and I'll roll you over and use the thermometer with the big bulb."

David spent three days in the Lamesa Hospital. During this time he discovered that the hospital dietitian chicken-fried everything except the oatmeal. The Highway Patrol sergeant visited him once to tell him his car had been towed in and was being repaired. David signed the authorization, but the car, which he'd bought with enormous pleasure six months before, had ceased to amuse him. He thought of it as belonging to someone else, to the man who had lived once in Houston. At night he dreamed of C. C. Cotton, Sr., and always awoke sweating. Cotton was usually dressed in his Minotaur outfit, but during David's last night in the hospital, he appeared in the costume of Ko-Ko, the Mikado's Lord High Executioner, a headsman's ax in his hands, a snickersnee at his belt, his reptilian eyes made up to seem Oriental.

The hospital's charges were not high, and he paid them with two of his hundred-dollar bills, wondering what the Other Arrangements Lady would have to say to that. Miss Kovacks came to say good-bye and helped him to put on his trousers. She had had his clothes cleaned and bought him a new shirt. "I suppose your luggage was in the car," she explained.

"One small bag," David said. "I left in a hurry."

"Is there what the television shows call an A.P.B. out on you? Did you rob a savings and loan association somewhere? There's usually a nice reward for turning in people like that." Once more, she laid her hand on his forehead. With all those fine shiny instruments, David thought, she took temperatures the way his mother did. The bandages were gone, except for a rectangle of gauze and tape over the stitches.

"No, nothing like that," he said. His head felt clear, but his legs were weak. He sat on the side of the bed. It would be just like C. C. Cotton, Sr., to set the police and the Texas Rangers on his trail, David reflected, just to harass him. "Here's a picture of the man, Captain. Been my partner for seven years. You can't imagine my surprise when I entered his home—the door was open—and found him committing bestial acts with one of my black-and-tan coonhounds. Can't tell where that sort of behavior might lead to. It's best you boys hunt him down and turn him over to a lunacy commission." Yes, that would be like C. C. Cotton, Sr.

David put on his clean jacket and said good-bye to the nurse, taking one of her cool hands between his. "Take it easy," she said. "If you start seeing double again, lie down. Dr. Cave says you ought to have the stitches removed in another week."

"Farewell, Nurse Cavell. When the dirty Huns come to take you to the firing squad, tell them you meant only to bring surcease of sorrow to the wounded."

"I count that as real flattering," she said. "Most of my patients, the only nurse they ever heard of was Florence Nightingale. I always thought of her as sort of stuffy, with dirty fingernails."

On his way out of the hospital, David stopped in briefly at the small office near the emergency room to talk to the nice lady in the gray suit. "Hello, there," he said. "I made other arrangements."

She smiled at him sweetly. "I'm glad to hear that," she said. "You come back real soon now."

David went into the warm, sandy Texas sunshine. He walked several blocks, slowly—his legs were still shaky—and realized that he didn't know where he was going. In his jacket pocket, he found a copy of the repair authorization for the car, Lamesa Motors on Sam Houston Street, but he didn't know where that was and walked on. In the center of Lamesa, he noticed, the cars still parked diagonally, a holdover from the horse days.

David entered the Busy Bee Café Steaks Chops. He had spent most of his life in Texas, much of it traveling from small town to small town. Until the Ptomaine Explosion of the sixties, when million-dollar thatched palaces with Polynesian names and glossy monster-burger havens sprang up all over the state, every Texas town had just one place to eat, and it was called the Busy Bee, the Elite, the New York, or the Texas. There were, he admitted, some called the Western, but one found them only in East Texas.

It was lunchtime, and the Busy Bee was full of farmers, whom it was polite to call ranchers. In Texas, anybody with four chickens and a dead Chevrolet in the front yard could say, "I got me a little spread up by Brownfield." It was all part of the Texas Dream. He'd had the Dream himself and had nearly awakened to find it clutched in his hand.

He had some fried chicken and a glass of milk, bought a *Time* magazine, and read it while he ate. It surprised him to learn that things in the world were still gimping along as usual, assuming that *Time* was reporting events correctly. The President had chewed out a man from the Associated Press for asking a question during a news conference. French farmers had struck over the price of shallots. An Italian starlet had appeared on the beach at Cannes wearing a dress which covered her body completely except for breasts and pubis. The Israelis and Jordanians were still exchanging gifts across their border, the Jordanians favoring hand grenades and the Israelis leaning toward bangalore torpedoes. A dermatologist had read a monograph recommending unrestricted sexual activity as a cure for adolescent acne, apparently unaware that, despite current teen-age behavior, acne still prevailed. The Pope had said he thought "population explosion" an unfortunate and misleading term. A musical-comedy version of *Death of a Salesman*, starring Ethel Merman as Willy Loman, was given a mixed review, the critic liking the general idea but feeling that Mary Martin would have been more comfortable in the part. Nowhere in the magazine was there a sentence beginning, "Ill lay: David A. Reed . . ." but he didn't expect to find it. He had been mentioned in *Time* only once, four years before, when he and C. C. Cotton, Sr., had pulled off a beauty in Wyoming.

Someone called his name, and he felt a heavy but gentle hand on his shoulder. Cruz Tafoya, looking even more of a farmer than the other customers, loomed beside David like a friendly moose. "I see you're out of it now," he said. "How was the hospital?"

"Fine, fine," David said. "I'm sorry. I remember your face, but not your name."

"That's okay," Cruz said. "I'm surprised you can remember anything. Cruz Tafoya. The whole thing is Juan de la Cruz Tafoya y Evans, but that sounds too *hidalgo*, and I sure as hell ain't no *hidalgo*. How's your head feel?"

"I hardly know it's there."

"That's the best way. I'm glad those two *pendejos* on the ambulance didn't kill you. You had lunch? Yeah, I see you had lunch. Why don't you come over and sit in a booth with me while I take a little something? What you drinking there? Milk? That's the best stuff. The coffee around here tastes like goat piss. Miss, give my friend here another glass of milk, please. Come on, man. You're not going anywhere right now. Talk to me while I eat."

They sat facing each other in the booth while David sipped his milk and Cruz ate two bowls of chili, complaining about its lack of character. David noticed that Cruz's right index and middle fingers were missing, and the hand was scarred badly. "Jesus," Cruz said, "if my grandmother could see me eating this slop she'd work my ass with a half-inch *látigo*. I've tasted oatmeal that's got more bite to it. This goddamn Texas. I don't know why I come here. Next time I'll go to Kansas or Oklahoma or one of those places. At least they don't pretend."

"You're not from Texas, then?" David was trying hard to make polite conversation, but he couldn't seem to keep his mind on it. This man, Tafoya, was a stranger. He'd pulled David out of a wrecked car, but he was a stranger.

"No. Jesus! Texas! No, I'm not from around here." He pointed to a direction with his chin, thrusting it out quickly with a tightening of lips, the way Mussolini did in old newsreels. "Northwest of here. New Mexico. You know Santa Fe? North of there. You know Taos? South of there. Pozo Verde, it's called. Real nice country. There's about eighty, ninety people around Pozo Verde, every goddamn one is related to me except three. On the map they call it Pozo Verde, but you got to have a big map. Around there we call it Los Tafoyas. Beautiful country, man. Dry as hell. All the calves are born with their tongues hanging out. But sometimes it rains, you know. It's not a real desert. There's grass, and when it does rain, *hijo de la chingada*, you never smelled anything so sweet in your life. Wet grama grass, and wet dust, and wet cow-flops and the wind that comes off the mountains—Jesus, you just want to stick your head down in the dirt and wave your feet around." Cruz took three more enormous bites of Texas chili and shuddered. "Right straight out of a can. Maybe I'll pour some cream on it and pep up the flavor a little bit."

"It sounds very pretty, very nice, that place you live in," David said.

"Nice, pretty, my big brown behind," Cruz said. "God made every other place in the world for practice, and when he'd learned how, he made the country around Pozo Verde. That land was created by a goddamn expert, man. You ought to come see it."

"I'd like to very much," David said. He had finished his glass of milk and saw no reason to sit around talking nonsense with Señor Tafoya y Evans. "Yes, I'll certainly make a trip up there sometime and see Pozo Verde. I've been to Albuquerque a few times, and yes indeed, it's very fine country. Well, Mr. Tafoya, I thank you for the nice glass of milk, and for helping out when I . . . when the car turned over out there. Yes. Thank you so much." He began to stand, and Cruz put a thick hand on his wrist.

"Just a minute, Mr. Reed. Jesus, I never saw a man could shovel so much horse hockey without working up a sweat. Sit down. In the first place, you owe me thirteen dollars and fifty cents. Here, you want to finish up this chili? You been an invalid the last few days. This stuff is for nursing mothers."

David, still standing, but hunched over the table, said, "I'm sorry. Thirteen dollars?"

"And fifty cents. *Trece cincuenta.* That's for the damage to Billy Joe Shields's fence. I talked to old Billy Joe this morning, and got him down from twenty-five hundred. He told me you'd scared one of his bulls so bad he went sterile, and I told him that was a bunch of crap, there weren't any bulls in that field. And then he said gas leaked out of your car and poisoned the grass and ten steers have the dry heaves, so I told him his lousy Texas grass is so poor that a little gasoline would improve it, and finally we decided on thirteen fifty. So I paid him, and now you pay me. Here's the receipt, if you don't believe me. I could have repaired that fence for four dollars, but Billy Joe's got so much money he probably strings it with platinum wire. Hell, man, don't stand up all bent over like that. Sit down."

Cruz handed David a completed receipt form bearing the legend, "Rec'd of Cruz Tafoya, Mexican bandit, $13.50, Wm. J. Shields." Beneath the printed blanks was scrawled, "I hereby release D. A. Reed from any liability for damage he caused my property, but if I catch him on my land again there's going to be trouble. W.J.S."

"There, you see?" Cruz said. "You're all squared up with the local big shot. The cop ain't gonna give you a ticket either, so you can leave town as soon as you pick up your car. Now you only got one problem, Mr. Reed. Where the hell you gonna go?" Cruz looked at him, amiably but with determination, and David saw for the first time that staring out of the dark-skinned face, a miracle of jumbled genes, were two Norwegian-blue eyes. He was nearly as disturbed by the eyes as by Señor Tafoya's genial meddling in his affairs.

"Mr. Tafoya, I really appreciate all the trouble you've taken with me, pulling me out of the car and paying that rancher." He pulled out his billfold and gave Cruz a ten and a five. "Here's your money, by the way. But none of this is really . . . I don't know how to say this without being rude. This is really not your concern any more. I'm fine, now. I don't need a, ah, a guardian angel or anything."

Cruz nodded his head slowly. "Guardian angel. Well, you sure as hell haven't got one, Mr. Reed, and I'm not running for that particular office. Maybe if I tell you three words, maybe then you'll stop looking at me like I was crazy. Will you listen to three words from me without covering yourself up like a naked Girl Scout?"

David found that his ears were roaring. Recovered technically from his mild concussion, yet still feeling fragile and delicate as a Christmas tree ornament, he knew he was simply not prepared for whatever this was, whoever this man was. Once again he felt a helpless, baby-in-Mama's-arms sensation. It was Cruz Tafoya in the Minotaur suit now, and whatever he had in mind, he approached it so obliquely that he might have been speaking Old Cretan. David said, "What three words?"

"Clyde Clifton Cotton," Cruz said, and watched him with his blue eyes.

The roaring in his ears stopped so quickly that the silence was more painful than the noise. David turned convulsively in the booth seat and looked over the back panel, expecting with panicky fear to see C. C. Cotton striding through the café door preceded by a pack of mastiffs, followed by a phalanx of attorneys. C. C. Cotton wasn't there. A rancher stood by the cashier's counter, buying the Fort Worth *Star Telegram* and a roll of antacid tablets. The thought, carried by a wave of paranoia, that the rancher was an agent of C. C. Cotton, flashed into his mind, to be dispelled immediately by another: that paranoia was a dangerous form of lunacy and, surely, if he recognized it as paranoia, it couldn't be the real thing. The paranoid kills in self-defense: "I'll get him before he gets me" is the usual, logical justification. With enormous relief, David found that he had no desire to kill the rancher with the newspaper and the heartburn pills. He watched until the man had left the café, supplied with news and balm, and then turned back to Cruz's azure stare.

"What?"

"C. C. Cotton. Come on, man. You know what I'm talking about. The minute I said your name to Billy Joe Shields he recognized it and told me."

"How . . ."

"Aw, you got to stop thinking there's a plot. There is no plot. Billy Joe's known Cotton for years. In Texas, everybody up in that tax bracket knows everybody else. As soon as you and Cotton split up, it was all over Texas, at a certain level. Hell, even I would have heard about it sooner or later, although it takes news like that a long while to trickle down to us peons. Jesus, man, you're pale. You want an aspirin or a candy bar or something?"

David shook his head. "Who the hell *are* you? Did Cotton send you after me for something?"

Cruz grinned at him, a vast, creased slash transforming his face into that of a Latin Santa Claus. It was as though someone had lit a candle inside a pumpkin. "I always thought it was us greasers who were suspicious. You are a very nervous man. Maybe that wreck did tear your brains loose from inside your skull, and now you're hearing voices and seeing witches."

"Who are you?"

"I already told you who I am. And why would Cotton send somebody after you? To do what? If I got the story straight from Billy Joe, you're the last man Cotton wants to see. He wants you the way I want scorpions in my bed. Oh, sure, Cotton got hurt some, but you got hurt worse."

"Do you know Cotton?" There was still a terror in David, but it was fading; Cruz did look, after all, benign.

"I met him once, about eleven years ago. There was a public land auction in Albuquerque, a big piece of land, some for sale, some for state lease. Right next to my land. I didn't want it. I got more land than I need anyway. But I wanted to see what kind of man was going to get it, so I went down. Old C. C. Cotton was there, with a couple of lawyers and one of his sons. He bid on it for a while, but then he lost interest. Billy Joe was there, too, and he introduced us. I don't think Cotton much liked shaking hands with me, but he wasn't in Texas, then. No, I don't really know Cotton, but I keep reading about him. And I'm not a private detective, and nobody *sends* me anywhere. I send people places sometimes, but nobody sends me."

"But you have been looking for me, haven't you?" David asked. "Why? What am I to you?"

Cruz shook his large head slowly. "No. You seem to think you're the center of something. You think everybody's coming at you or looking for you. No. I been in Big Spring and Midland for two days with my boy, buying some things and talking to some people. Just farmer business. When we got back here this morning, I said what the hell. You looked so screwed up the last time I saw you, with the blood all over your clothes and your eyes crossed and that pretty car of yours lying on its side like a dead horse, I said to myself, 'Maybe that poor gringo needs some help. A friend. Somebody.' So about once every ten years I act like a busybody and go poke my nose in somebody else's well. I looked around a little bit, went to the hospital, went to the garage, finally came in here. If I'd missed you, okay. None of my business."

"But you went to see that rancher, Shields. You didn't have to do that either."

"Ah, now that's something else again. I told you already, that man is a well-known mean son of a bitch. He's got a lot of land and a lot of money, and he pays most of the taxes around here, so you might say everybody works for him. If I hadn't gone over and busted him up a little bit, you'd be in the *juzgado* right now, and pretty soon you wouldn't have no car and no money, and the judge would have put 'Fence Breaker and Trespasser' on your behind with a hot branding iron, just because Billy Joe told him to. When I first started talking to him, I was just doing what I'd do for anybody. But when I gave him your name, and he told me who you were, then I really started dealing. You got enough trouble, man. You got bad trouble."

"No, really . . ." David began.

"Don't give me no *cago*, Mr. Reed. It isn't like the F.B.I. and the Texas Rangers wanted you for peeing on Sam Houston's tombstone. It's the other way. Nobody wants you for anything. It's like you got leprosy. Maybe you go to Kansas or Chihuahua or Helsinki or someplace, you'll look all right. But here in Texas your nose falls off, and women faint and men turn their backs and the kids throw horse apples at you. You are *malas noticias.* You speak Spanish?"

"Some."

"You sore at me for talking to you like this?"

David thought about that and decided that no, he wasn't angry. He was past anger and past embarrassment, past humiliation. For so many years—were they happy? He wasn't sure—he had seemed so potent to himself. Being in control, in command of things and people, had seemed so easy and pleasurable that he had often wondered why everyone wasn't in the same kind of position. And during the last few days the old field-marshal sensation had gone so completely that he couldn't remember the feeling of power, the rich smell of victory, the joy of watching a routed opposition flee across the plain, dropping weapons and articles of uniform as they ran while he, David A. Reed, the field commander, and C. C. Cotton, Sr., the gray strategist, sent the troops in to mop up, loot, scavenge, ravish the broads, and get happily stoned on enemy brandy.

He thought again of the article in *Time,* and of the photograph in the "Business" section. Cotton, in his wrinkled linen suit, looking benevolent and relaxed; himself younger and much leaner, the lines of tension on his face, standing a little behind and to the left of the old man, as a good executive officer should. He could recall every detail of the operation, and none of the emotion. How had he felt that day in Cheyenne? Wonderful? Great? Splendid? Tip-top? First-rate? Immortal? It was gone now. Somehow, the feeling of victory had lasted through the defeat, and when the enemy had relieved him of his sword he had still felt like a conqueror. But when the reaction, delayed, had finally come, when he awakened foggily in his overturned gray Mercedes, he knew his legs would never again cooperate in a victory prance. Now, today, he wasn't sure he could make a fist.

"No, Mr. Tafoya, I'm not sore. I'm sure your motives, whatever they are, come from a deep sense of kindness, or morality. And I thank you for your help. If I have leprosy, it's good to know that you're either immune to it or don't care if you catch it from me."

"Don't be so quick with your thanks," Cruz told him. "I used to think Father Damien was the biggest cretin the Church had produced, after Simeon Stylites. I still think so. No, it's just that I'm not in the same business as them, so to me you don't have leprosy. Me, I just run some cows and a few sheep and try to keep my relatives from screwing me. Let's go get your car." Cruz stood up and walked to the counter to pay his bill. David sat numbly in the booth for a few seconds, shrugged his shoulders, and joined Cruz. They walked together through the dusty heat to Lamesa Motors.

The Mercedes sat aristocratically among the Ford trucks and long dusty sedans. After repairing it, the garage mechanics had washed and polished it, giving it its due as a member of the royal family that included Rolls Royces and certain low-slung Italian vehicles. They had hammered out the scrapes and crumples and repainted it; now the two senior mechanics stood beside it, grinning, waiting for approval. As soon as he saw it, David knew he never wanted to sit in it again. He had outgrown it, as he had outgrown strained carrots and pajamas with feet.

"How much do I owe you?" David asked one of the mechanics.

"Let's see. Got your bill right here. Body work, mainly; hammering, repainting, replaced a headlight. We had to realign your wheels. Two hundred and twenty-five sixty-eight."

"You pay it," David said to him. "You pay the repair bill and it's yours. The papers are in the glove compartment."

The mechanic's face wrinkled, as if he were about to cry. "Mister, you're kidding. You don't want to sell that car. That's a beautiful car. It's only got about eighty-five hundred miles on it. Do you know how much a car like that is worth?" He was showing genuine distress.

"I know how much I paid for it. Do you want it?"

The mechanic turned to Cruz. "Is he crazy?" he asked, his voice rising to a forlorn screech. "That car ain't depreciated hardly any. Maybe down to five, six thousand. Jesus."

"What are you doing?" Cruz said to David. "Having a little bridge-burning?"

"Now, don't you start," David said. "It's my car. I can sell it if I want to."

"What's the matter? It's got Cotton's fingerprints on it? You gonna make a big dramatic renunciation? You gonna be a monk and eat wild berries?"

"No, I'm just going to start afresh," David said. He knew it sounded pompous the minute he said it, and it was a comfort to him that he recognized the fact. If you know you sound pompous, he thought, then maybe you're not as pompous as you sound. "The car reminds me of things I don't want to remember."

Cruz slapped him on the shoulder. "Sometime I'm gonna give you my talk about witchcraft and animism, and how it isn't possible to put a curse on something unless you can find some fool to *believe* there's a curse on it. But right now you look too shaky for it. At least sell it for enough so you can walk out with money. How about three hundred? That way, you'll have seventy-five dollars to start a new financial empire with."

"All right," David said. "Can you give me three hundred for it?" he asked the mechanic.

"Christ Jesus yes," he said. "Let me go to the front office and get a blank check. Holy God son of a bitch, you just stay right there and don't disappear." He danced out in his blue coveralls.

When he had signed the car over to the mechanic, David left with Cruz and walked with him toward the center of Lamesa. He felt better, not as wobbly as before, and the bright sun seemed to clear some of the remaining mists from his mind. It was good to be rid of that big, heavy, gray, beautiful, childish automobile, which he had driven—worn—like a Junior U.S. Marshal Badge and Decoder Ring.

"Did I do the right thing, do you think, Mr. Tafoya?"

"You gonna come stay with us, you better call me Cruz. Out there, nobody calls me Mr. Tafoya except the priest. I don't know if you did the right thing. You're the man that's trying to get rid of his witches, not me."

They walked another block to the bank and stood in line at the teller's window.

"What did you mean about my coming to stay with you?" David asked him. "I can't do that."

"Why not? You got gringo prejudices?"

"I don't even know you."

"So what? I don't know you either. You have any big plans? You gonna settle down here in Lamesa, Texas, and be a chicken farmer?"

"Are you inviting me? Is that it?"

"There's no profit I can see in kidnapping you," Cruz said. "I'm inviting you. Call it a trade. I'll give you some good meals and a bed, and you can tell me the secret of making big money. No charity. Okay?"

"That's kind of you, Mr. Tafoya."

"Cruz."

"Cruz. I accept. Just for a few days."

"Anything you say, *cuate*."

David cashed the mechanic's check, putting the seventy-four-plus dollars in his wallet, next to the rest of his earthly riches. "Maybe the car made him happy, the man I sold it to. It made me pretty happy when I first bought it. I can remember walking into that showroom in Houston and pulling out fourteen five-hundred-dollar bills, and some hundreds, and slapping them down, wheeler-dealer style."

"Impressive."

"No, it wasn't. Not really. Not in Houston. If you're really a wheeler-dealer, you never walk into a showroom. Your secretary orders a new Bentley or two for you over the telephone. Or, better yet, you send the dealer a cable from someplace like Viña del Mar or Klosters. The salesman could tell I was a pipsqueak right off the bat, carrying all that cash around. That's just not the way it's done."

"I wouldn't know," Cruz said.

They were in the center of Lamesa now. A single electric traffic signal hung over the center of a four-way

57

intersection, the lights on all sides showing amber. A few automobiles rolled by on the hot streets, their windows rolled up to keep in the conditioned air, but most people were indoors where they belonged. Neither Englishmen nor mad dogs were out in the noonday sun of Lamesa, Texas. Cruz halted at the battered Nash pickup, parked diagonally near the Alamo Theater.

"Get in," he said to David. "I'll go pick up Luis and we'll start back." He vanished into the movie house.

In the truck, hot and dry as a kiln, David sat in the middle of the cracked leather seat, his feet resting on the central hump over the drive shaft. The glove compartment gaped open, revealing road maps, a pistol, a flashlight, a copy of *The Passionate State of Mind,* and several Wonder Woman and Daffy Duck comic books. He decided it was never too late to improve one's mind and leafed through Wonder Woman. By moving her arms about rapidly she appeared able to deflect bullets, which ricocheted off her metal bracelets. Four sinister men in fedoras fired at her, hitting nothing but her wristlets. Then she waded into them, cold-cocked three and tossed the fourth out a window. "That's what happens to all crooks who try to destroy America!" she said. David leafed backward through the magazine. They had robbed a bank, the essence of un-Americanism, and Wonder Woman had punished them.

David rubbed his eyes. He felt sure that he would dream, that night, of C. C. Cotton in a Wonder Woman suit.

Cruz and his son Luis walked out of the movie theater, Luis blinking his eyes like a startled gopher. Cruz settled himself heavily behind the wheel, while Luis sat at David's right.

58

"Hey, you been reading my books," Luis said sharply. "I didn't say you could read my books."

"My son, Luis," Cruz said. "Luis, this is Mr. Reed." David offered his hand, but Luis reached across him and picked up the comic books.

"This one's tore," he said. "You tore my Daffy Duck."

"My son, Luis, is the last of the old-time grandees," Cruz explained.

Stung by what he dimly recognized as sarcasm, Luis burst into a babble of language. It was clearly not English, but only the repetition of the word *"chingado"* made it possible for David to recognize it as Spanish. Slurred consonants, gargled syllables, and abrasive vowels filled the pickup. David's ears began to ring with din and incomprehension.

Luis was panting when he stopped his tirade. David said, "I'm sorry about the book, Luis."

"He's not sore about the book," Cruz told him. "He's sore 'cause I took him out of the movie. Tarzan was in the river wrestling with this crocodile, and Luis wanted to see how it came out. I told him the crocodile never wins, but he wanted to see for himself."

Luis slumped against the door and opened a Wonder Woman. Cruz backed the pickup carefully out of the diagonal slot, pushed the window vent all the way out to catch any breeze, and pointed the truck northwest.

They drove twenty miles without speaking. Then Cruz pointed, with his chin, to a section of barbed-wire fence along the highway. "That's where your car went through and rolled," he said. "They fixed the fence already. You know, I still don't understand what made you go off the road right here. You fall asleep?"

"I think I swerved to miss a jackrabbit," David said.

"You're lucky you didn't kill it. Old Billy Joe would have sworn it was his and added another five hundred to the bill."

Luis gargled another spate of Spanish, with a sound like tearing canvas. As before, only the word "*chingado*" came through to David.

"Come on, boy. Talk English," Cruz told him. "This man doesn't know what you're saying. That's bad manners."

"It don't matter," Luis said. "Never mind."

"Come on."

"I said maybe the crocodile might of killed Tarzan. Anyway, I pay my ninety-five cents, so I got the right to see the whole movie. And old Jane was swimming in the river, too, and her clothes was sticking to her real tight."

Cruz shook his head. "You know that crocodile wasn't going to kill Tarzan, because if Tarzan gets killed, how the hell are they gonna make any more Tarzan movies? And if all you can think about is Jane's tits, I'll stop in Hobbs and buy you a copy of *Playboy*."

Luis slumped further in his seat and stuck out his lower lip. "I still like to know how the picture ended up. The natives had the White Goddess all tied up to a pole and they were gonna burn her ass. And the monkey tried to untie her but he couldn't work the knot, so he was running back to Tarzan and tell him, and this lion got to chase after him."

"I saw that one," Cruz said. "What happens is, the lion catches the monkey and eats him, and the natives burn up the White Goddess. Tarzan kills the crocodile and then runs away with a lady elephant."

Luis thought it over. "What happens to Jane?"

"She goes off with a band of baboons and teaches

them how to use a sewing machine. At the end of the movie, all the baboons are dressed up in the clothes they made, and they line up with Jane and sing a song about free enterprise."

"Well, shit," Luis said. "If you already seen it, how come you didn't tell me about it? I could of save my ninety-five cents."

Chapter 5

THERE ARE SIGNS at the border, of course. The first one says, "Y'all come back to Texas, heah?" and the second one says, "Bienvenidos a Nuevo Mexico." But a blind man can tell when he crosses the border because the quality of the highway surface goes immediately and dramatically to hell.

Eastern New Mexico, the area that shares a long, uninviting frontier with the Texas Panhandle, is flat and dry, covered patchily with a species of bitter grass that for thousands of years supported herds of gaunt, hungry buffaloes who died young of vitamin deficiency. Jackrabbits run two to the acre in a good year, a local saying goes, and good years run two to the century. Apaches and Comanches once roamed this waste, fed on the skinny buffaloes, and developed a reputation for corrosive meanness unparalleled in the history of human character.

In the year 1540, a swaggering Spaniard named Capitán-General Francisco Vásquez de Coronado marched northward from Mexico along the Río Grande, turned eastward, and came to a dispirited halt in this ruined desert. He was on a royally sanctioned raid for gold, land, converts, and women, and was authorized to steal anything that wasn't too hot or too heavy to lift, but eastern New Mexico defeated him.

Coronado's dusty troops leaned on their pikes, sweating in their leather armor, and gazed at the buffalo skeletons, the heat waves shimmering over the brown grass, the little knot of Comanches just out of musket range screaming obscenities at them. The friars were too tired to burn the distant heretics even if the soldiers had been able to run them down with their gasping horses.

The Capitán-General wiped his sweating face and said he didn't think His Gracious Majesty Carlos the First would give three hairs of his royal goatee for the whole miserable prairie, issued orders for a fast Te Deum, and raced his troops back to the Río Grande, where they could soak their feet and play with the jolly Pueblo Indian girls.

Today, along the pocked and ragged Federal highway that crosses the eastern plain of New Mexico, a state agency with a sense of history has erected signs that read: "Coronado's Route."

But Coronado and his men were the first and last Spaniards to see this awful landscape. If the Spanish explorers and colonists knew anything, they knew a good piece of country when they saw one. They settled along the Río Grande and the high mountain valleys, in the rolling pastures and the spruce forests. They made what was, for their rapacious times, a fairly easy truce with the farming Pueblos, staved off hostile Indians with some success, and left eastern New Mexico to the Texans.

Now, at sundown, Cruz Tafoya drove westward toward the mountains through that part of his native state which New Mexicans now call Little Texas. He was always more ill at ease in Little Texas than he was in the genuine, official Texas, despite its reputation as Mex-hating. The Texans, at least, had got all the Latin remnants out of power, ground down, beat up, and scared, and consequently treated them with a sort of easy, superior affection, the way a man treats an old sheepdog.

The Little Texans, however, were something else. On the surface they seemed like any other Texans: fundamentalist, insecure, twangy-talking, towheaded, church-going, dry-voting show-offs with watery blue eyes and an almost worshipful admiration for light-colored rayon socks, the Reverend Billy James Hargis, and money. But the terrible land they lived in, and the burning knowledge that much of the good land to the west still belonged to people with Spanish names, made them mean as the Comanches they'd driven away a hundred years before.

As the dust-filtered red sunset faded, David Reed could make out ahead the first black peaks of the Southern Rockies. The prairie flatness lifted gently, angling upward toward the foothills. Luis, who had been noisily asleep since the truck crossed into New Mexico, sniffed some hint of water and vegetation with his coyote's nose and started awake. The headlights picked up a streaked signpost announcing the next town. The last one, David remembered, had been Wicksburg. This one was Los Vados. The state line was a hundred miles behind them, but the truck had just crossed the real border.

Cruz pulled up the old truck next to a gas pump, ordered a tankful in Spanish, herded David and Luis into a nearby café and demanded *chiles verdes rellenos de queso* for everyone, with beer.

"I don't want none of that," Luis said. "I want a hamburger and a Dr. Pepper."

Cruz shook his head in heavy despair. "Jesus," he

said. "I don't know how you can eat that stuff all the time." He turned to David. "You like chili? I don't mean that Texas slop. I mean the vegetable, the pepper."

"Very much," David said.

"You got *some* brains, then. It's all full of vitamin C. If you eat nothing but the mountain diet, you'll live to be a hundred and ten, have forty fat children, and be able to run down an elk. But you got to eat it all: the chili, the beans, the squash, the tortillas, the cheese."

"No steaks?"

"You goddamn Texans and your steaks." The waitress set the beers and the Dr. Pepper before them. Cruz raised his glass. "To C. C. Cotton," he said, grinning. "May he get arthritis and the shakes at the same time."

David ate the stuffed chilies slowly and with pleasure. In the past seven years he'd spent many months in New Mexico and southern Colorado and Arizona, on Cotton's business, learning a fast, rough Spanish and developing a taste for the spicy food and the sweet, cool land of the mountains. He couldn't blame Cotton for buying all of it he could get his hands on.

"You said you met Cotton at a land auction," David said. "That piece of land next to yours. Who bought it?"

Cruz took another swallow of beer and wiped his lips. "A man from Hollywood," he said. "Rosen-something. He didn't come to the auction; just left it up to his agents. I think maybe he had a tax problem, and his lawyer or his accountant told him to buy some land, put some cows on it, and try to lose at least a hundred thousand a year. There's lots of stupid reasons for buying land, but if you can find one stupider . . ."

"It's good business," David said, "if your bracket's high enough. You see, a heavy loss gives you a . . ."

Cruz held up his hand like a traffic cop. "I know how it works," he said. "I got lawyers, too. But I like to make a profit on my ranch and pay my taxes on that. My ranch doesn't lose money too often. When it does, it's because I did something dumb, or because something happened I couldn't help. I don't lose money on purpose. Now don't you shake your head at me. I ain't C. C. Cotton or old Rosen-something. You know, I don't think he's ever even seen that piece of land. He's got a hotshot professional ranch manager working it for him, and all he gets is a profit-and-loss statement every six months. He's never even smelled the steer manure on it. Never drunk out of his own wells. Never hunted deer on his own land."

David nodded. "There are a lot of people like that," he said. "They think land's a thing, like a stock certificate. I used to think so, too."

"Tell me about it sometime," Cruz said. "Maybe I could learn to wheel and deal like Cotton. I've been sitting on my little patch for too long, probably. I ought to branch out." He smiled. "Do you think I could buy eastern Montana?"

"If C. C. Cotton's willing to sell it," David said.

Cruz clapped Luis on the back. "Let's roll, *hijo.* We still got eighty miles."

David was asleep, his head lolling against the pickup's blasted upholstery, when they arrived. In his dream C. C. Cotton, wearing a black robe and the white wig of a British judge, loomed over him from the bench and bellowed, "That's right, you beastly knave. Cower in the dock as you should. You're a wretched fellow, the wretched product of a wretched line. You make a black, filthy mark on the pleasant landscape. You are a stench in the civic nostril." David noted, without wonder, that

Cotton had lost his Texas diction and was speaking in the crisp accent of C. Aubrey Smith. "It is the duty of this court and, I might add, an extraordinarily happy duty, to put you into the bleakest and most odious cell in Her Majesty's system of prisons, from which there is no flight, for the remainder of your miserable life. Bailiff, remove this noisome hulk."

Strong hands gripped David's arms. Cotton stood, removed his wig with a flourish, and replaced it with his white Stetson.

"And if you ever screw up one a mah deals agin," he continued, his usual accent regained, "Ah'm gonna kick yoah ass up between yoah shoulduh blades and . . ."

"We're here," Cruz said, shaking David's arm. "You sure are a noisy sleeper."

David climbed wearily and stiffly from the truck. The black night air was cold, almost frosty. Every star capable of being seen by the human eye was visible; together they were bright enough to cast shadows.

"Where are we?" David asked, steadying himself against the side of the truck as Cruz fumbled in the glove box for the flashlight. He could see no lights, no house, no trees, nothing but black.

"Here," Cruz said. "We're here. Home. My place." He stepped out of the truck and snapped on the light.

All David could see, at first, was a well, a circle of stones three feet high, surmounted by a wooden framework, a crank, and a bucket. Cruz turned the flashlight away, and David saw a patch of tan wall, part of a carved old door and a stained Dutch oven, sitting on rough flagstones. He followed Cruz and his beam of light toward the door.

"Your son," David said. "Where is he?"

"His house. Dropped him off. Three miles back."
Cruz stopped at the heavy door, jangled a ring of keys,
dropped the flashlight, swore. A light turned on over the
door, a small yellow bulb of anti-insect wattage encased
in an antique bull's-eye lantern. A woman opened the
door and said, "Papa."

"Lupe," Cruz said, "this is . . ."

"You were pretty noisy," she went on. "You woke me
up. You woke everybody up. Why don't you put a muffler
on that truck? It sounds like a half-track."

"Now listen, *hija*. Let me introduce my . . ."

"Just a second," Lupe said. She vanished behind the
door and re-emerged carrying a funnel-shaped object.

"Please, Lupe," Cruz said. "For God's sake, don't do
that."

Lupe raised the funnel to her lips and spoke. Her
voice, magnified by a battery-powered bullhorn, boomed
and blasted into the black night.

"ALL RIGHT, YOU COWS. BACK TO SLEEP."

"Now that's *enough*, Lupe."

She lowered her bullhorn and smiled at David. He
could see that she was no more than twenty-five, lean
and long-boned, wearing a pair of men's pajamas.

"Lupe, this is Mr. Reed. David, my daughter, Guada-
lupe María."

"How do you do, Miss Tafoya," David said. "I'm
sorry we woke up the stock."

Lupe regarded him carefully. "East Texas, hey?" she
said. "It is a great honor to welcome such a fine gentleman into our home. We are very simple people here." She
began a rawboned curtsy.

"Oh, for Christ's sake, Lupe. Stop all that crap."

Cruz turned toward David. "Go on in," he said. "Lupe, get off your knees and make us some coffee."

Lupe completed her curtsy and walked away. Before she disappeared through a door she turned and bowed. "*A tus ordenes*, Papa."

Cruz tore off his hat and threw it from him into the gloom of a long, high-ceilinged room. "Goddamn that girl! She *knows* how that kind of bull scrapes me."

Cruz snapped on a light and beckoned David into the room, a great *sala* that looked like no ranch house David had ever seen, excepting the wagon-wheel chandelier and the portrait, over a massively ornate fireplace, of a breeding bull. The carpets, dark reds, blues, and golds, had kept whole Persian villages occupied for decades. The furniture covered nine centuries and twelve countries. In one corner, tastefully covered by a Navajo saddle blanket and a saddle, was a Bechstein grand piano. "It's out of tune and has some busted strings," Cruz said. "My mother used to play it."

Exhausted and bewildered as he was, David managed one circuit of the vast room, running a finger over the surfaces of a Sheraton desk, a Louis XIV chair, a sixteenth-century Flemish money changer's table, a sturdy Sears, Roebuck sofa of no particular period, and a nearly life-sized bronze Buddha on whose head reposed a ten-gallon hat with an arrow through the crown.

"Sit down," Cruz said, and sat down himself on the sofa. David sank into an old leather armchair and rubbed his eyes.

"If that girl wasn't so old and so mean," Cruz said, "I'd put her in a convent and let the good sisters kick a little sense into her. She's spent the last three or four years finding out what chaps my ass and then deliberately chapping it."

"I don't know what you mean, Mr. Tafoya."

"Cruz."

"Cruz. She certainly seems pleasant to me. I mean, it isn't often these days that girls curtsy."

Cruz groaned and lay back on the sofa. "Curtsy," he said. He raised his voice an octave and mimicked his daughter. "*A tus ordenes,* Papa." Then he began to laugh, and shook and bellowed on the sofa until his eyes filled and tears ran down his face. "David, that goddamn girl has a certified, double-checked I.Q. of a hundred and fifty-five. She made Phi Beta Kappa at Bryn Mawr in her junior year. She has an M.A. from Berkeley in Victorian Literature, whatever the hell that might be, and she spent four days in a Berkeley jail for calling a policeman a 'prickamouse.'"

As David sorted out this information, Lupe returned with a tray of coffee, fresh cream, sugar, and English muffins. The coffee service was seventeenth-century German silver.

"I hope the coffee is to your taste, señor," she said to David.

"You can cut out the hockey right now," Cruz told her. "Mr. Reed isn't going to buy it."

"Thank you for the coffee," David said. "What's a prickamouse?"

Lupe glanced at her father. "You have to tell everybody, don't you?" She turned to David. "It means something like 'pipsqueak,' I think, but that stupid cop didn't listen past the first syllable."

"Go to bed, Lupe," Cruz ordered. "And buy some nightgowns, will you?"

She ignored him. "Are you staying long, Mr. Reed?"

"As long as he wants to," Cruz said.

"Okay, okay. Just asking." She turned to go, and paused. "Papa, the guru was over today and says there's plague in Utopia."

Cruz looked puzzled. "What do you mean?"

"Clap in the commune," Lupe said.

Cruz sighed. "All right. I'll go over tomorrow. You don't have to talk in code."

"And don't forget," she went on, giving a fair imitation of Little Caesar, "Mr. Big's coming for a meet tomorrow night."

"Very funny. Go to bed."

"Good night. Good night, Mr. Reed. You stay cool." She strode out on her long bare feet.

"Cruz," said David, "maybe I'd better not stay here. It was very kind of you to ask me, but I think I'd better go tomorrow."

"Where are you going? What you going *in?* Huh? No, you stick around for a while. Don't let that girl bother you. I'll straighten her out. Underneath all this funny stuff she's got some manners somewhere. She's just all excited about something. It'll pass."

David sipped his coffee and watched Cruz. The older man's face was brown, but it was mostly sun-brown, a deep ranching tan. His hair was thick and black, but wavy—no Indian to speak of in the background. Luis, the son, was a sallow young man who, despite his dusty Levi's and his big hat, could have been a drugstore *ranchero* from any of a hundred towns on either side of the border. But Lupe had the look of caste of a Spanish duchess—the bony face and tall, tight body; the stiff-backed walk even in rumpled men's pajamas and bare feet.

"Your daughter," David began. "She doesn't seem to like me."

Cruz's shoulders rose a few inches and dropped. "You're an Anglo. Worse, you're a Texan."

"How would she know that?" David asked. "The Texas is gone from my voice. I worked like hell on it, but it's gone now."

Cruz poured more coffee for David and himself, bit hugely into an English muffin, and went on. "She can hear it. She listens for Texas in an accent the way a Southerner looks for signs of colored blood."

"Tafoya y Evans," David said.

"Sure," Cruz said. "My mother was an Anglo, a little Welsh lady whose father came out here to mine coal. Lupe doesn't like the idea, but there isn't one goddamn thing she can do about it. Right now she has . . . convictions, I suppose you'd say." Cruz peered closely at David. "You look pretty tired. You tired?"

David shook his head and, as he did, realized that he was about to fall out of the deep chair from exhaustion. "Yes," he said. "I am a little tired."

"Good. Get some sleep. You got some pajamas in that little suitcase of yours?"

"Pajamas. Toothbrush. Schick. Mum. Crest. Old Spice. Jockey. Hickey-Freeman. Florsheim."

"Yeah," said Cruz. "You're tired."

Chapter 6

THE GOVERNOR LIKED HIS OFFICE, which was round. He didn't care for the Executive Building—which was also round—but he had worked hard, spent more than two hundred thousand of other people's dollars, and said some humiliating things to get himself into the round office in the round building.

He was the first governor of New Mexico in more than forty years with a Spanish surname. He had explained during his campaign, when he spoke in Little Texas, that he felt no more Spanish than Eisenhower had felt German; the line got as big a laugh as a greaseball was able to get in Little Texas. The governor's English, of course, was impeccable. Indeed, it was graceful and sometimes elegant, the result of four years' stupefying debates at the University and fifteen years' advocacy before New Mexico judges, many of whom were senile and deaf, a few of whom were asleep on the bench.

When the Governor campaigned in the north counties he spoke only Spanish, not the Spanish he had polished at school but the rough dialect his father had spoken, in which v's turned to b's, n's were added where they didn't belong, and consonants were swallowed as regularly as beans.

The *nativos* admired him. They assumed he was on their side, though they would have been stumped to explain what their side was, simply because his name was Manuel Tafoya. They positively knew that he was rich, or would be before he left office, because the governorship is a signed, sealed, and framed license to steal from the state treasury. Any man who got that close to the pot of *reales* and failed to divert them to his own use was a simpleton.

The Anglos of Little Texas admired him because they assumed he was in their pocket, a captive Mex in the Statehouse, beholden down to his toes for the round-figure campaign contributions, the victory vote margins in the eastern counties, the invisible lassos tossed over Tafoya's shoulders by the Cowboys, the Oilboys, and the Cottonboys, or, as they thought of themselves, the Good Ol' Boys.

The plump, sweating man who sat across from the Governor was a clown. He was born a clown, grew up a clown, worked hard at being a clown, shunned all non-clown activities, patterned his behavior after the great historic clowns of the world, and thought of himself as a statesman.

Carlos Tafoya was sure, for example, that his campaigning had put his brother in the Governor's chair. In fact, his big, loose mouth had cost his brother four counties, three of them in the Spanish north. If he began a rambling speech with a sound, appropriate premise, his logic went haywire and he terminated the speech with a tangled conclusion. If his address started on shaky assumptions, his logic flowed clear and reasonable so that he painted himself into a granite corner. He spoke eloquently to the Petroleum Institute of the need for higher taxes to cover welfare payments. He admonished a ragged crowd of marginal farmers in Cañon Feo, many of them third-generation recipients of Aid to Dependent Children, to get off their butts and find honest, high-paying work. He regaled the Albuquerque chapter of B'nai B'rith with a series of Ikey and Abie jokes, guaranteed to amuse. He excited the Citizens for Clean Air and Water with a vision of the industrial future of New Mexico, wherein every town would boast a paper mill, a coal-burning power plant or— if the state were really lucky—a nerve-gas factory.

Manuel Tafoya, who was running as hard and well as he knew how, tried to convince Carlos to temper his awful honesty with discretion, but Carlos was too hysterically exuberant to listen. He believed himself a kingmaker who, after the coronation, would be named Grand Vizier. He mistook the looks of stupefied annoyance on his audiences' faces for rapt approval.

Eventually, the candidate sent his brother on what he called a "fact-finding trip" to Vermont, mended his torn fences, and won the governorship in what even his own party described as a squeaker. Carlos was allowed to return to New Mexico in time to vote.

After the election, Carlos went back to his law office to continue his career of failing to fix traffic tickets, speeding his clients into prison or bankruptcy, and writing confused, easily broken wills. His only connection with statecraft was negative. When the Governor had a difficult decision to make, he always asked Carlos's advice, thanked him for his counsel, and did the opposite. After slightly more than a year in office, Manuel Tafoya was developing a reputation as the wisest governor in history and was beginning to think about the Senate.

Now Carlos sat and smiled and sweated, unbuttoned his shirt collar, spread his stubby arms in incomprehension, and answered the Governor's embarrassing questions with folksy proverbs.

"A Man Must Do What a Man Must Do," Carlos said by way of justification. "The Work of the Spirit Is the Spirit of the Work."

"You stupid bastard," the Governor said. "Do you realize you kidnapped those men? Never mind the other charges they can hit you with. You kidnapped them."

"We let them go," Carlos said. "We didn't hurt them. The End Justifies the Means." Carlos smiled his empty, worried smile. "You Can't Make an Omelet Without Breaking Eggs."

"Carlos," the Governor said, "what in the *hell* are you doing tied up with that bunch of nuts? I didn't know you'd even met Primo."

Carlos looked wounded. "I'm his counsel." he said. "I'm his legal advisor. I'm the counsel for the whole Compañía. In Questions of Law, Only a Lawyer Knows the Answers. You know, Primo's not an educated man. He's a Man of Vision, but he doesn't speak good English."

"I know," the Governor said. "He doesn't speak good Spanish, either. The crazy son of a bitch is illiterate in two languages. Jesus, Carlos, I sat in here and talked to that man for three hours last June. Do you remember that time? Twenty farmers from the upper valley, half of them drunk, and Primitivo Rael yelling at me about Justice and

Land and Liberty and Jesus Christ and Adolf Hitler and President James K. Polk and the Archangel Michael and the Gadsden Purchase and Christopher Columbus. I felt like I was fighting off a swarm of bees with my hat."

Smiling, Carlos nodded. "That's just the point," he said. "Primo Knows What's Right, because He's a Man of the People. But he gets the details all mixed up. That's why he needs legal advice. That's what I'm for."

"And you advised him? You told him to take a gang of country boys into the campground and kidnap the Ranger and that tourist?"

Carlos took a handkerchief from his back pocket and wiped the sweat from his cheeks and eyes. "You don't understand, Manuel. That wasn't a kidnapping. We didn't hold him for ransom or send any notes or anything like that. This was a perfectly legal citizens' arrest. Ultimate Power Resides in the People. A Burro in Uniform Is Still a Burro." After a pause he said, "Primo wasn't there anyway."

A light on the Governor's telephone turned red, and he picked up the receiver, listened, grunted, said, "A few more minutes," and hung up. "That was Warschauer. He's fighting off the Associated Press, United Press International, both Albuquerque papers, the Las Vegas *Optic*, the Carlsbad *Current-Argus*, and some television people. They want a statement."

"What are you going to say?"

"I'm going to say, 'No comment.' And you, you silly bastard, had better get yourself a lawyer before you say one goddamn word to anyone. I mean, you get a *good* lawyer. Get somebody, for Christ's sake, who's read the law on kidnapping and citizens' arrests, anyway."

"I'm a lawyer," Carlos said. "I'll be my own counsel if it comes to that. If You Want Something Done Right, Do It Yourself."

"I'll quote *you* one, *estúpido*. A Man Who Acts as His Own Lawyer Has a Fool for a Client. Now, that door leads to my bathroom. In the bathroom is another door that leads to some stairs which go down one floor, and then there's a door. Are you listening to me? You open that door and you'll be in the Game and Fish Department storeroom. From there you can probably find your way outside."

Carlos buttoned his shirt and straightened his tie. "A Man Goes His Own Way," he said. "A Man Follows His Own Star." He opened the door to the Governor's bathroom and left, the smell of his sweat still strong in the big office.

Manuel was, as he usually was, cooperative and amiable with the press and said nothing which could conceivably come back to haunt him. Newspaper stories with headlines beginning "Governor Mum On . . ." pleased him the most. Those that began "Manny Scores . . ." or "Tafoya Lauds . . ." usually meant he'd lost his poise somewhere during an interview and babbled an indiscretion. This interview, he decided when he watched himself on television that night, was a textbook example of friendly, noncommittal neutrality, tempered with fairness and wisdom.

Q. Is your brother a member of the Compañía?
A. (Smiling) Do you mean Carlos, Cruz, or Pete? (*Laughter.*)
Q. Carlos.
A. I honestly don't know. He belongs to a number of

organizations: Rotary, Elks, V.F.W. . . . . (*Laughter.*)

Q. What are your feelings about the Compañía?

A. I know very little about it.

Q. Do you approve of its activities?

A. I'm afraid I don't know much about its activities.

Q. Did Primo Rael tell you about his plans to invade a national monument and kidnap a Ranger?

A. In the first place, words like "invade" and "kidnap" are best left unsaid at this point. The . . . the question is apparently a Federal matter. I am neither a Federal officer nor a practicing attorney, nor do I have . . . do I know of the details. Aside from what I read in the papers. (*Laughter.*)

Q. Did Primo Rael, when he talked to you, threaten to do anything like this? Like that business up at Cumbre?

A. Mr. Rael threatened nothing. Mr. Rael presented to me a petition signed by two hundred and seventy-three people. I believe all the news media in the state got copies of the petition. I know the *Standard* ran a copy of it.

Q. Well, what did he want you to do with the petition, Governor?

A. I believe Mr. Rael misunderstood the . . . the powers of a governor. Some of the points in the petition were quite far-reaching. They were completely outside my powers. My province.

Q. Mr. Rael said that the Spanish-speaking citizens from the upper valley were discriminated against by the Anglo power structure. Do you agree?

A. I agree that Mr. Rael's petition said it. (*Laugh-*

79

ter.) And I agree that, on a personal level, some discrimination of various kinds exists in all parts of the country. Racial and religious prejudice is an ugly part of life in America, an aspect of our life with which I have no sympathy. As for the Anglo power structure, I am the Governor of this state, and my name is Tafoya. (*Laughter.*)

Q. Is the Compañía what you would consider a legal organization?

A. I'm not sure what sort of organization it is. It isn't a political party, because it isn't registered with the Secretary of State. I don't believe it's a commercial or industrial corporation; it has requested no license to sell or dispense any goods or services. It isn't a registered lobby. Perhaps it's a social club.

Q. Primo Rael says it's a revolutionary group.

A. I don't think the state supplies licenses for that sort of activity. (*Laughter.*) Of course, if it's change in the statutes the group wants, they are perfectly welcome to attempt to make the changes, so long as their attempts are not violent, and are within the framework of the law.

Q. Is your brother . . . your brother Carlos, that is, legal advisor to the Compañía?

A. I have no idea.

Q. When you talked to Rael, did you form any opinion of him?

A. It was a brief meeting. I would say—remember, this is an opinion only—that he was sincere but misinformed. Or underinformed.

Q. Are there going to be indictments?

A. So far as I know, neither Mr. Rael nor any member of his organization has broken any state law.

Q. Federal indictments?

A. Ask the Feds. (*Laughter.*)

Q. Governor, are you planning to announce your candidacy for the United States Senate?

A. I am very busy trying to be a good governor right now.

Chapter 7

WHEN DAVID FOUND THE KITCHEN the next morning, Cruz was already there, in a broad alcove looking out on an untidy flagstoned courtyard in which a few chickens pecked among the weeds. He could see now the configuration of the house, a hollow square of adobe built around the court, the far side broken by a gated entrance wide enough to admit a wagon or an automobile. It looked like a movie set for Fort Apache, the effect marred somewhat by several marble statues of naked Greeks standing about gazing at the mud walls with empty eyes, and a crippled manure spreader.

A stern, gloomy woman in the kitchen chopped onions at a wooden table as David walked through to join Cruz. She nodded at him briskly, and her blond-white bun of hair bounced. *"Muy buenos días, señor,"* she said.

David was surprised to hear Spanish emerge from so Nordic a face, and said "Good morning" in English.

"She doesn't speak the lingo," Cruz said. "Sit down. You hungry? Sure you are. Have some coffee." Cruz poured dark coffee from a gray speckled camp pot into a delicate bone-china cup and handed it to David. "Sleep okay?" he asked.

"Yes," David said. "Jesus, yes. I didn't even dream." Cruz was looking at him with his innocent blue eyes, probing his soul in the friendliest manner. "I've been dreaming a lot since . . . recently."

"Yeah," Cruz said. "Yeah, I'll bet you have." He sipped his coffee thoughtfully. "Ham and eggs all right? Little red sauce on the eggs?" Without awaiting an answer, he turned to the blond woman in the kitchen. "Ingeborg, *jamón y huevos con salsa para el señor.*" Ingeborg nodded again, and her bun bounced.

"Ingeborg?" David asked.

"Lupe found her. Woman named Gloria used to cook for us. Old Abundio's widow. Lived on the place all her life, since my grandfather's time. She died a couple of years ago. Must have been a hundred and ten. Good cook, but old-fashioned. Used to grind her own goddamn corn on a stone *metate*. Couldn't break her of the habit. Used to get little pieces of rock grit in her tortillas. Wore everybody's teeth down. Anyway, she died. Lupe got her back up, said we couldn't have any more *nativas* doing the cooking. Said it was slave work. Demeaning. That was some piece of *cago* she picked up in California. You follow me?"

"I think so," David said.

"So I told her to go find an Anglo to work in the kitchen. Thought I had her buffaloed. Not Lupe. Smart girl. Mean as hell, but smart." Cruz pulled a frayed cigar from the pocket of his blue workshirt, sniffed it, wrinkled his nose and returned the cigar to his pocket. "Terrible things," he said. "But not as bad as cigarettes. I can hold off a little while longer."

Ingeborg set a plate of broiled ham and *huevos rancheros* in front of David, the sauce pungent with onions and garlic and *chile colorado*. Cruz poured another cup of coffee for him.

"Lupe flew down to Mexico City," he went on, "and came back a week later with Ingeborg. She'd found her in the Swedish Embassy. The butler's daughter. Spoke perfect Mexican Spanish and Swedish, naturally. It tickled hell out of me. All Ingeborg knew how to fix were potatoes and herring, and something called *gravlax*. Lupe had to spend a month with her, teaching her how to cook something that didn't call for fresh salmon. Funny. Lupe was boiling mad, especially when I told her she was running wetbacks, like any Anglo rancher." Cruz chuckled to himself and mopped up the last of the *salsa* with a piece of toast.

David finished his breakfast and thanked Ingeborg in Spanish. She received his remarks with a dim Baltic reserve.

"After that breakfast, I'm ready to go to work," David said.

"No hurry," Cruz told him. "Look around first. Plenty of things to see. Plenty of time."

"Yes," David said. "And there's something else. What is it exactly you want me to do for you? I'm not a very good hand on a ranch. I worked a couple of summers when I was in school, a ranch near Mauldin, Texas, but I've forgotten most of what I learned."

"I don't need any hands," Cruz said. "I got lots of hands. Mauldin. Was that Charlie Cobb's place? The C Bar C?"

David was surprised. "That's right. Do you know him?"

"Met him," Cruz said. "Bought a bull from him a few years ago. Anyway, you don't have to do any manual labor unless you want to. You're probably out of shape after spending all that time sitting behind one of C. C. Cotton's desks. Lawyer's spread."

"I'm not a lawyer," David said. "Cotton kept a whole law firm in business all by himself. I was more like a confidential secretary."

"Uh-huh," Cruz said. "I know what you were. But I don't want a lawyer. I have one already. I just want somebody to help me a little with the paper work. There's a lot of goddamn paper work on a ranch." He arose from the breakfast table and motioned for David to join him. "Ingeborg?"

"¿Jefe?"

"Seven, no, eight for dinner tonight," he said in Spanish. "Two fish, six steaks." Ingeborg's bun waggled in acknowledgment. "Come on, Daveed. Let's go look at the property."

By Texas standards, Cruz Tafoya's ranch was contemptible, but it had been in his family for more than two hundred and fifty years and had a certain sentimental value. In flatter country it would have been a neat rectangle ten miles by twelve; here its profile was jumbled and craggy, its contours hard to trace without surveyor's instruments. The western boundary ran along the ridge of the Rockies, above timberline; the eastern edge of the ranch was in gently undulating pasture land. There were living streams, three of them, that coursed from the melting snowfields in the heights, and there were windmill-powered wells to supplement the natural water. Cruz ran between one and three thousand head of cattle on the ranch, depending on the weather and the water; he admitted to David that he had never bothered to count the sheep.

"It's a gorgeous piece of land, Cruz," David said, as they sat together in the Nash pickup high in the summer pasture, watching the Herefords forage among the pines. "What is it, may I ask? A hundred sections?"

"You can ask," Cruz said. "It's a hundred and twenty. About twelve miles east-west; ten miles north-south. It used to be a whole lot bigger, maybe five hundred sections." He wiped his neck with a bandanna. "The whole Juan Tafoya Grant was about that. My grandfather lost it, most of it. The usual way. The usual swindle." He looked at David. "You know what I'm talking about?"

"I know," David said. "When I worked for Cotton I got to be a sort of expert on it. What was your grandfather's trouble? A bad survey? Taxes?"

Cruz nodded. "Both of them. And you know, he wasn't dumb, my grandfather, not like some of these sad-ass illiterate inbred *estúpidos* with their 'proud Spanish heritage' and their quarter-acre chili patch. Oh, hell. Never mind them. I'll tell you my theory sometime, but not now. Anyway, you and Mr. Cotton are the real experts on those people. They were your specialty."

"That's unfair," David said. "My specialty was land—judging it, evaluating it, bargaining for it, paying for it. With Cotton's money, of course. I never got enough money together to buy an acre of pea patch for myself."

"You're not going to tell me C. C. Cotton was cheap, are you? Didn't he pay his help?"

"Yes," David said. "He paid his help very well. He paid them beautifully. He paid *me* beautifully, too. I worked like hell for him, but I still got the feeling that there was a leak in the main money pipe and I was standing underneath with a bucket. Sometimes I thought he was being careless with it, but that's foolish. Cotton was

86

never careless with money. He was buying loyalty. He was too smart to try to buy love—nobody could love that old bastard—but loyalty was something else. Do you want to know how much mine cost?"

"If you want to tell me," Cruz said. "Whatever it cost, I can't match it. And anyway, even if Cotton was paying you a million a month, it wasn't enough. As I heard it from Billy Joe Shields, you screwed old Cotton up real bad." He glanced at the sun, pulled a watch from his jeans, and stood up. "Let's go see some people," he said. "It'll give you an idea what kind of a dumb operation I run here."

Cruz jounced the old truck down from the high pasture to the rolling prairie, where flocks of sheep munched the brown grass. He stopped once to talk to an old man who emerged from a wood-and-canvas lean-to to greet the boss in Spanish. A dead coyote hung from the slanted roof, tied there by its hind leg.

"I shot a wolf," the old man said.

"You did good, *viejo*," Cruz told him. "You're my best man."

"He knows it wasn't a wolf," Cruz said as they drove away. "There haven't been any wolves for a hundred years. But it makes him feel good. He's a *vasco*, you know. A Basque. The best shepherds in the world. If it had been a wolf, he'd have been happy to feed the wolf his arm rather than lose a sheep. That was old Echeagaray. Been here since before I was born. All my other *vascos* are up there in the sixties or seventies too. When they die, I don't know where the hell I'm gonna get any more. The *vascos* are disappearing just like the wolves."

David watched the swirling, eddying sheep, the stupidest mammals—next to horses—domesticated by man.

"Why do you run sheep?" he asked. "Sheep and cattle aren't supposed to mix."

"I know all about that," Cruz said. "The sheep eat the grass down to the roots, and the cattle can't get feed and starve. People have been telling me that for forty years."

"Well . . . ?"

"I do it because I'm a dumb Mexican, and dumb Mexicans like to run sheep. It's a family tradition. Everybody expects it of me, so I do it. Also, it works. I run about twelve hundred Herefords and somewhere around eight hundred Merinos and Rambouillets, and they all make money for me, most of the time."

The rough truck road paralleled a bluff, a steep escarpment eighty feet high that blocked off all view to the north and extended eastward as far as David could see. By turning in his seat, he could see that the bluff ran west to the mountains, like the Great Wall of China. "That's quite a little barrier," he said. "How do you get your animals over it?"

"I don't," Cruz said. "Right along that bluff my property stops. My grandfather, and all the other Tafoyas back to the eighteenth century, had grant land for fifteen miles beyond the bluff. It was called the Upper Grant. Down here where we are is the Lower Grant. It was all one piece of land, but really two separate ranches. The foreman up there, and all his hands, didn't see my grandfather more than two or three times a year. The Tafoyas themselves all lived on the Lower Grant, in the big house. They had one hell of a communication problem, too."

The road veered away from the bluff, to the south, and David saw that the top of the ridge was shaggy with tall ponderosa pines.

"The land up there," he said. "That's the land you lost?"

"That's it. Almost four hundred sections. I never owned it, but I miss it anyway. Before there were telephones or telegraph lines, the Tafoyas would ride down here to the base of the bluff and build a signal fire out of green wood. Then they'd wait for somebody up above to see the smoke. When a head showed over the edge, they'd yell back and forth at each other for a while until the message got passed. It worked the same way, of course, when somebody up there had something to say to somebody down here."

"That's very charming," David said.

"You bet it was. It was a pain in the ass, too. But that's the way they did it, from 1719 until the gringo bastards stole it."

The truck topped a gentle rise and David saw, in a narrow valley, a vividly painted dome, like a gaudy igloo, with thin woodsmoke rising from the curved roof. Behind the dome was a plowed field in which a few struggling cornstalks and tomato vines withered.

"The house of the future," Cruz said. "Ugliest thing I ever saw."

"Do people live in that thing?"

"Sure. My tenants. Used to be forty of them, but the population's dwindled some. This, my friend, is the Noble Savage Garden of Eden Farm, an enterprise of love, or so they tell me."

As the truck stopped, an enormous but emaciated blond youth stepped out of the dome, bending deeply at the waist to clear the low door. His beard, filthy and straw-colored, flapped stiffly in the light breeze.

"Hello, sir," he said, flashing the peace sign.

Cruz returned the signal. "You better give him the sign, too," he told David, "or he'll think you're a policeman."

David formed a V with his index and middle fingers and was relieved to see the giant smile.

From behind his seat Cruz took a cracked leather bag and got out of the truck. David remained where he was, uneasily watching the young man and the small, unutterably filthy girl who peered at him from the door of the dome, a naked baby straddling her hip.

"Your crops look like hell," Cruz said. "Aren't you irrigating?"

The giant smiled again. "We got behind," he said. "Some of the cats left. The ones that knew how."

"Where is everybody?"

"They took the bus into Santa Fe. It's Food Stamp Day."

"Yeah," said Cruz. "Now what's the trouble? Lupe says you're clapped up again."

"It's probably nothing. It stings a little when I . . . you know."

Cruz set his bag on the ground and opened it. "Never mind the delicate talk," he said. "It's not your style. Now drop your pants."

The giant seemed shaken. "Right here?"

"Right here. Drop 'em. Let it all hang out. The man in the truck is my colleague. If he sees something he's never seen before he'll throw a brick at it."

Cruz worked, not too gently, with a cotton swab and a microscope plate while the giant gritted his teeth and looked at the horizon, as if pretending there was nothing going on below his line of vision. When he buttoned his Levi's he gestured toward the girl in the doorway.

"What about her?"

"If you have it," Cruz said, "then you all have it. This" —he waved the slide—"is going into the lab this afternoon, and I'll know by tomorrow." He paused, his face tightened by a mild look of disgust. "Where'd it come from? You were all clean two months ago." He sniffed the breeze cautiously. "Well, maybe not exactly clean."

The giant shifted his feet. "There was this new chick. From San Diego."

"Jesus," Cruz said. He backed off a pace and looked at the young man carefully. "How are you feeling otherwise? Looks like you lost thirty pounds since I saw you last. What are you eating?"

"Number Seven."

"What the hell is Number Seven?"

"Brown rice."

"And . . . ?"

"That's pretty much it. Brown rice. You can really groove on it. It's austere."

"You bet your ass it's austere. I don't much care any more whether you starve to death or not, but you better feed that baby some real food." Cruz closed his black bag and got back in the truck. The giant put his shaggy head through the window on David's side; he smelled like a very old horse.

"Like, I thought we might all cut out from here pretty soon," he said. "Farming's a bummer."

"How would you know?" Cruz asked. "You never gave it a try. This is good land. Plenty of water. Why didn't you work it?"

The giant shook his head. "All the cats are leaving. Why should I bust my ass for a tomato?"

"A year ago you were going to turn this valley into a paradise."

The giant shrugged. "So we changed our minds. You got to be flexible." He leaned further in. "You hear about the Compañía? What they're doing now?"

"I've heard of it," Cruz said. "They all have their heads screwed on backwards."

"No, man. I mean what they're *doing*. Those mothers have freaked. They're burning places, man. They're settin' things on fire up there, you know? A barn—whoosh! A house—boom! Man, that is action. That is good action. You know?"

"I didn't know. Where did *you* hear about it?"

"On the tube. I got a little, you know, battery-powered rabbit-ear set inside."

Cruz smiled indulgently at the young man. "Television. You people really got your lives pared down to the primitive essentials, like you said in your sales pitch."

The giant spread his arms. "Aww," he said, like Gary Cooper kicking horse apples, "you know. We got to keep informed. And the old lady likes the soaps. Anyway," he leaned forward again and rested his arms on the truck window, "some of us are thinking, maybe, you know. Go up there, up north, and help. Burn some of those Texas types out. Shake up the straights. Get the land back to the people, you know? The rightful owners."

"Well, good luck," Cruz said. "*Muy buena suerte* with the Compañía. I can't think of anything those guys would like to see more than you and your little band of honest dirt farmers."

The giant's smile faded. "What're you being sarcastic for, man? What's wrong with us?"

"You're an Anglo, for one thing, but that might be all right if they knew you. And you're a hippie . . ."

"I am like hell a hippie."

"To them you are. Anybody who wears his hair longer than Harry Truman is a hippie. And it's ten to one you've got a dose, and they don't need that up there either. They got plenty of their own."

"You put me down. You really put me down. Man, I'm a *friend* of your people."

Cruz said, "Uh-huh," without conviction. "If the lab gets a positive, I have to report you all to the Public Health Service. It's the law." He started the engine.

"Love is beautiful," said the giant. "Peace."

"I think I'm gonna throw you and your people off my property. I don't want my sheep getting gonorrhea."

"You put me down, man," the giant said, and turned toward the dome.

Cruz drove away, muttering, "My people," he said. "My people. Christ almighty. Those kids. They're so good. They're so kind. They're so *dumb*."

"You're a doctor," David said.

"What? Oh, yeah. I was. Well, I still am. I still got a license, but I don't practice much. That back there with the swab, that's work for vets."

"What kind of a doctor are you? Were you?"

"A plumber. General surgery." He displayed the maimed right hand. "I cut these off on a power saw, and then I figured anybody that clumsy better quit while he's ahead. I could still cut and slash, but I couldn't tie those fancy knots any more. You know, every time my boy stumbles over something or knocks all the dishes off a table, I think, 'That's the Cruz Tafoya coming out in him.' You want to see Luis's house?"

"If you want me to. Cruz . . . what the hell am I doing here?"

Cruz looked at him blankly. "Looking over the ranch, *cuate*. How you gonna work for me if you don't know the ranch?"

"Come on, Cruz. There's nothing I can do for you. I'm no foreman."

"I got a foreman. It's the paper work . . ."

"Crap. Excuse me. You run a funny kind of personal operation here. I don't even think you're serious about it. Cattle and sheep on the same spread, for God's sake. That's suicide. Basques. A hippie commune. What is it? A hobby? Are you an eccentric millionaire?"

Cruz grinned at him, and again the brown face was lit by the inner candle. "Hey, you're doing okay. You're asking some questions. Yessir, I think you're gonna get your ass out of that wheelchair and take a few halting steps."

"Please stop it, Cruz. I . . . look, I know you know about Cotton and that business. You know I'm all screwed up. What is it? You feel pity for me? What?"

Cruz drove for another mile without speaking. He stopped the truck, finally, within sight of the old adobe house he lived in, the brown walls shaded by deep green cottonwood trees.

"If you laugh at me, I'll kill you," he said. "Really. I'll kill you."

"I won't laugh."

"My wife's been dead for fifteen years. My boy . . . well, you met him. He's a half-wit. I don't even think I love him any more. Lupe, she only comes back to rest in between revolutions and shit like that. We got nothing to talk about, me and Lupe. You've seen the ranch. It's all I have to do, and it runs itself. This land is so rich that nobody can screw it up. It really makes money; I know you don't believe it, but it really does. Even now, when it's not even half as big as it used to be, I can't help making fifty or sixty thousand dollars a year on it. I only work for the exercise, so I don't get too fat and have a coronary. I . . . well, Goddamnit, that's it."

"You mean you're bored?"

"No!" Cruz shook his head angrily. "No, not bored. Not . . . David, I just want somebody to talk to. I'm lonely. You're not gonna laugh, are you?"

"No. But why me? I'm just a gringo you found in Texas with blood on his head. You don't know me."

"Oh, yes I do," Cruz said. "I know you. You're the man who felt so sorry for some ragged-ass *nativo* that you cost C. C. Cotton a few million dollars in royalties."

Chapter 8

POEM from "Youth Speaks," a regular feature of *La Lucha* (*The Battle*), weekly newspaper published by La Compañía de Tierra y Libertad:

Hay Te Watcho
By Mike Morales
(9th Grade, Apodaca Jr. Hi, El Tejon)

There's going to be a *gran chisguete*
Cuando yo get out of school
Porque yo soy the brother of Pancho Villa
And getting shot at *no me importa.*
This is *mi tierra,*
And I'm going to spill some *sangre* on it.
Hay te watcho, anglo son of a bitch,
Porque yo vengo.

Editorial in the Albuquerque *Standard:*

Compañía Flaunts the Law
The so-called Companyia de Tiera y Libertade, a revolutionary organization which has as

it's aim the taking over of all land in the Southwest for Communistic purposes, led by a fiery orator Primivito Rale, has once more struck at the heartland of American free enterprise.

This organization flaunts the law of this sovereign state, and should be outlawed forthwith.

Former Police Chief Lemann, who was dismissed from the force for speaking the truth about this Marxist group, said it all when he said: "This group flaunts the law. This is a law-flaunting group. No group, no matter what its political or philosophical aims, should flaunt the laws of our forefathers, who included such great Americans as Thomas Jefferson and Andrew Jefferson. They never flaunted the law, but worked within the system."

We agree.

Letter to the Editor of the Albuquerque *Standard:*

Dear Sir:
You meant "flout" in that dumb editorial, don't you? And who is Andrew Jefferson?

Cipriano Moya

(ED. NOTE: Yes, of course we meant flute, and we feel that readers who would rather quible than discuss the real issues bring in a note of levity which has no place in these pages.)

Chapter 9

FATHER PEDRO TAFOYA Y EVANS, a small angular man with a nose the color of Welch's grape juice, arrived at six, gave Cruz a perfunctory *abrazo*, greeted Ingeborg in Spanish and told her he prayed constantly for her conversion from wicked Lutheranism, returned to the big *sala*, poured himself four fingers of Scotch, and was introduced to David.

"My brother the father," Cruz said. "Pete is a man of great piety and great capacity."

"How do you do, Mr. Reed," the priest said. "Pay no attention whatever to Cruz. Beneath all those layers of cynicism and worldly preoccupation lies a genuine sinner." Father Pete swallowed his drink in a single, smooth gulp and handed his glass to Lupe. "My dear child, could you get me another. You're not only the most beautiful of my nieces, but the kindliest."

"It's your liver," Lupe said, taking his glass.

"I've been on retreat for two weeks," he said. "It was a period of total self-denial. Also it's a dusty drive down here."

Lupe refilled his glass and gave it to him. "You ought

to smoke grass instead," she said. "It's better for you." She turned to David. "How's yours, Mr. Reed?"

"Still working on it," David said. "You serve good bourbon."

"We keep some around for the odd Texan," she said.

"Ah, you're from Texas," Father Pete said. "I would never have guessed it. Where did you learn to speak English?"

"Remedial Speech class at Rice University," said David, who'd had that needle before. "I kept pebbles in my mouth for three years."

"Can you do the accent?" the priest asked. "It always breaks me up. I think it's funnier than Yiddish."

"Shore Uh kin," David said. "Ah kin say purt near anythang yew lahk in Texiz, but Uh cain't talk Meskin fer sour dawg hockey."

Father Pete was into his third drink when Carlos came in, rumpled and sweaty and bulging out of his suit. He gave David a wet hand and looked at him with nervous confusion. "Yes. Mr. Reed. Reed? Is that right? Yes. Carlos Tafoya. That's C-a-r-l-o-s. It means Charles in Spanish."

"What's he doing here?" he whispered to Cruz a few minutes later. "What's that Anglo doing here? This is supposed to be family."

Cruz put his hand on the fat man's shoulder and addressed him gravely. "It's a conspiracy," he said. "There's nothing we can do about it. He's a spy for the English-Speaking Union."

From the driveway came the shriek of metal on stone, the sound making everyone start except Cruz. "There's Luis," he said. "He hit the goddamn well again."

"I pray for that boy all the time," Father Pete said.

99

"Isn't there something a doctor could do for him, Cruz?"

"You can't cure stupid."

Luis entered carrying his son, a sturdy little blond boy of eighteen months, whom he handed to Lupe. "I'm sorry, Papa," he said in Spanish. "I can't stay for dinner. But I have to talk to Carlos a minute."

"Where's Marta?" Cruz asked him.

"She's not coming. We had another fight. That's one mean woman."

Luis and his Uncle Carlos isolated themselves in a corner and whispered together. Lupe brought the baby to David. "My only nephew," she said. "Miguelito Tafoya y Romero, this is Mr. Reed."

"Hi, Miguelito. That's a pretty long name for somebody your size."

"And it's a pretty funny name for a kid with hair that color, too," Lupe said, "but I don't care. I could eat this boy up." She nuzzled and hugged Miguelito and bit him lightly on the behind. "Mmm. I'd like to try these *nalgas*. Medium rare with a little *salsa picosa* on top."

From the corner, where Luis and Carlos stood together, came a ripple of snarling laughter and a burst of *"chingao"*s from Luis. Carlos was sweating again and wiping his neck with a handkerchief. The two men shook hands. Luis turned and walked swiftly toward the door, his booted foot catching on a table leg, causing a silver bowl of tortilla dip to wobble dangerously. He went out without even a surly good-bye.

"I'd better give him back his son," Lupe said. "He might notice he's missing in a week or two." David followed her outside. Luis stood by the old well, looking at the new wrinkle in his Mustang's fender. The car, no more than a year old, looked as if enraged Iraqi villagers had tried to stone it to death. All the glass was starred and opaque, except the windshield, which was missing. Even the top had dents and scratches and metal rips. Luis kicked the stone well in rage and whimpered at the pain.

"*Oiga,* Luis," Lupe called. She held the little boy up. "*Tu chico. Le olvidaste.*"

Muttering, Luis walked back and collected his son. "*Chingao* well," he said. "It's always in the *way!*"

"I'm sorry I didn't get to meet your wife," David said. "I hear she's very pretty."

Luis looked at him with suspicion, seeking any sign of lurking Anglo sarcasm, but saw none.

"Yeah," he said. He spun around, nearly dropping Miguelito, and stamped back to his car. "Shit!" he said, and kicked the fender.

A big car, moving fast, drove into the open space around the well, leaving a fine curtain of dust behind it. Luis backed his crumpled Mustang out of the way in a squeal of rubber and gravel and roared off, the broken muffler bouncing beneath the rear bumper.

"Is this more family?" David asked.

"Sure," she said. "Spics breed like hamsters. Didn't they teach you that back in Texas?"

A state patrolman, freckled and bulky in a sharply tailored blue-gray uniform, got out of the car and walked around it to open the rear door. "Hello, Miss Lupe," he said.

"Mac, you *chota* bastard, how are you? Who you got in there? Heinrich Himmler?"

"Now, Miss Lupe," he said. "Don't you start." He opened the door and Manuel Tafoya climbed out, wearing the slightly iridescent sort of suit that looks good on television. He said, "Lupe, my dear," and saw David. His face arranged itself into an expression of genial, yet serious, sincerity, and his right hand rose into shaking position as though operated by wires from above.

"Good evening, sir," he said. "Manuel Tafoya."

"This is Mr. Reed, Uncle Manny," Lupe said. "He doesn't vote in New Mexico."

"Mr. Reed," the Governor said. He squeezed David's hand.

"You're the Governor," David said. "My God, of course! You're the Governor. It's an honor to meet you."

"Ah, yes. So they tell me."

"I'm really embarrassed," David said. "I knew your name, but I didn't put it together."

"He got his head busted a few days ago," Lupe explained. "He can't put *anything* together." She turned to the policeman. "Mac, are you having dinner with us?"

"No, thank you, Miss Lupe. No, I've eaten. I'll just get the dust off the car."

"I'll tell Ingeborg to bring you a beer," she said, and steered David and the Governor into the house.

The Governor gave an *abrazo* to his brothers, even to Carlos, though Carlos got the hug on only one side. The genuine *abrazo* is a monosexual, nonvoluptuous embrace associated with two or three back-thumpings. There is none of that slobbery kissing the French insist upon, but the participants do rest their chins on each other's shoulders—first the left shoulders, then the right. The *abrazo* is performed most efficiently between men who are approximately the same size; great disparity in height, as when Lyndon Johnson leaned over to deliver the ritual squeeze to the President of Mexico on the International Bridge at Juarez, makes the *abrazo* look like assault with intent to rape.

102

As the Governor hugged his brothers, he repeated the ceremonial Spanish words of greeting: "*¿Cómo estás? ¿Qué hubo? ¿Qué tal?*" and followed this with a brief, whispered communication.

To Cruz: "Who the hell is this Reed?"

To Carlos: "I got some good news for you, *estúpido.*"

To Pete: "Pray for me. I think I'm in the toilet."

The priest said a brief grace before dinner. He slurred his consonants somewhat, but felt confident that God, if He was bothering to listen, would be able to decode the thick speech. With his mountain trout he drank a sixth Scotch, chased by Moselle.

"Uncle Pete," Lupe said. "When are you going to break loose and marry one of those sexy parish nuns? Sister John's nice."

Pete delicately removed his trout's backbone and waggled it at her. "The Holy Father," he reminded her, "has spoken clearly and *ex cathedra* on that matter. We're still supposed to keep our thoughts and our hearts away from fleshly things, and stick to bingo."

"The Holy Father's almost eighty years old," Lupe pointed out. "It's no skin off his nose. What would you do if he came out against Chivas Regal?"

Pete picked up his Scotch and observed its clear, amber tone. "I'd begin to have doubts," he admitted.

"Mr. Reed," the Governor said. "What brings you out here?"

"Well, sir," David began, "I'm, uh . . ."

"Possibly a confidential matter, eh? You needn't tell me, Mr. Reed."

"No secret," Cruz said. "He's a fugitive from Texas. He's got the Rangers on his tail." He went back to his steak.

Ingeborg came in from the kitchen with a second platter of onion rings and told Cruz there was a policeman in the kitchen poking around in the refrigerator, and did it have anything to do with her immigration?

"Give him something to eat," the Governor said. "Give him a beer."

"Give him an extra steak, Ingeborg," Cruz said.

"If you're really a Fugitive, I'd prefer not to Break Bread with you," Carlos said. "I'm an Officer of the Court, and I've Sworn to Uphold . . ."

"*Cállate, estúpido,*" the Governor told him.

"He's not only a fugitive," Cruz went on. "He understands Spanish, too."

"Ha!" the Governor said. "No wonder he's a fugitive. Of course, I've met the Governor of Texas. Fine gentleman. He even shook hands with me. It's wonderful the way politics will make people do things contrary to their convictions." He turned back to David. "I'm serious, Mr. Reed. What does bring you here? No offense intended, sir, but when a new and unknown Texan arrives in New Mexico in any capacity other than touristic, we lock up our wives and daughters and bury the silver."

"I suppose I'm sort of a tourist," David said.

"He's working for me," Cruz said. "He's going to help me in a few business ventures."

"I didn't know you had any business ventures, Cruz," the Governor said. "Outside of administering our magnificent family estate here, which you operate like a rustic madhouse."

"Never mind all that," Cruz said. "And if you don't like the way the place is going, you can come down here and shovel the sheep crap yourself, and turn your office over to Pitt the Younger here." He indicated Carlos with

104

a steak-laden fork. "My plan, if you don't louse it up for me, is to take a little cash out of the bank and buy Texas. David, here, knows the owner."

"Good for you, Papa," Lupe said. "Can I have Wichita Falls for my very own?"

"I don't know, *chica*. Before I buy, I want to make sure that Carlos and his mob don't have some kind of a prior claim on it."

Carlos looked up from his trout, into which he had been tearing messily. "Sure it's ours," he said. "But we're not ready to Take on Texas. It's More Complicated. There are many Technical Considerations."

"Carlos," the Governor said. "Let's drop the whole thing for a while. The Compañía is a nightmare. It's a waste of time. It's a fraud and a swindle, and everybody in the state is on my ass, pardon me, Lupe, from every direction. All I wanted to do was have a nice, quiet administration, pave some roads, wangle some dough out of Uncle Sam, make some nice speeches about brotherhood and the American way, and either go on to Washington or back into practice."

"Primo's a Great Man," Carlos said. "He's a Man Whose Time Has Come."

"You tell 'em, Uncle Carlos," Lupe said.

"Not you too, Lupe," the Governor said. "Oh, Christ. Mr. Reed, do you know what we're talking about?"

"It's the land thing, isn't it? I read a little about it in the Houston papers. They're not taking it too seriously there."

"They wouldn't, in Texas, but things are different here. I have to try to please everyone."

"You have to Do Justice," Carlos said.

"There's nothing just about burning out some poor son

of a bitch rancher who's trying to hold a lease and raise a few cows and pay his taxes."

"The Compañía has nothing to do with that," Carlos said. "That's a Spontaneous, Grass Roots Activity. The People are Rising in Fury."

"They really are burning?" Cruz asked. "My tenant, the Freak, told me something about that this afternoon. I thought it was just something his clap-softened brain had invented."

"Yeah, they're burning," the Governor said. "Somebody shot forty of J. B. McCulloch's steers last night and tore down a lot of fence. They got onto Berntsen's property and killed his dog and scared the hell out of his wife and destroyed his pump house. They burned all of Whitt's alfalfa and poured gasoline in his watering tanks and broke his leg for him with a shotgun butt." He sought sympathy from David. "These are small ranchers, Mr. Reed. These aren't the ranch combines that own half a county. These are just people who thought they had clear titles or good leases on a few hundred acres."

"They stole it," Carlos said. "It's not their land."

"Damn it, Carlos, think of your law. They stole nothing. They bought the land from the people who bought the land from the people who bought the land from the people who may—I say may—have acquired the land in a slightly fishy manner from the people who stole it from the Indians in the first place." The Governor sipped his Burgundy. "Hell, man, I'd like to see some redress myself. I know there was some screwing back in the eighties and nineties, semilegal and illegal . . ."

"*Some* screwing?" Lupe said. "It was a twenty-year orgy. They brought in dancing girls to peel the grapes.

106

They had champagne and Spanish fly coming out of the fountains."

"This is getting to be a very noisy and bad-tempered party," Father Pete said. "Is there any more of this Moselle?"

"Probably in the kitchen," Cruz said.

"Don't bother Ingeborg," the priest said. "I'll get it myself." He arose, quite steadily, and picked up the empty wine bottle. "I don't have much influence with the Archbishop these days, but I wonder if he'd consider consecrating this for Masses." He wandered away from the table.

Carlos was pouting and sweating. "We didn't do it, Manny. The Compañía didn't burn those farms. We are going to Stay Within the Framework of the Law."

"I know what you're thinking about. You're trying to get some sort of civil test going, aren't you? You and Primo want to challenge ownership somewhere and leave it up to the Federal courts. Lots of newspaper and TV play."

"What's wrong with that?" Carlos asked. "That's legal."

"Not the way you're doing it, it's not. Why don't you just file a suit, somewhere? File a battery of suits? Tell the Department of Agriculture that the Peralta National Forest is sitting right in the middle of the old San Gabriel community grant—which it is—and raise hell with your affidavits. Or file a private suit in behalf of the Senas and the Chavezes, and challenge the title of D. D. Snow's ranch? Hell, Carlos, there's plenty of honest work for a bleeding-heart *nativo* lawyer."

Carlos set his jaw and shook his head. "No. It takes too long that way. Our way works faster."

"Talk to him, Cruz. Lupe, you're a smart girl. *You* talk to him."

"Hell," said Lupe. "I agree with him. Right on, Uncle Carlos. Power to the peons."

Pete wandered back into the dining room, a new bottle of Moselle in his hand. "I believe," he said, "that Ingeborg is going to come in pretty soon and announce her engagement to the policeman. They were giggling together in mutually incomprehensible tongues, and he was showing her how his handcuffs work. Their children will be a race of titans." He sat down and filled his wineglass.

"That *chota* better not steal our Swede," Lupe said. "I had a terrible time finding her."

"Mr. Tafoya," David said, looking at Carlos. "I'm a little hazy on what your group wants. Do you want *all* the old grants resurveyed?"

"Everything," Carlos said. "Everything."

"Sir, I'm not trying to interfere. I'm not even a citizen of this state. But that's going to be a hell of a job."

Carlos set his jaw again. "Everything. Primo wants everything back like it was. You don't know anything about it. Justice Will Prevail."

"If I remember right," David went on, "you're talking about public and community grants made in New Mexico by the Spanish Crown."

"Mainly those," Carlos said. "Anyway, you don't know anything about it."

"He appears to," the Governor said mildly.

"Every village had common land for farming and grazing," Carlos went on. "Now it's all Federal land. The people have to pay a fee. A *fee!* To graze on their own land!"

Silence went around the table clockwise, like old port.

"For Christ's sake, Carlos," Manny said. "I have to pay a fee—pardon me again, please, Lupe—to go to the *caballeros* these days."

"That's not funny," Carlos said. "It's unfair."

" 'Life is unfair'—John F. Kennedy, 1917–1963," the Governor said.

"I don't suppose you'll try to deny those community grants *used* to belong to the villages, do you?"

"No, and I don't deny that Amarillo, Texas, used to belong to the Comanches. Things change. Times change. Get the romance out of your soul and operate from a position of reality. You sound like a firebrand, not a lawyer. Your flash point's too low. Leave the mystic oratory to Primo."

"Excuse me," David said. "Are you really trying to bring back the old *ejido* system?"

"Sure," Carlos said. "Why not? It worked for three hundred years."

"I think it's a sweet idea," Lupe said. "I see it all like an old painting. All the women are wearing *rebozos;* all the men are wearing big straw hats. Every few minutes somebody leads a burro through the plaza, for color. It would be sort of like Williamsburg with tacos."

"You used to be with us, Lupe," Carlos said.

"I used to believe in the tooth fairy, too."

"I don't think it's possible," David said, "but good luck."

"You don't know anything about it," Carlos repeated.

The Governor broke in. "If the Americans stole the land, it was a case of thieves stealing from thieves. Don't quote me, Mr. Reed."

"Those Anglo bastards stole it," Carlos said.

"They didn't steal it all, *hermanito*," Cruz told him.

"I still got some. Come on, let's go in the *sala* and drink a little brandy and talk about something else." He pushed himself away from the table. "I got some Armagnac that goes down like maple syrup."

"I'll be in pretty soon, Cruz. I have to talk to Carlos a minute," the Governor said.

When the others had left, Manny Tafoya poured a cup of coffee from a silver pitcher. Carlos sat across from him, black sweat stains under his arm, waiting for another lecture from his brother. He had a law degree from the University, just as good as Manny's, and he hated the Governor's superior attitude. Manny wouldn't even *be* Governor if it weren't for Carlos's counsel and speeches and wire-pulling. *No hay justicia.*

"You're off the hook, Carlos," Manny said. "I had to spend three very bad hours with the U. S. Attorney, but you're out of the privy for a while."

"We don't need your goddamn help," Carlos said.

The Governor ignored that. "You got to listen to me, man, or there's going to be one hell of a big *chisguete* and I'm going to forget you're my brother, and you'll be planting radishes at the Los Lunas Honor Farm or sewing mailbags at Leavenworth. Are you listening to me?"

"Go ahead."

"You're trying to force a civil suit with the Feds. They're not going to do it. They will if they have to, but they've got other things to worry about. The U. S. Attorney told me that neither he, nor his boss, nor the Congress, nor the Supreme Court wants to open up that grant business again. They figure they settled it back in 1904. It's a big can of worms, and they're not going to open it again."

"They have to. We'll make them open it."

"Uh-uh. They'll wait until Primo pushes those poor

rubes into some real barbarism, and then they'll hang criminal indictments on you. Trespass, assault, destruction of Government property—whatever. But right now, you're all right. That Park Service Ranger says he won't testify. He's scared for his wife. He's scared if he starts getting his name in the papers the Park Service will call him a troublemaker and ship his ass off to Rocks and Rattlesnakes National Monument in the middle of Nevada. That other man, that tourist, is back in Iowa hiding under the sink. He won't even talk to the mailman."

"That wasn't a kidnapping anyway, I told you."

"Yeah, you told me. Now I'm telling you. Take some money, maybe a couple of thousand, out of the Compañía treasury and send a cashier's check to the Ranger, at Cumbre. No letter, no reason. Just send it. Call it good will."

"You're crazy. We don't have that kind of money. Our members give us a dollar or two a year, dues. That's all. We're a Movement of the Poor and Repressed."

"Oh, bullshit, Carlos. Your advertising costs alone must be twenty thousand a year. I never heard of a Movement of the Poor and Repressed that could afford dollar-apiece silk-screen posters, and every time I go north from Santa Fe I see one of the damned things staring at me from a tree. 'Tierra o Sangre,' for God's sake. Grow up, Carlos, and stop playing Pancho Villa."

Carlos sat and chewed his lip for a while, finished his coffee, finished his wine, wiped his mouth and his damp face on a napkin, and belched.

"Okay, Manny. You're smarter than me and you're the Governor. But I really believe in this, and I can make some money out of it too, and make it honest. There's almost a million acres of land we're trying to get back. Good land and bad land. Private land, Federal land, state land. Land with ranches on it and forests on it and towns on it. If we got to chase two hundred thousand people off it, we'll do it. We don't want to kill anybody or hurt anybody. Primo'll do what I say, because he knows I'm a good lawyer and I won't get him into trouble. I ran your campaign real good, and I'm doing the same for Primo. This thing is going to work."

The Governor leaned back and lit a cigar, looking at Carlos through the smoke. "Little brother, I know just about how stupid you are, and I don't think you're this stupid. So you're lying to me. There's something else this is all about. You know it's impossible, what you're talking about, so you're making noise and smoke and working for something else. Anyway, right now you're not in any official trouble, and that's the last favor I do for you until you go back to your regular work in barratry and champerty and subornation. Next time you go up against the coyote pack, I'm just gonna sit back smiling and let them chew on your behind. Now, let's go in the living room and have some of Cruz's Armagnac and act like a family."

Chapter 10

INGEBORG BURNED EVERYTHING but the orange juice the next morning. Officer Macauliffe, who weighed, as she pointed out to Cruz, more than a hundred kilos, was going to escort her to a rodeo the following Sunday, on his day off. He would teach her English, she said, and she would teach him Spanish and, if their friendship ripened, Swedish.

The priest had spent the night in a spare bedroom. David and Lupe put him to bed, removing his shoes and loosening his clerical collar. "Poor man," she kept saying. "Poor, sweet man," and tried to explain why her uncle drank so heavily. "The other priests are all concerned with the celibacy issue, and the right of priests and nuns to marry, and the rule against birth control, and they're organized and raising hell with the Pope. Not Pete. He believes everything the Pope says about that. What bothers *him* is the doctrine of the Corporal Assumption of the Virgin. He claims it's nonsense. He says no one in his right mind could believe a thing like that. It's contrary to the laws of physics and biology, he says, and he refuses to teach it."

Now Pete was drinking coffee with David and Cruz, his eyes horribly bloodshot, his hands shaking like aspen leaves, discussing the ferocity of his hangover with Jesuitical clarity.

"Mine is not an ordinary *goma*, Mr. Reed, nor even the *goma doble*, which comes as the result of drinking too much of one thing. In the *goma*, one has the fear that one's head is full of tiny men who are endeavoring to extract coal from the brain with pickaxes and occasional dynamite blasts."

"I've had that one a few times, Father," David admitted.

"Now," the priest went on, "with the *goma doble*, there is the more terrifying feeling that one's head will actually fall from the shoulders and hit the floor like an overripe cantaloupe. And, further, while it lies there on the floor, it will still hurt."

"I can remember one of those," David said. "It was when I was at college. I went with some friends to Matamoros, across the border from Brownsville, and drank something called tequila sours."

"Enough of those would certainly do it," the priest said. "Now what I have, and I look upon it as just punishment—a form of expiation—is a *crudo*. Pardon me for using Spanish terms, but English just doesn't have the nuance of vocabulary in this field."

"Quite all right."

"Well, a *crudo* comes from overindulgence in a variety of liquors—Scotch, Moselle, and Armagnac, for example." He shuddered and bit into a piece of dry toast. "With the *crudo* you get something extra. Aside from the pain in the head, and the red eyes, and a tongue that tastes like the paper in a very old magazine, there is a sensation of morbid dryness. It is, let me see if I can describe it, it is as if you had been baked quite slowly in a kiln, and all the moist parts inside your body had become dry and brittle and were slowly flaking off and falling down inside and filling up your legs. That's what I have, Mr. Reed, may God have mercy on me."

"You drink too much," Cruz told him. "When you die they're going to remove your liver and make harness out of it."

"That's what *my* doctor says, too. It's frightening the way you people stick together." Pete finished his coffee and stood up shakily. "Thank you for bed and board, Cruz. It was a lovely party. I wish Mother were here to see how well the brothers are getting along. Kiss Lupe for me. I have hope for that girl. She's working her way back to the Faith in her own manner, I suppose. Didn't she say a few years ago that she was a Taoist?"

"Not quite. She was a Maoist."

"Ah, well. The same sort of thing, I imagine. Goodbye, Mr. Reed. Please try to get this wicked man to confession."

"I'll do what I can, Father. At least it's a clear-cut assignment. Cruz, go to confession."

"If I told Father Serex what was on my mind he'd rupture an artery. Pete, tell the Archbishop to send us another priest, will you? The crazy Belgian is making all the hands nervous. He thinks they have nothing else to do around here but mumble Hail Marys. You ever try to brand a calf with your hands full of beads?"

When the priest left, Cruz telephoned a laboratory in Albuquerque, said "Goddamnit" several times, and returned to the breakfast table. "Can you do something for me?" he asked.

"Sure. Anything. I don't think I'm much good as a paid companion."

"Well, I got a V.D. ward on my hands. Go down and pick up Lupe—she's at the school; I'll draw you a map—and go into town with her. She knows where. I'll write out an order for you. Oh, hell, I need the truck. Can you ride a horse?"

"All us Texans can ride a horse."

"Okay. Goddamnit, now I can't kick those bastards off. I have to keep them together or they'll scatter clap all over the country."

"You run a hell of an operation here, Cruz. I didn't know ranching could be so exciting. There's nothing about the clap in your back issues of *Southwestern Stockman*."

"I wouldn't know," Cruz told him. "I never read that junk. I run the ranch on intuition and native cunning."

Cruz lent him a gentle roan mare with an unsynchronized, spine-crunching trot, gave him a map and an order for several quarts of penicillin, and sent him off down the gravel road. David felt useful for the first time in several weeks, but he wondered what sort of a figure he cut in his wrinkled blue business suit. After a few hundred yards of the mare's stiff-legged gait, he noticed a familiar ache in the thighs. He recalled that he hadn't been astride a horse since that pleasant summer at Charlie Cobb's ranch.

Three miles later he was standing in the stirrups as best he could, clenching his teeth and trying not to scream. The mare was apparently unable to walk or to canter. He passed an adobe house, marked on his map as Luis's house, and saw a woman hanging clothes on a line in a littered back yard. A little blond boy toddled behind her; he recognized Miguelito just as the woman, for no reason that he could understand, spun around and slapped the child on the side of the head. As David bounced past, he heard the little boy crying and saw Marta's pretty, savage face. As he watched, she slapped Miguelito again, knocking him down, then turned toward David with a smile of garish lechery to say *"Buenos días, señor."*

David nodded jerkily and averted his eyes. He had never seen a child treated with such nonchalant cruelty. A few yards farther on, near a collection of rural mail-boxes, he turned his mare to the right, jolted over a rise and down into the village of Pozo Verde, or Los Tafoyas, Cruz's company town.

Lupe's little green MG was parked in the dusty school yard, in the shade of a flaking adobe building no different from the twenty adobe houses strewn along the road, recognizable as a school only by a jungle gym and swings. Ten women, among them Lupe, were perched on ladders leaning against the building, slathering soupy mud onto the walls. David rode the painful mare into the yard and said "Whoa." Then he tried *"Alto,"* and the horse lurched to a stop.

"Good morning," Lupe said from her high rung. "If you've come to help with the plastering, you're out of luck. This is women's work. It's one of those cultural traditions they can shove."

David dismounted in agony and leaned against the mare, while Lupe climbed down from the ladder, muddy to her elbows.

"Why are you riding her?" she asked. "She's a fanny-buster."

"I know. I know. Your father provided the mount. Here." He reached in his pocket and handed her Cruz's written order to the medical supply house. "I feel like Balto bringing the serum to Nome."

Lupe read the order and made a face. "Dumb slobs," she said. "They really let me down. Why don't you come in with me? I'll show you around Fun City."

"Albuquerque? I always thought of it as Lubbock reborn."

Lupe rinsed her hands and forearms at an outside faucet and gave brief orders in Spanish to the women mud-plastering the school.

"What about the old bone-breaker here?" David asked her.

"Slap her on the rump. She'll find her way home. And if she doesn't, it's no loss. That mare is cat meat. How's your butt?"

"What? Oh. Black and blue." David slung the reins over the saddle horn and popped the mare a good one. "Giddap," he said.

Lupe climbed into her little car. "Try '*Adelante*,'" she suggested.

"*Adelante*," he said, and the mare ambled away in her off-center trot.

Lupe was a superb driver, David noticed, her fingers light and firm on the wheel, her down-shifting smooth. She handled her car as if it were a lively and intelligent Arabian pony.

"You're good," he said.

"Hmmm? Oh. It's something you learn in California. Nobody walks out there. You want to drive?"

"No, thanks. I had a kind of sports car, but I drove it very sedately. The one time I gave it free rein it threw me."

Lupe turned out of the ranch onto a paved state highway and headed south toward Albuquerque. Seventy miles away the Sandías, the city's hump-backed mountain range, loomed mistily out of a girdle of smog. David pointed to it.

"Progress," he said.

"Los Angeles has already been invented," Lupe pointed out, "and it didn't work, but the Albuquerqueans had to try it themselves." She groped behind the bucket seat with her right hand and pulled out her bullhorn. "ALL RIGHT, ALBUQUERQUE," she bellowed out the window. "COOL IT."

"Where did you get that thing?"

"From a police equipment catalog. Forty-nine fifty with wrist strap. Here, you take it and yell something out the window. You'll feel better. It clears the sinuses."

"I'd like to take that horn back to Luis's house and tell Marta, nice and loud, to stop beating her little boy."

"Oh, no," Lupe said. "You didn't see that, did you? Damn that woman."

"She was cracking him on the head when I went by her house. I suppose I should have stopped her, but it wasn't my business."

"Marta's one of the Mean Romeros, from Vado Ancho. Most of the Romeros in the area are Good Romeros, or at least Okay Romeros, but there's a nest of mean ones there, and the line almost always runs true. Leave it to Luis to marry one of them."

Lupe stopped at a suburban supermarket and bought a Styrofoam ice chest and twenty pounds of crushed ice. At Rio Grande Medical Supply she and David packed it with a hundred and twenty ampoules of thunder-and lightning penicillin, the 600,000-unit model designed to stun gonococci. Lupe also charged two gross of throw-away syringe needles.

"Damn freaks," she said as she threaded her little car through Albuquerque's manic traffic. "It's my fault, I guess, but they promised."

"What's your fault?"

"I invited them. About fifteen of them were trying to get a commune going in Marin County. Nice kids—a little grimy, maybe. They were going to try organic farming and discover the secret of the Great All. I went out one day with a sociologist on the faculty. We sat around with the kids and smoked some really good grass and drank fruit juice with lots of pulp in it. One of the boys played 'The Marine Corps Hymn' on the sittar. I think it was the soundest antiwar statement I ever heard. Two of the girls did an interpretive dance while someone else read aloud from Ronald Reagan's inaugural address. I don't know. It was a funny, sweet evening. The boy in charge of the operation was an ex-Mormon who'd grown up on a farm near Bountiful, Utah. I figured he knew what he was doing. Anyway, I invited them down to the ranch. They were getting hassled very badly in California."

They were in the outskirts of the city again, a scarred, asphaltic landscape spiky with smokestacks, littered with plateaus of junked cars. Lupe's face contorted in distaste. "It was so beautiful here when I was a little girl. It was the last beautiful place in America."

They stopped for sandwiches and beer along the road, and David bought the Santa Fe paper to read while Lupe was in the ladies' room. The world, he was comforted yet depressed to learn, was still out there. It was even beginning to creep into New Mexico, though haltingly. He read a story headed, "Tafoya Noncommittal on Grant Problem." In it, the Governor said that he sought justice for all citizens of the state, irrespective of cultural, racial, or religious background; that he deplored violence no matter by whom perpetrated; and that he was looking into the matter.

"Your uncle," he said to Lupe when she returned, "is apparently a great statesman and diplomat. I think he'll go far."

Lupe nodded and polished off her beer. "He's gone about as far as a *nativo* can. Even a half-Anglo *nativo*. When I was young I was proud of Uncle Manny; he was a mover and an operator. Later I thought he was a *vendido*, a sellout. He was always out bird-dogging for the Anglos. Now—now I don't know. It's nice to have an uncle who's Governor. I don't get as many speeding tickets as I used to. But he's such a compromiser. And things are changing in the state, finally. Oh, we're still twenty years behind everyone else—I know what you *tejanos* think of us out here—but there's some action, and Manny doesn't know how to handle it. Primo Rael came out of nowhere—well, actually, he came out of Portales, over in Little Texas—and Manny can't just keep saying to him, 'I'll look into the matter.'"

"You know," David said, "that's one of the things I like about New Mexico. Primo Rael's still walking around free and healthy. He may be a maniac, but he's alive. I think if he'd tried this in Texas he'd be . . . in jail."

"He'd be dead and you know it. He'd be the main course at a barbecue."

"Maybe," he said. "Probably not. Texas isn't as barbaric as it used to be. There's a symphony orchestra in Houston, you know. And there's an opera house in Dallas, with indoor plumbing and all."

121

"Sure there is. And who do you suppose cleans out the urinals? You're really just like all the other damned *tejanos*. If you're not busting up Mexicans yourself you're closing your eyes when the Texas Rangers do it."

"The Rangers don't have jurisdiction in Mexico."

"Now you're quibbling. You know who I mean. I mean American citizens who speak Spanish at home and have Spanish last names and do all the crapwork. The only ones who ever made a name for themselves were Speedy Gonzales and the Frito Bandido."

Lupe arose suddenly and stalked to the counter, looking both furious and beautiful in her plaster-spattered Levi's and work shirt. She paid for both lunches, machine-gunned a question at the proprietor, and took from him a tabloid-sized newspaper he got from under the counter.

"Read this," she said to David. "Read the whole thing and then tell me what you think."

While she drove the pocky state highway toward the ranch, David read the latest edition of *La Lucha*—poems, letters to the editor, heavily biased articles about such familiar American landmarks as job discrimination, police brutality, genocide, fascists in government, getting it together, right on, punching out, keeping cool, revolutionary postures, and bloodbaths. Underlying almost every feature was the idea of land, earth, real estate, territory. The newspaper was partly in English, partly in Spanish, but mostly a slangy mixture of the two languages. Once he asked Lupe for the translation of an unfamiliar word. "*Chota?* Literally a suckling kid, that is, a baby goat. It's a derogatory term for policeman, particularly a Spanish-American policeman who beats on his own people."

When he had finished, Lupe said, "What did you

122

think? Never mind the makeup or the spelling. I know they're lousy. Just tell me what kind of feeling comes out of the pages."

"Anger," David said. "Anger and frustration. But it's so awful and amateurish. In some ways it's like any other underground paper, and in others it's like that old-fashioned Marxist nonsense from the *Daily Worker* back in the thirties. And this main article here, the speech Primo Rael made last month in—where was it? Agua Negro? That's really pretty creepy. I mean, a little of what he says makes practical sense, and some of it makes what I suppose you can call emotional sense. But most of it is gibberish. Just raving."

Lupe nodded, but didn't answer for several minutes. She watched the road carefully and drove her small car expertly, chewed her lip, combed her hair back with her fingers, glanced at David a few times as if trying to decide something about him.

"Primo has visions," she said. "And he hears voices. When you and Manny and Carlos were talking last night, I could almost hear you thinking 'swindle.' Primo's no swindler. He talks directly to God and God answers him in Spanish. God explains the past to him and foretells the future and issues orders for the present."

"Well, he's crazy then. Why doesn't somebody lock him up?"

"Up in the north counties he's not crazy. He's magic. He's given those people a picture of what life used to be like, before the Americans came here—rich farms and deep pasture and fat sheep. It's a false picture, I know. That's mean, hard land up there and it always has been. The Spaniards ignored those settlers, and so did the Mexicans, but . . . but they can't remember back that far. Primo remembers for them. He tells them they're a great people, a mystic race. Nobody's ever talked to them like that before. Nobody talks to them at all except around election time."

Lupe turned into the ranch, over a rattling wood bridge and a cattle guard. Only a crude plank sign identified the property—"Tafoya Ranch."

"You know Primo?" David asked.

"Oh, yes. He talked at Berkeley a year and a half ago, when he got his movement going. The students took a few days off—they're always doing that—and invited speakers from every organization you can think of—Panthers, Women's Liberation, Gay Liberation, Opium Products Incorporated, Theater of the Insane, Boy Scouts, the Pentagon, everybody. Primo sort of invited himself; no one had ever heard of him. He's a little man, quite dark—he's only first-generation in the U. S. and he has a lot of Zapotec Indian in him. He was dressed up for the occasion in those white cotton peasant pajamas they wear in southern Mexico. Nobody wears that costume in New Mexico, naturally; they'd freeze to death. But it was a good way to identify himself to the kids at school. They referred to him as Son of Emiliano Zapata. The speaker from the Panthers called him 'Whitey,' but of course they have pretty stiff color standards. So he talked—wild stuff, poetry, music. About two thirds of it was absolute bull. That's my part of the country he was talking about, and I couldn't recognize most of it. But it got to me anyway. If some eighteenth-century Tafoya hadn't done the King a favor and been granted this land, Papa would be a broke chili farmer drinking white port under a culvert every Saturday night."

They drove slowly through Los Tafoyas. The little church seemed deserted, the plastering job on the school was finished and beginning to dry, the residents had returned from their day on the range—men and boys, lean and dusty and tired. Lupe yelled jokes and greetings to many of them in clattering Spanish.

"Serfdom," she said to David as they approached Luis's house. "This is so damned close to serfdom it scares me."

She stopped the car in Luis's littered yard and got out. Miguelito, a little dried blood on his upper lip, was sitting on an overturned wheelbarrow playing with a horned toad. He smiled at his aunt and offered her the beast. Lupe picked him up, kissed him, and banged on Marta's door. "¡Oígame, tonta!" she yelled, and walked in. David heard screaming, then more yelling, all in a Spanish far too rapid for him to comprehend. Lupe stamped out of the house, her lips nearly white, and got back into the car, quivering. "That whore," she said. "That *puta*. She's got a goddamn man in there with her, both of them naked as mice. With that little *boy* right there."

"Where's Luis?"

"Hell, I don't know. She said he went off a few hours ago with some men and she was entertaining her cousin. Some entertainment."

"I couldn't understand what you were saying," David said. "I think I'm just as happy I couldn't."

Lupe got the car moving again. "I suppose I ought to get this stuff to Papa," she said, gesturing toward the ice chest. "I don't much care if those freaks turn up sterile, though. When the Mormon boy split I knew the others wouldn't know what to do. And I'd spent a week breaking Papa down, convincing him those idiots were serious about it. Damn. Everything I try goes to hell."

As they turned into the road toward the big house,

125

they could see a thick, black smoke rising, miles to the north, on the Upper Grant.

"Burning out their Russian thistle, probably," Lupe said. "Those snobby cows up there won't eat anything but watercress."

Chapter 11

CARLOS WASN'T WITH THE RAIDERS this time. He was, instead, irritating a municipal magistrate in Santa Fe by quoting long-winded and irrelevant law concerning civil rights, speedy trials, writs of certiorari and the rule of treasure trove. The magistrate didn't care. He wasn't a lawyer anyway.

Carlos's client, an unemployed swineherd named Salazar, had spent a comfortable night in jail and cheerfully corroborated the statements of two city policemen that he had drunk far too much blackberry-flavored vodka the preceding afternoon and committed a public nuisance on the mint beds in front of the fire station. By the time the magistrate had fined Salazar twenty-five dollars, and toyed with the idea of sentencing Carlos to death in the gas chamber, just to have the pleasure of watching his reaction, the men who hit the Upper Grant had finished their work and dispersed.

Luis Tafoya was with them, at once resentful and relieved that he had not been put in charge of the foray. He was uncomfortable at first in the role of Freedom Fighter for The Cause—the expression his uncle Carlos had used in his recruiting speech—but Carlos had stressed the likelihood of Luis's getting a ranch of his own, cheap, without having to wait around for Cruz to die.

Luis was a useless hand on his father's place, a clumsy and impatient *vaquero*, too arrogant to take advice from the skilled professionals, too uncoordinated to master the simplest skills of cowboying. But he was tenacious. Most ranch hands who mashed their thumbs while shoeing mounts or seared themselves with white-hot irons while branding calves would have realized eventually that they were in the wrong profession and changed jobs. Luis kept going. Someday, he knew, he'd be ramrodding the whole ranch himself. He'd work in the ranch office, hire only Anglo cowboys, and chew them out whether or not they merited it.

"Don't count on your papa," Carlos had warned him that night at Cruz's dinner party. "He might leave you the ranch, but he might not. He's tricky, you know that."

"He don't like me," Luis said.

"So do yourself a favor," Carlos went on. "Scare those *chingao* Anglo sons of bitches off the land. They scare easy anyway. They're all *maricones*. It's all *raza* land. It's ours by rights. Scare them off and we can buy it cheap."

"I ain't got no *chingao* money," Luis pointed out.

"I'll lend you the *chingao* money," Carlos said. "You're thirty years old, Luisito. It's time to be your own man."

Now Luis rode in the back of a pickup with a dozen others, all wearing domino masks over their eyes or bandannas over their faces. A burlap sack, draped with apparent carelessness, covered the license plate. When the truck stopped at the cattle guard he hopped out, opened the gate, and swung it wide. This ranch had a real sign, the kind he wanted some day. LEN-JAR-ROSE RANCH. REGISTERED HEREFORDS AND SANTA GERTRUDIS. CHAMPION GRAND

Duke Cadwallader of Hilldale at Stud. Registered Quarter Horses. For Fishing Permit See Ranch Manager.

Luis climbed the pole where the telephone line cut in from the highway. He climbed it carefully, as he had no lineman's belt and was afraid of heights. At the top he unhooked the long-handled wire cutters from his belt, dropped them accidentally, swore, climbed down (tearing his blue jeans on one of the steel pole-steps), retrieved the cutters, climbed up again cursing, and snipped the wires. He was boiling when he returned to the ground a second time and kicked the pole as hard as he could. This had no effect on the pole, but deep in his right boot he felt a toe bone crack. Luis limped back to the truck and hauled himself in.

The owner of the Len-Jar-Rose had never seen his spread and didn't want to. Morris Rosenthal had made thirty million dollars in the movies by creating stories that featured a savage, psychopathic comedian named Lenny Jarvis who specialized in falling backward, flailing his arms, into ponds, swimming pools, horse troughs, and other small bodies of water. The sight of Lenny Jarvis getting wet struck some profound chord in moviegoers, and he and Rosenthal raked the money in for years, until their association ended. Jarvis, grown rich and preposterous, had tried to dictate story lines. He actually produced one movie on his own, based on custard-pie-throwing and a cleft-palate accent he had perfected, but the fans saw that the new comedy was too subtle for his talents. Nevertheless, Rosenthal remembered his old star with affection, and in part named his tax shelter after him.

Rosenthal's business advisor recommended livestock ranching, arranged for the purchase of the land, and found a competent manager for the Len-Jar-Rose. Twice a year Sam Applewhite submitted a balance sheet on the ranch's financial condition—it was always depressingly profitable —and quarterly he dispatched to the owner 1,500 pounds of prime, four-inch-thick sirloins, cut, trimmed, aged, and frozen on the premises.

Sam heard the pickup approaching and reached into his desk for fishing permits. The eight streams that coursed the ranch foamed with rainbows, Dolly Varden, cutthroat, and German browns. Licensed fishermen who paid an extra dollar for the private ranch permit could catch unheard-of monsters in the pools. Sam himself had pulled a seven-pound native trout from a stream only three feet wide and had had to eat the brute himself. The cowboys were steak eaters and believed that fish was food for bears.

Standing on the porch of the adobe ranch headquarters, Sam waved to the truckful of men. He noticed the masks and bandannas, thought "The return of the Dalton Gang" to himself, and raised his hands quickly when one of the riders pointed a .30-caliber Winchester at his head.

The driver of the truck, a Mean Romero from Vado Ancho, got out and walked up the porch steps. He patted Sam all over, looking for a weapon.

"I'm not armed," Sam said. "What the hell do you people want? We don't keep cash in the safe."

"Where's your stock?" Romero asked.

"My stock? You mean the cattle? Hell, they're up in summer pasture, way up there in the mountains, about twelve miles. If you're rustling you won't be able to get more than a couple head in that little truck of yours."

Luis limped over to the foot of the steps. "You own this place?" he asked.

"No, sir," Sam said. "This ranch belongs to Mr. Morris Rosenthal of Bel Air, California. I'm the manager."

"Where's the hands?"

"Most of them are up with the cattle. There's some down the road, at the corrals. Some of them are probably bunked in right now. The bunkhouse is next to the corrals."

"Do they have guns?" Romero asked.

"There's some rifles in the bunkhouse," Sam admitted. "Now don't you go shooting any of my men."

Luis, Romero and two others conferred briefly in Spanish. Twelve miles, they decided, was too long a piece to drive on unfamiliar land, four to five thousand head of cattle were too many to kill with their limited supply of ammunition, and some of the cowboys with the herd might have rifles with them for coyotes or cougars.

"Where's the corrals?" Romero demanded.

Sam gestured with his head. "About a half mile down this road. If you people will tell me what you want, maybe we can . . ."

"What you got in your hand?" Luis asked.

"Fishing permits."

"Piss on your fishing permits."

They left a man to guard Sam, piled back into the truck, and drove to the corrals. Only the old adobe stables and tack rooms remained from the days when Tafoyas had owned the ranch. Succeeding owners had put in cinderblock houses for the married hands, a long frame bunkhouse for the bachelors, a cookhouse with dining hall attached, and a solid barn. There were more people about than any of the men expected—women and young children, mainly, but at least a dozen hands. Romero split his

131

men into two ill-disciplined squads and ordered them to herd everyone at gunpoint into a branding pen. The cowboys sleeping in the bunkhouse emerged blinking and confused, but quiet. The women made a few sharp-tongued remarks, and the children either cried or giggled. Only the blacksmith protested, a nearly senile cowboy of the sort known throughout the West as a codger. He had learned Spanish forty years before along the New Mexico–Chihuahua border and now employed an interesting string of pejoratives about the raiders, focusing on their lack of sexual aptitude, their cowardice, and their preference for sheep over women. Luis, whose vocabulary of abuse in Spanish was pretty much limited to *"chingao,"* was impressed by the richness of the old man's expression. Romero, however, took personally the attack on his *machismo* and clubbed the blacksmith near the temple with the butt of his carbine.

They brought all the saddles out of the tack rooms, including Sam Applewhite's beautiful old McClellan and his ceremonial Western with hammered Mexican silver ornaments, put them into the barn, and poured gasoline on the saddles and the bales of cured hay. Romero lit a Fourth of July sparkler and threw it into the barn from well outside. When the greasy smoke started to climb, some of the women in the branding pen began to scream.

It was incredibly noisy as the burning barn crackled and roared and the stallions reared and kicked in their stalls, terrified by the fire and the blood smell. In the corrals and stables, the men shot all the horses, the working stock as well as the quarter-horse racing animals.

Champion Grand Duke Cadwallader of Hilldale was a lover, not a fighter, and he stood dumbly while Romero essayed a few graceless veronicas before him, using a blanket from the bunkhouse as a cape, and shot him between his stubby horns. His short forelegs crumpled and he pitched forward onto his nose, a ton of prime beef and paternity, cooling off quickly in his air-conditioned stall.

Luis used his pistol, a massive .357 magnum, to put a hole in the engine blocks of all the vehicles—pickups, Jeeps, and land cruisers, as well as a few private automobiles. He was a poor shot, but at a range of two feet he couldn't miss. The people in the branding pen were silent now.

At the ranch headquarters, Sam was still standing with his hands in the air; the young man guarding him spoke little English and couldn't understand Sam's request to lower his aching arms. When the truck returned to pick him up, Sam yelled, "What did you do? Did you kill any of my people?"

"We didn't kill no *people*," Luis told him.

"You stupid bastards," Sam said. "You crazy Mexican sons of bitches." A few tears began to well in his light gray eyes. "That was a sixty-five-thousand-dollar bull." The pickup began to move away as Sam said, "God damn every one of you." Sam was fifty-five years old, gray-haired, six and a half feet tall. His monogrammed Western shirt and his Levi's were ironed and crisp. His dove-gray Stetson sat perfectly straight on his head. His Tony Lama boots shone black in the late afternoon sun. He looked, Luis thought, like every *chingao* Texan Anglo *hijo de puta* he'd ever seen in the movies. He pulled his heavy pistol from its holster, braced both hands on the bouncing tailgate of the truck, aimed for the "S.A." sewn over Sam's breast pocket and shot a ragged hole through the fishing permits in Sam's hand.

Chapter 12

"DOES THAT HURT?" Cruz asked him.

"No. Ouch. *That* hurt."

"You're all fixed up, *cuate*. That man in Lamesa did a nice job. It's gonna be visible, but distinguished-looking."

"You can tell people you got it dueling in Heidelberg," Lupe said.

"What do you charge for pulling out stitches?" David asked.

"A medical man of my international reputation can't sell his talents cheap. Call it fifty dollars a stitch. Better make it seventy-five. I'm splitting the fee with my attractive colleague here."

"That's an outrage," David said. "All she did was hold my head steady. Anybody could have done that. You didn't have to fly your attractive colleague in from Zurich."

Cruz threw the tweezers into his black bag and snapped it shut. "If you're going to question my decisions, you can get yourself another physician. Absolute trust is a major part of the doctor-patient relationship. Absolute trust and a willingness on the patient's part to pay through the nose."

David eased himself painfully off the Sears, Roebuck couch in the *sala* and walked about the room like an old man. "All right," he said, "I trust you and I'll pay. Now what can you do for a sore behind?"

"Not my field," Cruz said.

"Dr. Shultz of Nuremberg is the leader in that area, I believe," Lupe said.

"Ah, yes. Shultz. An excellent man. We can have him here in twenty-four hours."

"All the best people go to him," Lupe explained. "Garbo. The Churchills. The Kennedys. The Earl of Snowden."

"Let's go cure some clap," Cruz said. "You want to come along, David?"

"No, thanks. That's not *my* field."

"Oh, come on, David," Lupe said. "There's nothing to it."

"I'm not a doctor."

"Neither is Lupe. But if that's worrying you, repeat after me: 'Blood is thicker than water.'"

"Blood is thicker than water."

"*Now* you're a doctor. That was the Hippocratic Oath."

David retrieved the penicillin from Ingeborg's refrigerator, repacked it with ice in the Styrofoam ice chest and carried it to the waiting truck.

"Would you stop by the school a minute, Papa?" Lupe said. "I'm supposed to get some books in today. I asked the man at the Depository to leave them on the *portal*."

Cruz nodded and started the engine. The truck's bouncing sent waves of fresh agony through David's thighs.

"Nothing you can do about it," Cruz said, "except get back on a horse and ride it out. I'm sorry about that mare. I forgot about her gait."

"Quite all right. Lupe, how does that school work? Is it state-supported or what?"

"It's accredited," she said, "but Papa pays for it, maintenance and so on. The state provides the books. It's just for the little kids. After sixth grade the students go off to Santa Fe."

"You pay the teachers' salaries? That's awfully generous of you."

"There's only two teachers," Cruz said, "and one of them doesn't get a salary. Mrs. Mondragon gets three thousand dollars a year. Lupe gets a chance to sell left-wing ideas to unformed minds."

"I teach straight academics," she said. "They don't start on Lenin until the third grade."

Lupe and David carried the books into the bright schoolroom and set them down. The walls were brilliant with children's art; stories and poems were tacked everywhere, in English and Spanish.

"That's a fine idea," David said. "In Texas the kids can get bopped for speaking Spanish anywhere on school property."

"It's happened here, too. Over in Little Texas, Spanish is considered some sort of speech defect. Nancy Mondragon and I conduct all our classes in both languages, English one day and Spanish the next. When we graduate them they're fluent in both."

"Very civilized."

"David . . ."

"Yes."

"Are you *really* a Texan?"

"Yes, ma'am. Born and raised in Beaumont. Cheered for the Rice Owls. Carried whiskey in a paper sack into the restaurants and ordered mixers. I even wore high-heeled boots for a while, but they hurt my feet."

Cruz began to honk the truck's horn.

"Do you mind my asking what you're doing here? I know that sounds rude, but I'm curious. Papa's just enigmatic when I ask him."

"I'm not really doing anything, Lupe. I suppose you could say I'm accepting your father's hospitality while I recuperate from a traumatic experience. I screwed up a business deal for my boss and got canned."

Cruz hit the horn again, and they went back to the truck. Lupe locked the door behind her.

All the Gardeners of Eden were at the dome when they arrived. The approved transportation for the counterculture, three antique school buses with a riot of flowers painted on them, were parked in the withered garden.

Lupe pulled out her bullhorn. "ALL YOU FREAKS OUTSIDE. SHORT-ARM INSPECTION."

The blond giant, crouching low, came out of the dome. "You don't have to be crude," he said.

"Get everybody outside," Cruz told him. "Everybody."

There were twenty-six adults, twelve of them women, and five children. They formed a ragged semicircle, hirsute, wan, dirty, their sloppily tie-dyed clothes stained and dusty, the fire of the great experiment long faded from their eyes.

"Are any of you sensitive to penicillin?" Cruz asked

137

them. "If you are, or you think you are, speak up. It can kill you."

No one answered him.

"Gonorrhea," Cruz went on, "is a lot worse than a bad cold, no matter what you think. I am assuming that you are all infected. Today, or tomorrow at the latest, I want all of you—the children too—to go to the Public Health Service Laboratory in Albuquerque for blood tests. The tests are free. You have to go. It's the law, and it's one of the few good laws I know about. If you find this embarrassing, you should have thought of that before you started playing musical sleeping bags."

One of the girls spoke up. "Why the kids? They couldn't have it because kids don't ball."

"Kids use towels," Cruz said. "Have you ever seen a baby with a gonorrheal infection of the eyes? Now, I will treat the men out here. The girls can go back inside and Lupe will treat you in there. After you've had your shot, give your full name and age to Dr. Reed here."

"You a doctor?" one of the girls asked Lupe.

"No," she said, "but I'm hell on the long dart. Inside, ladies."

"One more thing," Cruz said. "This will take several days. You will all have to continue blood tests until you're found free of infection. Until then I want you to refrain from sexual intercourse. Abstinence won't kill you. I've practiced it myself for years."

The women went inside with Lupe. Cruz gave David a notebook and a ball-point pen and gestured to the giant. "You first," he said. "Drop your pants."

"What's your name?" David asked him after Cruz had given him the injection.

"They call me Krishnamurti."

138

"What's your real name?"

"Tell him," Cruz yelled over. "That's the law too."

"We all took new names," the giant said. "I'm Krish-namurti."

"Okay," David said. "What was your name before this incarnation?"

"Myron Kaminsky."

Cruz was giving the last shot when Lupe came out of the dome. "Papa," she said, "somebody raided the Upper Grant yesterday. Burned the barn, killed some animals. They almost killed an old man."

"Holy Jesus. Who told you?"

"It's on television. Manny's having a press conference tonight."

"That won't do any goddamn good. He never says anything."

"That's the way to go, man," the giant said. "Burn asses. Varroooom!"

"Listen, friend. Up until seventy-five years ago that land up there belonged to *my* family. If anyone should want to get it back, it's me. And I don't want it bad enough to hurt people. If you want to do the world some good, learn how to plant vegetables."

Old Echeagaray was waiting beside the road as they drove back. He held up a dead bobcat, and Cruz stopped the truck beside him.

"I shot a lion, *jefe*."

"I don't know what I'd do without you, *viejo*," Cruz told him.

Luis was sitting in the *sala* when they arrived, his bare foot propped on a hassock.

"What the hell happened to you?" Cruz asked him.

"I hurt my foot. I stubbed it."

Cruz examined it and wiggled the middle toe. "It's broken," he said. "You're going to have to stop kicking automobiles."

"Just fix it, old man."

"Nothing I can do unless you want a cast. Just stay off it. Don't wear shoes till the swelling goes down. It'll knit."

"You might stay home a little more," Lupe said. "Miguelito needs your company."

"You can soak it in cold water," Cruz said. "Or maybe I mean hot water. Hell, it doesn't matter."

"Marta don't like me hangin' around the house."

"Do whatever you want, Luis. Don't ask me to get mixed up in your marriage."

Luis limped out. "I wish I could love that boy," Cruz said. "It's terrible not to love your own son." He shook his head. "I wish he'd turned out a little more like you, Lupe. Not that you're any prize."

"I still have all ten fingers," she pointed out.

"You hear how my daughter talks to me? She's a twenty-six-year-old scorpion."

"If you gentlemen will excuse me," Lupe said. "I'm going to take a shower. After looking at a dozen unwashed fannies I'm feeling a little unsanitary."

"Would you be offended," David said, when she had gone, "if I told you that I like your daughter?"

"Lupe? How could anybody like Lupe?"

"Somehow I do."

"I told you, she's a jailbird. She's a radical. She's a nut. She wears men's pajamas."

"She just teaches school. My mother taught school too."

"You know the Compañía? That crazy outfit that hit

140

the Upper Grant? Well, it was probably them, but they'll never prove it. Anyway, the first thing Lupe did when she got back from California was join it. Primo Rael was running around in all directions, but Lupe got him organized. She set up a treasury. She started their little newspaper. She wrote editorials. She even wrote Primo's goddamn speeches for a while. Then she figured they needed a lawyer and she convinced Carlos to take the job. That was the worst advice anybody's ever been given, by the way."

"Did she ever quit?"

"Well, yes, she did. She *said* she was disillusioned, but I think that's a lot of *cago*. I think she just got bored. Right now she's probably putting together something like the Mexican Mafia."

"I like her anyway," David said.

"Wonderful. Marry her. Take her away. She'll have you throwing bombs at the Bank of America inside a month. You can spend your lives in adjoining cells. I'm beginning to wonder now if maybe I didn't have this on my mind when I pulled you out of your Mercedes. 'Aha, here's some stunned sucker who'll take Lupe off my hands.'"

Ingeborg managed to get enchiladas together for lunch, but her mind was still on Officer Macauliffe. Lupe talked happily to David about the school, which would open in a few weeks, and invited him to be a guest lecturer. David said he could give them a brief talk on either petroleum geology or real estate law, but he didn't think the fourth-graders would be terribly interested.

"We could have used you back in 1895," Cruz said.

"How did your father lose the land, Cruz?"

"It was my grandfather. Oh, it was happening to a

lot of people back then, but it happened to him worse. The Government was confirming all the private grants—it took about thirty years—but to confirm the grants there had to be accurate surveys first. Have you ever seen a royal Spanish charter?"

"Lots of them," David said.

"Then you know how they're written—'From this rock to that tree to that creek and then back to this rock.' The Spanish were pretty sloppy in their land descriptions, and when the Americans came they insisted on something a little more technical. You Anglos got no poetry in your souls."

"Maybe not, but we know how to use a transit."

"Okay. The original Tafoya grant seemed pretty clear. It used good landmarks. 'From the middle of the Pacheco River where it is joined by the Cuervo River west along the Cuervo to the spine of the cordillera and then north to the *colina*, east along the base of the *colina* to the Pacheco River and then south to the original point.' No mistake about that. Bounded on two sides by rivers, on one side by a' mountain range and on the other by a bluff."

"Didn't the grant give any distances—leagues or *varas* or anything?"

"No it didn't, and that was the *chisguete*. That bluff you saw on the north edge of the ranch: that wasn't the goddamn *colina* the charter referred to. There's another one about twenty miles north, much higher, maybe a hundred and fifty feet. *That's* the one that marked the true northern boundary. My grandfather was trying to get the whole five hundred sections confirmed. The Government confirmed only a hundred and twenty. The rest of it reverted to the Territory, it went up for auction, my grandfather tried to buy it back, but he was outbid. I don't suppose I have to tell you the man who bought it was the surveyor's brother-in-law."

"All veddy legal," Lupe said.

"I don't know," Cruz went on. "Maybe five hundred sections is just too much land for one man to own. But hell, he was responsible for a couple of hundred people and God knows how many sheep. It was everything to that man. It was his life. My father was just a boy then. He told me that the day after the auction my grandfather took his favorite stallion and rode the Upper Grant all day, just rode across it, up into the mountains, along the streams, through the woods and the pastures—a middle-aged plump man on a black horse, not speaking a word, tears on his face, saying good-bye to his land."

Chapter 13

FROM the Albuquerque *Standard:*

SANTA FE—State Police are investigating a series of violent, armed attacks on pirvately-owned ranches and frams in three northern counties, which resulted in widespeard loss of livestock and other porpety.
of livetsock and other propertu.

Acting State Police Chief Joe Sierra said his men are "checking out all leads," and added, "We Hope to make some arrests very snoo."

Governor Manuel Tafoya, in a sepcial television broadcsat, scored the violence and called upon all citizens of New Mexico to "remain calm and avoid emotionalism." He announced that his office was looking into the matter.

Militant land-grant leader Privatino Rael, whose organization claims owndership of thousands of acres of old Spanish grnats, denied that his group was in any way repson

144

denied taht his grop was in any way responsible
no medical reason to douche unless a physician
advises it. The mucosa lining the normal vag-
for the violent raids.

Chapter 14

NEWS STORY by Tobias Lujan, part-time correspondent for *La Lucha:*

Last Saturday, over in Rossville, where the Gringo Power Structure still exploits and grinds down our Chicano brothers and sisters and degrades our proud heritage and makes us speak the "hated language" (English) in school and every place else, some brothers and sisters were picketing Larry Dugan's groceriteria and supermarket because the manager and assistant managers are all Anglos and the brothers and sisters have lousy jobs like Check-out Boy and Clerk. It was a real peaceful demo, nobody was hurting anybody, all the brothers and sisters were doing was to carry some signs and singing. They were NOT blocking the sidewalk and they were NOT hassling any of the customers and they were NOT damaging any private property, and none of those things Mr. Dugan said were being done. Dugan is a well-known Chicano-hater and racist and liar, and very in with the

Power Structure in Rossville, which is all Anglo and *tejano*.

Then Officers Herbie Blessing and Mike Larimer from the Rossville Police Department, two very well-known pigs who have a history of being brutal to the Chicano people, and Officer Tony Lobato, a Tio Taco that all the brothers and sisters hate because he is a *vendido* and a lard-ass, came up to where the poor people were having their demo and they told them to move on, they were blocking the sidewalk. Then Dugan came out of his store and he told the pigs that Benny Roybal, who was leading the demo, was a communist and trying to ruin his business. So Roybal came over and said he was within his rights, they were only picketing and that's allowed under the Anglo law, and said he wasn't a communist, he was a registered Democrat and a Catholic. Officer Blessing warned him he was wising off, and then he yelled to the people to take their ——— signs and moved on, and Officer Lobato repeated the order in Spanish and poked Roybal in the belly with his stick. Then Roybal's wife, Gloria, accidentally dropped her sign because she was nervous the *chotas* were going to hurt her man, and it fell and hit Officer Lobato on the head.

Anybody could tell it was an accident, but the two Anglo pigs, who love to bust heads and have injured a lot of brothers and sisters in the past few years, waded into the crowd with their sticks. There were a lot of women in the demo, and some young people who were just learning to stand up for their rights as citizens, and how do you think they felt when they saw these so-called officers of the law breaking the law themselves and denying people their rights?

Some people got their heads knocked open and were bleeding, while the pigs were swinging their sticks left and right. They didn't care who they hit, just as long as they hit a Hispano, and then some more police cars drove up and half the pig force came out and began knocking on skulls and macing the poor people. The *vendido* Lobato tripped or slipped and fell through a plate glass window, causing breakage. This was the incident the pigs called Damaging Private Property.

Eleven of our Raza brothers and sisters are now in the can with all kinds of incorrect charges brought against them—resisting arrest and disturbing the peace and assault—when all they were doing was protesting unfair racist treatment and standing up for their rights.

The Rossville and Albuquerque papers, which are owned by the rich Anglo racists and written for the rich Anglo racists, wrote very inaccurate stories about this incident, and this is the only true account. *La Lucha* once again has the only correct and unbiased account, where both sides are presented fairly.

SUBSCRIBE TO *LA LUCHA* AND GET ALL THE FACTS. *¡VIVA CHICANISMO!*

Chapter 15

"SOUTH WALES on a Sunday," Lupe said. She untethered her horse, a shiny roan gelding, and led him to another patch of sweet mountain grass.

"What's that supposed to mean?" David asked.

"Nothing to do." She sat beside David and took another drumstick from the leather food bag. "I don't even want this drumstick."

"Have another beer," he suggested.

"Pour it in one of the pans and give it to Rocinante," she said, indicating David's horse. "The poor brute's a beer freak." She nibbled her chicken. "My grandmother," she went on, "lived fifteen years after her husband died. She never left the ranch. She called it gadding. 'And how would it look now if a respectable widow of my years went gadding about?' So she sat around the house and knitted eight hours a day, big gray greasy sweaters and scarves full of sheep tallow, and got that tight-lipped look whenever one of her sons had a drink. Poor, sour old lady. Respectable, of course—God, she was respectable! —but sour. She'd look up from her knitting sometimes and say, 'South Wales on a Sunday.' I think it expressed the ultimate in boredom."

"No Welsh in my family, as far as I know. French, Dutch, a little Caddo Indian."

"Typical Anglo," Lupe said, and smiled. "You're well off. The Welsh are a dwarfy, dark, broody people. Every two or three generations the Tafoya men marry outside the clan. It's good genetics, I guess. A lot of this state's trouble is inbreeding. There's a village in the Sangre de Cristo mountains inhabited by twelve-fingered half-wits. Anyone with the normal complement of digits is considered ill equipped."

"It sounds like the Big Thicket," David said. "That's a swampy patch in East Texas. The people there run to pink eyes and hip deformities. New Mexico's not the only survivor of the stone age."

"You're just saying that to be nice."

David knocked crumbs from a cake pan, filled it with Coors beer, the *vin ordinaire* of the Southwest, and offered it to Rocinante. She sucked it in noisily and nickered with appreciation.

"Why do you stay with that horse?" Lupe asked. "You rode her all during roundup; jolt, jolt, jolt for nearly a month."

"We're used to each other. I have calluses built up in the right places. It's a kind of unbalanced line: a big one on the inside of my right knee, a little one on the left thigh, and a few more in places I'd rather not specify. It's no worse than riding a bicycle with a triangular wheel."

A cool wind, a wind with October snap in it, came down the ridge of the mountain, shivering the evergreens and the golden aspens. Rocinante and Lupe's gelding, Volapié, champed the grass. David took a plastic cup

150

from the food bag, knelt beside the stream, and scooped up some water. It was clear and delicious, stinging cold. "The water's safe to drink, I suppose."

"So far," Lupe said. "I've drunk it all my life and only had typhoid twelve times."

"Can't ask for better than that," he said, and drank another cupful.

Despite his years of city living, car-driving, desk-sitting, and bourbon-drinking, David had found Cruz's roundup profoundly satisfying. The hands started early. They had worked the cattle down from the summer pasture at a creeping, gentle pace so as not to run the T-bones off them. David was not surprised to learn that Cruz did it the old way—no Jeeps, no walkie-talkies, no helicopters; just cowboys and quarter horses. The hands communicated over the long distances by whistling, a piercing *vaquero* code of signals that he had heard about, but never heard.

He insisted on joining the roundup. Cruz said no; the concussion was too recent. David persisted. Cruz smiled and gave in. David chose Rocinante, the lurching mare, because she was sweet and gentle and responsive and, like him, handicapped.

His saddle sores abated, finally. He was thrown twice and fell off, for no accountable reason, twice more. He killed a rattlesnake with a rock. He sprained his shoulder, spent several sleepless nights in a bedroll chewing aspirin for muscle soreness, sunburned the backs of his hands until they curled up like a falcon's talons, ate beans and steak and bacon and tough biscuits and tougher tortillas. He sweated off eleven pounds of office flab and retaught himself the youthful art of spitting for distance. He learned, with disappointment, that he would never be skilled with a rope. He learned with pleasure a dozen New Mexican *vaquero* songs, some of them astonishingly sexual and explicit.

Cruz himself seemed uninterested in the roundup. He left all technical decisions to the *capataz*, a stringy, savage little man named Juan María Perez who punished each minor mistake or clumsiness with a lash of Spanish abuse, but spoke to the cattle as if they were beloved children. Perez watched David closely the first few days in the mountains, realized his crew was burdened with a dedicated but barely competent gringo amateur, and merely cautioned him not to get hurt.

Perez saved his cruelest words for Luis, who shambled up the cordillera two days late, hung over, his sharp face marred by one of Marta's scratches, still favoring his broken toe.

Luis watched the herding, slouched arrogantly in his saddle. The slow movement of the stock seemed to infuriate him. He screamed at the nearest hands to hurry it up, but they ignored him. They had ignored him on every roundup since he was fifteen years old. Luis charged his mount into one of the placid heifers and whipped its flank with a rope end. His horse reared. Luis whistled and yelled, "*¡Ándale!*" A dozen nearby head began to trot nervously downhill.

Perez rode over to him and gently put a hand on Luis's arm. He knew one didn't strike the boss's son. He said, "As I told you last year, Luis, and the year before that: that animal is beefsteak and beefsteak is money. Our horses are built for exercise. Our cattle are built for eating. There is no hurry. The buyers will wait. Your father will wait. Let the animals fatten as they descend. Do you understand?"

"It's too slow."

"Perhaps, Luis, but I set the speed of the animals because I am *capataz*. That is what your father pays me for. When you work under my direction you accept my orders. You do not have to work under my direction. We would all do a better job if you stayed home."

Luis jerked his outthrust chin toward David, who was trying to convince a bawling calf, by reasoning with it, that it should return to its mother's side. "What about him? I suppose that Anglo *pendejo* can give me orders, too. He's been polishing the old man's *palo* all summer."

Perez removed his hand from Luis's arm, and turned his horse. "No, he has no authority. He volunteered to help us. He hasn't much skill, but he takes all orders willingly and does his best. He also has a fair baritone voice, and he has taught us a wonderful song about the Harlot of Jerusalem. So far he has not given me one ounce of shit. You have not been with us five minutes, and from you I have received a bucketful. Now stay with us and help us, if you wish, or return to your wife and child. And take care not to fall from your great horse."

Luis remained, muttering and dark-faced. Few talked to him, and they did so only when absolutely necessary. Cruz rode up to the main herd sometimes, though he was usually busy with a small crew in the valley readying the dry-pens. When he arrived, Luis would straighten from his gloomy slouch and try to look cheerful and efficient. He would mumble something to the nearest hand, receive no reply, and laugh as if a joke had been exchanged. Then he would sneak a look at his father.

Cruz always spoke to all the hands. He would say,

"You're doing fine, *hijo*," to his son, and ask David sympathetically about his sore behind, never failing to recommend a visit to the fashionable Dr. Shultz. He treated the sprains, cuts, scrapes, and bruises of the men and cured David's clawed hands with gobs of U.S.P. lanolin, which, he explained, was pure sheep tallow, its price raised to astronomical levels by the wicked drug manufacturers.

Lupe rode Volapié up to the camp one evening after school. She wore a long riding skirt in deference to the older men, who believed that women in pants were an invitation to mortal sin, and sat perkily on a sidesaddle. She brought her bullhorn, but Perez was quick to forbid its use. "The animals will gain weight only if they have calm spirits," he explained. "If you yell at them, they will think they have done wrong. They will feel confused and remorseful."

She shared dinner with the men—steak, beans, and coffee—and told David that, from a half mile away, she was honestly unable to distinguish him from the real cowboys.

"Hey, Perez," she said across the fire. "How's the gringo doing?"

Perez constructed his answer as he swallowed a mouthful of beans. "Within the limits of his natural capacity," he said in Spanish, "he is the best hand I have."

When the herds arrived at the pens in the valley, most of the men dispersed. Those remaining cut out cows and calves, who would winter over on hay, while a small crew began to weigh yearling steers and heifers. Despite their trek from the cordillera, the cattle were rested and as fat as grass could make them.

Cruz and Mr. Munn, the buyer from Colorado—a traveling representative for a feedlot syndicate—were talking about thirty cents a pound when David got to the pens, freshly showered and dressed in his blue suit. Cruz introduced them.

"We're talking thirty cents," Cruz told him.

"It was twenty-nine and a half last year," the buyer said. "A satisfactory arrangement to all parties." He turned to David. "That's for what we call the 'meat frame,' Mr. Reed. Mr. Tafoya's animals provide what you might call a skeleton or armature of beef, and we put the weight of meat on them at the feed lot."

"Interesting," David said.

"Thirty and a half might be better," Cruz said. "Wetter year. Better grass. Better animals."

The buyer averted his head to watch the hands as they herded eight soporific steers onto the scales. Perez adjusted the weights. "*Seis mil, ochocientos noventa y seis,*" he called to the buyer's tallyman, who was recording weights.

"I'm not sure my employers could find thirty and a half possible, Cruz. We might negotiate thirty and a quarter. Corn's not cheap this year, as you know. There's blight."

"They're good animals," Cruz said.

"They're an adequate frame," the buyer said.

"Well, let me think about it."

"I believe thirty-*two* and a quarter cents a pound might be equitable," David told the buyer, who turned white under his sunburn.

"Now, David," Cruz said, "just let us . . ."

"Corn is high, as you say, Mr. Munn," David acknowledged. "That's why I didn't mention a price of thirty-three, which would be a fair minimum if your feed grains weren't pegged at a premium."

"Mr. Reed, are you empowered to, ah . . .?"

"Oh, yes indeed, sir. Cruz, may I talk to you privately for a moment?"

The two men walked a dozen yards away from the buyer, leaned on the corral fence, and huddled.

"What the hell are you trying to do to me?"

"I'm trying to make you some money. Will you trust me? Please?"

"Trust you? Jesus, man, that's almost half a year's income in those pens. You don't know anything about cows."

"Maybe not," David admitted, "but I know about buying and selling. And I've been trying to learn the jargon from your back copies of *Southwestern Stockman*. Please, let me try to get you a better price. Your heart's too soft."

"Jesus," Cruz said. "Jesus." He removed his hat and wiped his forehead with a bandanna. "Okay. Try it. But don't push too hard."

Munn had regained something of his composure when they got back to him and decided to take the whole thing as a joke.

"Thirty-two and a quarter," he said. "That's kind of an eye-popper, Mr. Reed. How about fifty cents a pound and a Swiss watch for each head? Or perhaps you'd like my right arm. You might find some use for it. I've grown tired of it, to tell the truth."

"Had lunch here today, did you?"

"Why, yes, I did, sir. Very nourishing."

"Steak?"

"Yes, sir. A nice little rib eye, medium rare. Side of *posole*. Can't fault the cooking."

"We slaughtered that animal yesterday," David said. "Fresh beef just off pasture. No aging at all."

"That so? Well, it *was* a little vealy. I'm surprised you'd slaughter an unfattened yearling. Seems unnatural."

"That meat's immature, I grant you, but choice. These animals are a lot more than a meat frame. Handful of corn a day, and they'll turn into prime in no time at all. They're not starvation cases, Mr. Munn. That's not gaunt beef. Thirty-three is more than fair, but we'll knock off three quarters of a cent on the corn-blight issue, and because we're good citizens."

The buyer blinked several times and shifted his weight. "Thirty-two and a quarter," he said, repeating the number in awestruck tones as if he were figuring the distance to Saturn in inches.

David pressed on. "Those eight head just moving off the scales weighed in at six thousand eight hundred and ninety-six pounds. That's eight hundred and sixty-two average, about fifty pounds over median weight in four Southwestern states, a good thirty-five pounds over valley stock. I'm sure you're familiar with the figures."

"Maybe so, Mr. Reed, but they still have to fatten."

"Fatten, yes, but not as much and not as expensively. This is the best grass-fed stock you'll find in New Mexico. Fat and happy and healthy and tender. Tender right now. You said so yourself. Thirty-two and a quarter."

"Impossible."

"Walt Gordon in Topeka doesn't think so. He's offered thirty-one and three quarters, and he'll have to truck them twice as far as you. We told him we'd think it over. We'd prefer you to get them because you buy from Mr. Tafoya more regularly. Isn't that right, Cruz?"

"What?" said Cruz, blinking. "Oh. Yes. I'd say three times out of four Munn's lot buys my stock. About that."

"Right," David went on. "So you're a regular customer, and we'd like to favor you. Let's talk thirty-two and a quarter."

"Corn's really high. Let's talk thirty-two."

"Cruz?"

"What?" Cruz said again. "Yes, all right. Thirty-two. Fine."

"Thirty-two, then," David said, and shook Munn's hand, which twitched nervously in his. "You're getting these beauties for nothing. It's rustling, that's what it is."

"Rustling," Munn said. "I didn't *say* thirty-two. I said I'd *talk* thirty-two."

"You're a hell of a trader," David said. "I hope your company appreciates it."

"Thirty-two cents a pound," Cruz said, walking over and shaking Munn's hand. "We'll have close to nine fifty, a thousand head probably. Get 'em counted tomorrow. You want to do that contract now, or you want a drink? I still have some of that single-malt Scotch you like."

"No, I think I'll go up and see Sam Applewhite right now." He drew a deep breath. "Sam's a reasonable fellow. Mr. Reed"—he turned to David and offered his hand again—"I took you for a city man."

"I am a city man. I'm just sort of trying my wings at this."

"Uh-huh," said Munn. "Well, I hope you never turn to crime on a large scale. Good-bye, Cruz."

"Good-bye," Cruz said. "Come again next year."

When Munn had climbed into his company pickup and driven away, Cruz looked at David for a long time. He was leaner and more sunburned, but he still looked like the man lying asleep in the overturned Mercedes.

"Where'd you learn to do that, *cuate?* That's the highest price I *ever* got for beef."

"They're worth it," David said. "Nobody got robbed. They're worth more, probably, but you said not to push."

"Who the hell is Walt Gordon? Did you just make up that name?"

"No, of course not. Gordon really does run a feedlot and a slaughterhouse in Topeka. He has five or six producing oil fields scattered around here and there, too. He and C. C. Cotton play poker together. Munn knows who he is. Everybody knows his own competition. I just, well, I took a chance. A bluff. No harm done."

Cruz turned back to the pens to watch the weighing. Munn's tallyman was still writing figures on his clipboard. Those cattle already weighed were getting their first drink of water of the day.

"What if he'd called your bluff?"

David shrugged. "Nothing. He'd have called me a liar and bought your stock for thirty and a quarter."

After dinner that evening—a roast cut from the slaughtered yearling, which, David and Cruz had to admit, *was* a little vealy—Cruz offered David a job.

"Doing what?" David asked. "You only dicker for your beef once a year."

"Like I said, there's a lot of paper work to running a ranch, and I usually let it slide. You can read a contract."

"That I can surely do."

"That thing I signed with Munn today. For all I know, it was a marriage license."

"No, it was okay. You sold X head at thirty-two cents a pound. That's all it said."

"See what I mean? You're useful. You know anything about taxes?"

"Try me," David said.

"Of course, I'll have to pay you. I hate to pay salaries. It takes all the friendship out of a thing."

"I come high," David said. "Cotton paid me sixty-five thousand a year, never mind the little fringes and bonuses and stock options."

"I was thinking more along the lines of two hundred and fifty a month, plus room and board."

"I'll take it."

"Of course, I'll have to get a letter of recommendation from your former employer. What was his name again?"

Now, sitting on the mountainside, Lupe said, "You're trying to make Papa rich. Why? He's already rich."

"That's not it," he insisted. "Buying and selling is a kind of game; a game I used to be good at. I've been out of practice for a while. It was just as much fun to horse-trade for a cent and three quarters as it was to mess around with multiples of a hundred thousand dollars. With other people's money, naturally."

"You made him nervous that day, but very happy."

"I was trying to earn my keep, Lupe. Nobody asked me to, I know, but I'd been slouching around here like an invalid aunt, sleeping on silk, drinking first-class whiskey, stoking myself with chow, and interfering in conversations. I'm really too heavy and too old to start learning how to be a cowboy. Perez was good about it, but no professional likes to see an amateur screw up his work. I was looking for a job. Now I have a good one."

"This isn't Texas," Lupe said. "New Mexico's a poor state. We're always fighting Mississippi for bottom honors —personal income, infant mortality, literacy. Really, we're twenty years behind everybody else in most things, a hundred years behind them in a few. They're teaching the kids with television in California. Here I'm spreading mud plaster on the schoolhouse by hand. My most recent textbooks date from the Harding administration."

"Bitter, bitter," David said. "You're forgetting the benefits." He pointed to the clear mountain stream. "You can still drink water that doesn't taste like something dipped from an old swimming pool. Try a glass from the Houston Ship Channel sometime."

They cleaned up their picnic and gave their horses a drink from the stream. As they rode down into the valley, in the early evening, they could see the abandoned domehouse, its gaudy paint fading, the failed truck garden brown and dry behind it. Once pronounced cured, the Gardeners of Eden had dispersed. In lieu of the last month's rent, they had offered Cruz two keys of marijuana, ten pounds of soya flour, and one of the babies, whose mother had lost interest in the novelties of child-rearing. Cruz had waived payment.

"Another of my great and decent projects shot in the ass," Lupe said. "I was apparently born to teach in a one-room schoolhouse. I'll be a skinny, horse-faced old lady with left-wing tendencies and nervous mannerisms. I'll keep a fading autographed picture of Eldridge Cleaver hidden in my top right-hand drawer. I'll . . ." She noticed again the brutal lurch of Rocinante, whose movements tossed David up and down in unsyncopated arcs. "Are you *sure* that doesn't hurt?"

"Not any more," he said. "Rocinante and I are as one. Moving poetry. And she has feelings, too. What if all the other horses got ridden, and Rocinante had to stay in her stall munching oats, feeling like a wallflower at the Senior Prom?"

"That's very sweet," she said, "but perhaps a bit too sentimental. You're wasting those fine attitudes. You're just another romantic Anglo bleeding heart. Is that why you had to leave Texas? Did you try to nationalize the oil business?"

"Naw," he said. "It's cuz Ah wooden mount long-hawns on muh Cadillac. They said Ah was uh traituh to muh clayuss."

"You're a closet Socialist, that's what you are."

"My mother voted for Adlai Stevenson. She said she did, anyway. I was going to turn her in, but she died right after the election. It would have been my duty, though."

"Yes, I can see that. I voted for Lawrence—Manny's opponent. He was nasty and crooked, but it was out in the open. You won't fink on me, will you?"

"What's wrong with your uncle? I liked him. I think he's a pro."

"Aaah. Manny." She waggled her right hand, as if she were snapping water drops from her fingertips, the gesture of contempt and dismissal. "If somebody hit Albuquerque with a thermonuclear device—not a bad idea, by the way—Manny would call a press conference and say he was looking into it."

They topped a gentle rise and saw the big house in

the distance, piñon smoke rising from the chimneys. The first fire of the fall.

"Give me and Native Dancer, here, a half-mile start, and I'll race you to the stable," David said.

Chapter 16

SAM APPLEWHITE, jeans pressed, boots shining, his gray Stetson held in his hands, stared at the floor and nodded his head slowly.

"Yes, I figured you couldn't, but I thought I'd ask."

"I'm sorry," Cruz said. "I know you're good. I know you're the best there is, but I just don't run that big an operation."

"Yes, sir. Hell, I probably ought to get out of it anyway. I'm fifty-five. I got a nice little place of my own in Oklahoma. Four sections. I can make do."

"If anyone can, you can," Cruz said. "Has Mr. Rosen—uh . . . ?"

"Rosenthal."

"Has he got a buyer? That's a hell of a property."

"No, sir. Well, I don't know. It's not even officially up for sale yet. I haven't heard anything."

Sam stood up and twirled his hat in his hands, slowly. "I'd even ask to sign on as a hand, but I don't speak any Spanish. Isn't that one hell of a thing? Don't speak a measly word, except maybe 'Coma si yama.' "

"I'm sorry, Sam," Cruz said.

Sam looked at his hat. "I thought maybe I might like

working for you because, well, if you'll pardon me for saying it, you're, uh, Spanish and all, and I figured maybe those kind of . . . raiders wouldn't, you know, bother you. Most of the other spreads, big spreads, are owned by white men. I mean, uh, Anglo fellas. Hell, you know what I'm getting at."

"Sure," Cruz said.

"I'm just too old for that kind of thing. Shooting that bull right there in his stall. Those quarter horses. Burning those saddles. Boots too. You know how a cowboy feels about his leather. Felt worse about that than we did about the Jeeps and the pickups."

"I know," Cruz said. "That was a hell of a mess up there. I wish we could have done more to help."

"I appreciate you and your hands helping with the cleanup. I wish to Christ I could figure what those son of a bitches were after. What they wanted. Scared all those people, shot all those animals. I mean, hell, if I knew why, maybe I could figure who. Then I'd go out and pepper a few asses. If that'd been my place I sure as hell would've."

"Anyway, they didn't kill anybody," Cruz said.

"Yeah, there's that. Hell, I'm not Tom Mix. I never was. I don't know what the hell's going on. I don't understand it and I don't want to fight it."

"I understand, Sam. I don't know what the hell's going on either. I'm too old, just like you."

"Had some good years at it, anyway. Except for the raid, this one was maybe the best. Sold four thousand head, pretty near. Got thirty-one and a half cents for 'em. Well, I'll be seeing you."

"Stay for lunch?"

"No—no, thank you. I got all kinds of work yet to do."

When Sam had left, Cruz drummed his fingers on the

top of his desk for several minutes, thinking wicked, impossible, greedy thoughts, all mixed in somehow with nostalgia. Then he called his accountant in Santa Fe.

At lunch he tried to concentrate on the food and the beer, but his left leg kept bouncing with a boyish glee of its own. He chuckled sometimes and smiled, and David distinctly heard him humming. Lupe finally put her fork down and stared at him.

"Are you okay, Papa?"

"Fine. Fine."

"Maybe feeling just a teeny bit *loco?*"

"Nope. Not *loco*. No locofoco on the coco. Thank you for asking." He hummed some more.

Lupe looked at David, found no explanation in his face, shrugged, and returned her attention to lunch.

"David," Cruz said, "I appreciate that additional one and three-quarters cents you got for me on the cattle."

"Glad I could be of service," David said.

"Very useful. Came to about fifteen thousand dollars."

"Which you need like I need another inch of nose," Lupe told him.

"Just a drop in the bucket," Cruz went on. "Little drop in a big bucket. Tum de tum. Gonna need a big, big bucket. Lots and lots of little drops."

"I'm sorry, David," Lupe said. "I was hoping you wouldn't see it when it happened. It's that damned streak of raving insanity again. We've traced it back to the seventeenth century."

"Not crazy," said Cruz. "Crazy like a *zorro*. Tum de dum de diddle-e-oh."

"It only affects the males," Lupe said.

"What's going on, Cruz?"

166

"I've saved a lot of money," Cruz said. "I've saved a real bunch. I didn't know how much *dinero* I had in the old *cajo*, you know what I mean, *cuate*? *¿Hay mucho oro en el banco, sabes?*"

"I know you're loaded," Lupe said. "I've just never heard you talk about money before, except when I ask you for a new car. You ought to be rich. You never pay anybody the minimum wage."

"Never mind that. He he he. You are looking at a *patrón*. Not just a little nickel-and-dime *patrón*. You are looking at a *gachupín*."

"I am looking at a madman," Lupe said.

Cruz paid no attention to her. "David, old *cuate, mi brazo fuerte*. I save my money, right? I keep that old Nash pickup instead of buying a lot of fancy tin. Once a year I go to Texas, okay? I buy what I have to have over there. Because it's cheaper. Yes? Save eleven hundred on a hay baler one year, save eight hundred on stock tanks another. Little drops. They add up."

"That's what Benjamin Franklin used to say."

"Never heard of him. One year—this year—I go to Texas, I pick up a corpse out of Billy Joe Shields's pasture, I dust him off, buy him a glass of milk, pretty soon he's made me an extra fifteen thousand bucks. I'm a genius. You're a genius too, I admit that, but I'm a real, big horse of a genius. I have working capital. I never realized that. I have . . . what did he call it? I have fluidity. The accountant called it that. It's a wonderful thing to have. I'm a genius."

"That's a good thing, all right," David said. "Are you planning to invest it in something?"

"Oh, no!" Lupe said. "Oh, my God, please no. Not

another one of those goddamn bulls. No. David, don't let him buy another bull. Four years ago he paid twelve thousand dollars for a faggoty bull. I swear. A gay bull."

"I don't believe it."

"She's right," Cruz said, laughing. "He was. Not sterile—we checked on that—but completely uninterested in cows. A cruel trick of nature. Twelve grand down the old *pozo*. A huge, beautiful *maricón* of a Hereford. Dandy Bruce, his name was." Cruz's laughter began to break him apart, and his eyes filled with tears.

Lupe was smiling, but grimly. "We tried to put a ring in his nose, but Dandy Bruce wanted to wear it in his ear. We couldn't even use him for artificial insemination. He died. He pined away. He *languished*. He was apparently in love with another bull who lived in Wyoming."

"No, no," said Cruz, wiping his eyes. "Not a bull. Now listen."

David and Lupe listened.

"I'm going to buy the Upper Grant."

"I told you. He's crazy," Lupe said, after a long silence which broke all the laughter.

"Not crazy. I'm gonna do it. You watch me."

"The Upper Grant's not even for sale," Lupe said.

"The Upper Grant is very much yes indeed for sale, *mi hijita*, and it is going to be what they call a quick sale because the gentleman who owns the ranch is all of a sudden up to his *nalgas* in boredom with the ranching profession. He has given Sam Applewhite a month's notice, and when a man gives Sam Applewhite a month's notice, you know that is a serious man."

"Four hundred sections," David said. "Now you're talking like a Texan."

"I am going to give the Texans lessons in *tejanismo*. I am going to show them how to wheel and then, when that lesson is absorbed by their tiny brains, I am going to show them how to deal. And when I get that four hundred sections—it is three hundred and eighty-seven sections, but I call it four hundred because I deal only in large, round numbers—I am going to remove the sign that says 'Len-Jar-Rose,' which is a childish thing to call a piece of land, and chop it into very small kindling and start a fire and roast one entire steer of perhaps twelve hundred pounds. I will start the fire on a Thursday and roast the steer on a Friday. Then I will invite, I will command, Father Serex to attend this *gran barbacoa,* and I will make him eat a pound of beef on Friday, and if he refuses because of medieval religious superstition I will dismiss him from his little toy church and hire an archbishop. A cardinal."

Cruz raised his glass of beer and smiled like a mountain lion.

"*Salud.*"

"*Buena suerte,*" Lupe said.

"One sip only, David. You're going to help me and I want you to be sober. Even a man so clever with one and three-quarter cents must have a clear head for grand finance."

In the *sala* they planned their approach. Lupe lay on a couch reading a magazine while Cruz and David made tentative marks on work sheets, scattered old ranch files around the coffee table, drank coffee and argued.

"We don't even know his asking price," David said. "We're working blind."

"We're working in a dim light, but we're not blind,

169

cuate. Look: 1895, that *piojo* with friends in Santa Fe, he bought it all for eighty-five hundred cash. In other words, for nothing. Sold it to a land and cattle company just before the first war, twenty-five thousand cash, another twenty-five in notes. Fifty. Nice profit. They sold it to a Texan in 1933. Depression. Still went for a hundred and twenty-five thousand. All cash. He put in improvements. Barn, stables, houses, wells, tanks, fence. I don't know exactly how much, but a lot. Those bastards always have cash. Hung on to it until eleven years ago. Died. Family didn't want it, so they auctioned it. Remember? I told you. I went to the auction in Albuquerque."

"You said you didn't want it. You said you already had enough land."

"You got a good memory, *cuate*. That wasn't the truth, exactly. I got scared off by the big money. I'd had three years of no rain. I'd had to sell breeding stock, at a loss. My wife had died four years before that, a long illness, osteogenic sarcoma, bone cancer. I was still depressed and still paying the goddamn hospital. I couldn't afford to bid. Okay? You forgive me the lie?"

"Sorry, Cruz."

"Anyway, the auction got very lively. Your noble and distinguished employer Mr. Cotton was there, but he stopped bidding at three hundred thousand dollars. Just listening to those numbers made my teeth hurt. It went finally for four hundred and eighty thousand. I talked to the man who got it. He said he was acting as an agent for a client. That's all he said, but in the paper next day they listed the buyer as this Rosenthal from Hollywood."

David studied the sale prices. "It's a good progression," he said. "Not too showy. Probably no minerals there worth going for."

170

"You mean gold?"

"No, I mean oil and gas. Did they explore it?"

"Sure. About twenty-five years ago, when that Texan had it, they drilled holes and set off dynamite. It was noisy as hell for a while. Used to wake Lupe up in her cradle. Scared the hell out of Luis. I guess they didn't find anything. There's no oil wells up there."

"A waste of money, all that seismic exploration," David said. "This whole slope has no action. I'd call it a classic dry-hole formation. Dig for a hundred years and you won't find anything but turtle eggs. It's mighty good cattle country, though."

Cruz grinned, lighting up half the *sala*. "You said it, man."

Lupe lowered her magazine. "What's it worth now, gentlemen? All that big money you're tossing around so lightly belongs to somebody else."

"Well," Cruz said.

"Well," David said. "We don't know, exactly."

"That's true. We don't know at all."

"But we can guess," David said. "We can make a pretty good estimate right now, before Rosenthal posts any notices or advertises."

"You see, you terrible girl, your old man's not such a *tonto*. I got some early information. We can get a bid in there first. Nobody knows it's for sale except me. Naturally it has to be a reasonable bid."

"It's going to have to be realistic," David said.

"Why don't you offer thirty-two cents a pound for it?" Lupe asked. "It worked fine on the cows." She went back to her magazine.

An expression of profound injury spread over Cruz's face. He waggled a maimed hand at Lupe. "They are an entirely different species," he said. "I have dissected cadavers of both sexes, and I can tell you that women are not human. They come from the moon. Here I am, with dreams of empire, and she lies there and makes jokes."

"There is a very strong *macho* stink in this room," she said. "When men start talking about money and land, it's trouble for the women."

"Quiet," Cruz said. "Mr. Reed is figuring."

David figured for three days. Through the courtesy of Sam Applewhite, he toured the Upper Grant for an afternoon and devised an estimate of the physical improvements. He drove into Albuquerque and talked to several realtors who specialized in ranch properties. They were wonderfully informative until they discovered he wasn't interested in their listings. In Santa Fe, he spent a productive morning in the library of the State Land Office, then had lunch with a bank vice-president, a former classmate at Rice. Without actually saying so, he let the vice-president believe that he still worked for Cotton and was informally offered the keys to the vault, at prime rates. He scanned newspaper files on microfilm, with special attention to retail beef prices at Piggly-Wiggly over a ten-year period. He made notes and drew rough charts and graphs, rented a calculating machine, perused an area of real estate law with which he was insufficiently familiar, and talked cows and values and prices and troubles with eleven ranchers, five of whom had been raided and were considering selling out, six of whom were afraid they might be raided and were also considering selling out.

He returned to Cruz's ranch exhausted, still lacking an important piece of basic information.

"Do you or Lupe know anything about Rosenthal?" David asked. "Anything at all?"

172

"He wants to sell," Cruz said. "That's all I know."

"You said he's never seen the ranch."

"As far as I know. I've never seen him around here. Applewhite's never met him."

"Are you sure it was a tax shelter?"

"Pretty sure. He just makes movies. He discovered that funny guy. What's his name?"

"Lenny Jarvis," Lupe said from the couch. "He's what they call 'a great comedian and a great human being.' I'm not a real fan of his, but I can't help reading about him. He gets into fist fights at nightclubs. I think he's the honorary chairman of the National Strabismus Foundation."

"Well, what about Rosenthal?" David asked. "I know he's got lousy taste in comedians, but I'd like to know more. Hollywood doesn't make much sense to me."

"Jesus, I don't know," Cruz said.

"Wait a minute," said Lupe. She left the *sala* and returned shortly with another magazine.

"Roberta Hill," she said. "A movie critic." She found the page and read aloud: "'. . . new film, *Horseapples* . . . barbarous tragicomedy . . . tragedy accidental . . . comedy infrequent . . .' Ha. Here it is. '. . . the forty-third straight filmic disaster by Morris Rosenthal, a producer whose name is spoken in hushed, reverent tones whenever the subject of vulgarity arises.' Is that any help?"

"It's something," David said, and went back to his figuring.

Eleven years ago it had sold for $480,000, less than two dollars an acre. A great bargain. But the family that sold it was bereaved, probably very rich, Texas rich. They were converting a complicated estate to cash. They didn't want the hassle, just the money. They may have sold at a loss. Rosenthal buys it, no doubt on the advice of one of those ice-cold business managers. Rosenthal himself doesn't understand what's going on, doesn't care. He has no appetite for that kind of operation. Doesn't know a cow from a buffalo. He probably chases starlets and buys French Impressionists.

Okay. Now, I'm either going to get it right or I'm going to outsmart myself, he thought. Stereotypes. Rosenthal. A German Jew. That's a guess. City people. City people from way the hell back. If he thinks of real estate at all, he thinks about buildings. Office buildings. Apartment houses. Not 250,000 acres of grass.

Now he wants out of it. Why? His manager's advice? Doubt it, because as long as he holds it, it's a good umbrella. The raid, then. They shot his bull, killed his horses, burned up his barn, scared his employees. That's a lot of trouble, and he doesn't want his investments to cause trouble. Who does? So sell it and sell it fast. Take a small profit or break even. No need to take a loss, and a loss is bad for the ego.

"Cruz, do you know whether or not the ranch has done well since Rosenthal bought it? I mean, do you think it's shown a profit?"

"I'm sure it has. His ranch manager is one of the best. Sam Applewhite's never lost a nickel for anyone. By the way, you got a half cent more for my beef than Sam did for Rosenthal's. You're up there with the champions."

Now. Figure. No quantum jumps because there's no mineral substratum. Is there? Can there be? No. Steady appreciation. Dollars down—what? Call it twelve percent. Profit, but not a big one. No operating losses to cover; on the contrary. Out fast, sell to the first solid bid. What? What?

174

David wrote two figures on a writing pad, leaned back and sighed. "Here's what I come up with," he said. "It's pure hunch, I'm afraid, but I'm awfully short of facts. And it's a big spread of money."

Cruz tore the paper off. "Eight hundred and twenty-five thousand dollars at the bottom. One million, two hundred and fifty thousand at the top. Ay-yi-yi."

"That's a lot of money, Papa," Lupe said.

"Can you swing that, Cruz? Lupe's right. That's a bundle. But worth it."

"Ay, Chihuahua!" Cruz said. "*¡Ay carajo!* Yes. I can swing the low figure with a little trouble, and I can swing the high figure with a lot of trouble. But I can swing it. Of course, I might have to mortgage the old homestead a little bit."

"I didn't think you had that kind of money lying around in a shoebox," David said.

"Don't kid yourself, *cuate*. I got most of it in cash. I got it in savings accounts and lockboxes. I'm just a simple native, and all I understand is money."

"I never heard of such a thing, Cruz. Nobody keeps cash lying around. It's unbusinesslike."

"What he *really* wanted to do," Lupe said, "was to convert it all to pieces of eight and bury it on a beach in the Grand Caymans."

"Go ahead and laugh at me. I got the money, and if you figured the price right, I can buy that son of a bitch. It's like I told you. I saved my money. A little drop here, a little drop there. Keep the Nash pickup and shop in Big Spring."

"Fine. Now, if it's okay with you, I'd like to talk to him myself. I'm going to start at nine hundred. Eight twenty-five's maybe a touch low. I'll tell him I represent

175

you, and he'll probably like that, because at his level people never talk to each other. Their representatives talk to each other. Anybody know where I can find him?"

Cruz shrugged. "Hollywood, California."

"I'll bet he has an unlisted number."

Lupe got the Albuquerque morning paper and found it on the entertainment page. "*Horseapples* is at the Zuni Drive-In. 'Morris Rosenthal Presents A Gargantuan Film.' That's Gargantuan Pictures, Incorporated. A nice, modest name."

David stood up and stretched, feeling brain-tired but satisfied. "Just a couple more things before I go in and goose the goat. Sorry, Lupe. A figure of speech. I'd like to use your office phone and do it alone. This will be just a tentative opening. I don't believe we'll decide anything concrete, but we might. He'll turn me over to his business manager. If he takes the bid he'll want a check for escrow and a letter of intent. But at first I want to be alone in there. With the goat."

"Sure," said Cruz. "Hell, yes. I'd probably start talking in Spanish. I haven't felt this excited since I cut my fingers off."

"Second thing. How do we know that the ranch is for sale? There's no public notice yet."

"Oh. I didn't think about that." Cruz slowly scratched the back of his neck. "Tell him," he suggested, "tell him it's ranchers' gossip. He won't know there isn't any such thing."

Lupe held the magazine in front of her face, but she couldn't make sense of the words. Cruz walked back and forth across the *sala*, rhythmically pounding his fist into his hip. They could hear only the drone of sound from

Cruz's office as David talked. When he came out, Cruz stopped walking. Lupe sat up.

"Cruz, I think maybe you've got yourself a ranch. Now wait a minute. Don't start whooping yet."

"I'm not whooping, *cuate*. I'm crowing." Cruz was prancing heavily around the *sala,* flapping his arms. "*Cu cu ru cu cu!* That's my rooster imitation. How you like it?"

"There's no kind of final deal, yet. We're just starting on it. He says he's interested and in a hurry and we have to do a lot of talking to his business manager . . ."

"*Cu cu ru cu cu!*"

"You sound like a goat with laryngitis," Lupe said. "Why don't you sit down and listen to what the man's saying?"

"Okay, man. What are you saying? *Dígame.*"

David spread his notes on the coffee table. "At first," he said, "I thought he was angry. He used very coarse language, one word in particular, and he used it three or four times in every sentence."

"Did he call you 'sweetheart'?" Lupe asked.

"No, he didn't. He called me 'Dave, baby.'"

"What did you call *him?*"

"I called him 'sir.' Anyway, I gave him some background. I told him your place adjoined his, that you were a reputable rancher, gave him some banking references, and sort of let it slip that the Governor was your brother. I'm not sure that helped too much. He let it slip that two kings and a shah had been his houseguests at one time or another. So then I . . ."

"How much?" Lupe asked.

"Oh. Well, he says he likes to deal in large, round figures too. A million dollars."

"A million dollars," Cruz said. "Hey, Lupe, what do you think about that? A million dollars. Your old man's a reputable rancher, and he's going to buy a little ranch for a million dollars."

"I wouldn't know about that high-finance stuff. You can always find me rubbing mud on the schoolhouse."

"Cruz, from what I could tell, he wants out. He was surprised we knew he was thinking about selling, but he bought the 'ranchers' gossip' idea. He says they have the same trouble keeping secrets in his business. The ranch wasn't losing money the way it was supposed to, he said, and it was f . . . lousing up his tax picture. And the raid had disturbed him, even though he didn't know any of the employees involved. He told me he's well known as a champion of civil rights out there. He doesn't buy domestic lettuce, and he's always careful to put one Chicano in every movie, and he feels the same way about the *schvartzers*. He spent quite a while telling me about his aggravations. He's got some troubles with the craft unions, he said, and one of his stars is a heroin addict, and his sources of production financing are drying up, and the Academy sons of bitches won't give him the Jean Hersholt Humanitarian Award, and somebody busted into his house and stole two of his Monets, and if there's one thing he doesn't need it's a bunch of knife-waving, tequila-drinking, serape-head spic bastards calling him a bigot. If they don't want him to own property in New Mexico, okay with him. By him, he says, it's all a big *tsuris*. Anybody know what that means?"

"A pain in the ass," Lupe said.

"David," Cruz said. "I really want that land back in the family. But is it honestly worth a million dollars?"

"Oh, yes. It's worth more like three million, but

Rosenthal's in a hurry—I thought he would be—and he's never seen it, so he doesn't have any feeling for it. I think you'll get it. We as much as shook hands."

"Goddamn," Cruz said. "Goddamn. I'm gonna raise your salary to two hundred and seventy-five a month."

Chapter 17

"I DON'T THINK you understand, Carlos," the Governor said. "I'm not shitting around with you brother to brother. I don't have any relatives right now. I have constituents, I have opponents and I have undecideds. And I have a funny feeling that inside of a year you're going to be making automobile license plates in the penitentiary tin shop."

"Manny," Carlos said, spreading his arms. "Manny."

"If you end up in the *juzgado,* I want to be damned sure I put you there myself. Don't forget that. If I stick your ass in the cage, it will mean votes for the honest and courageous Governor. If somebody else does it, you'll just be a further embarrassment to me. It's really possible, you know, that you could be a *further* embarrassment to me. You seem to have infinite capabilities."

Carlos wiped his face and neck. "Manny, there's nothing illegal, I swear to you. Where's your Bible? You have a Bible someplace in here? Would I lie?"

"You would. You have, many times, and you will again. Many times."

"Where's your Bible?"

"I don't want you to put your sweaty hands on my

Bible. The Chief Justice uses my Bible for swearing in incompetents."

"Manny. Jesus Christ, Manny. It is only the community grants. The Compañía doesn't have anything to do with the private grants. Primo doesn't care about them. Well, yes, he cares about them, but I've explained to him. There's too many of them. The owners lost them too many different ways. They sold them, a lot of them. Primo tells them their fathers and grandfathers shouldn't have sold them, should have been more careful. He talks about the Trust. The Sacred Trust. You know that. You've heard him. The people had no right to sell their lands cheap to the Anglos. All right. But they did, and it's too late to get them back. I think Primo understands that now. I tell him about the statutes of limitations. I believe he understands. The Compañía has no activities in that area. It's the community grants, the old *ejidos*, the lands that belonged in common to the villages. That's all he cares about now. Believe me, Manny."

The Governor got up and stretched and walked to his window. He looked out over the once-beautiful town of Santa Fe, now unhappily interred under asphalt, government office buildings, frame-stucco houses transplanted from Akron, Ohio, and billboards proclaiming it The City Different.

"Carlos," the Governor said gently, "you are a fat, stupid, lying son of a bitch."

"It's possible, Manny. It's really possible now. The Feds are all jumpy about everybody's civil rights. Christ, there isn't one group of people the government hasn't screwed at one time or other. They're breaking their necks in Washington to right all the old wrongs. Now Is the

Time. The Time Is Ripe. The People Have Spoken."

"The people have spoken through their hats, little brother. The Feds are not going to give up . . . what? . . . nine million acres of national forests in New Mexico just so the rubes up in Vado Ancho and Lago Seco can graze their stock free. The Department of the Interior is not going to part with one acre of Park Service *caliche*. The Government, however half-witted and conscience-stricken it may be, is not going to reinstate the seventeenth century to please Primo Rael."

"Taos," Carlos said. "The Taos Indians. Theodore Roosevelt took forty-eight thousand acres away from them in 1905. Now the Government's given it back, all back. Manny, it's possible."

"Yes, it is. The Taoseños raised hell for more than sixty years, and *then* they got it back, with the very clear understanding that it was not to be considered any kind of precedent. It doesn't suggest that they're going to return the Louisiana Purchase to France just because they bought it at panic prices. Hey, I just thought of something. Maybe the Russians would like Alaska back. Carlos, stop fooling Primo. Stop making his eyes water with lawyer talk. He might not know better, but you do. And tell him to call off his goddamn nighthawks. I got ranchers from all over the north camping in my waiting room. I haven't got enough cops to cover all that territory. I don't want a lot of pissed-off cowboys riding vigilante and stringing up Spanish sheepherders. You hear me?"

Carlos shrugged. "Kids. Wild kids. Fiery Latin Blood. They're not part of any group. They hear the talk, you know. And they get crazy ideas. They think it's open season on the Anglos. They've heard about the times when the Anglos held open season on them. On us."

"Go on, get out of here. Go file your briefs. Lock horns with the Feds. I don't care. Keep it in the courts and you can make any kind of fool of yourself you want to. I don't care. But if one more rancher gets hurt I'm going to mobilize our fire-eating, well-trained National Guard and send a squad right straight to your house to jab your fat ass with bayonets."

"Trust me, Manny," Carlos said on his way to the exit through the private bathroom. "Believe me."

"Where does the Compañía get its money, Carlos?"

"A dollar here, a dollar there. From the Little Man. It adds up."

"Bullshit," the Governor said. "Oh. Did you send money to that Park Service Ranger?"

"Twenty-five hundred, Manny. In cash. In an envelope."

"Well, he'll have a Merry Christmas, anyway. Goodbye."

My state, the Governor thought. Since 1912, since statehood, nothing happens. Lost, poor, forgotten and quiet. People from New York write letters to our governors asking what the rate of currency exchange is here. They think it's a foreign country. The blank space between Texas and Arizona. The cities blow up; New Mexico snores. Men fly to the moon; in New Mexico men can't get from Chimayo to Cordova without fording a river and breaking an axle. Forty-nine states and a colony. Goddamnit, we were such a happy, ragged-assed colony. When Lew Wallace was Governor, he had time to sit in his office and write *Ben Hur*, for God's sake. Why did it all have to come unglued now? All I wanted to do was to

183

go to Washington and ride my burro down the middle of the road.

He dialed the National Guard number himself. "Hello, General," he said. "How are all your fine young men? Trained to a fighting edge?"

Chapter 18

" 'YOU ARE A GREAT PEOPLE, but you are drinking the powdered milk of the Welfare Department. You speak the strongest and most beautiful language in the world, but you cannot read it or write it because the schools will not teach you.

" 'Your children should be fat and healthy, but they are weak and sick. You have no doctor. You cannot go to the doctor because the roads are poor and the bridges are broken. You cannot walk a hundred miles, but you cannot drive either because the finance company will not wait for its money and it takes your truck.

" 'You cannot get money because you cannot work. You cannot work because your land is gone.' "

"You read that beautifully, Uncle Manny. You have a good, strong, sonorous voice. Maybe you ought to go into politics."

"Why, thank you, Lupe. May I go on?"

"Shoot."

" 'Your fathers and grandfathers and great-grandfathers lost their land. They sold it for nothing in bad years. They could not pay their taxes, so the men, the blond men who came laughing from the east, the men with money bought your land for taxes. They came to your ancestors, to men who didn't see two *reales* from one year to another, and they gave them the green paper decorated with eagles and the portraits of Anglo presidents, and they bought the land, *varas* and *varas* of land, for the price of one chicken.'"

The Governor paused to sip some of Cruz's cider, and continued reading from *La Lucha*.

"This isn't boring you, is it?"

"Well, I've heard it before," Lupe admitted.

"I'll just bet you have," the Governor said.

"'What they sold is gone. It is gone forever unless you can buy it back with money. Your parents and their parents had no right to sell the land, but they sold it anyway, because they were poor and because they did not know what is right. They had forgotten that if you sell your land you sell your mother.'"

"'The powdered milk of the Welfare Department.'" Cruz said. "He makes it sound like arsenic."

"I wish I had as good a speech writer as Primo Rael," the Governor said. "Warschauer keeps sending in drafts full of phrases like 'at this point in time' when he means 'now.'"

"Rael makes a pretty strong speech," David said. "I liked the part about George Washington being a red-neck Anglo racist."

"One of my better touches," Lupe said. "Of course, I wrote two basic speeches for him. This one was for delivery in Spanish. The one he gives in front of the Rotarians is supposed to stress intercultural harmony and crap like that."

"Maybe you forgot," Cruz said. "If it hadn't been for intercultural harmony and crap like that, we wouldn't be here. Your grandparents committed intercultural harmony often enough to have four sons. Now, why don't you clear off the table and bring in some of that pie you made?"

"I'll help you," David said.

"No, you sit still. I wouldn't want you to compromise your goddamn Texas manhood. Let the women do the dishes and plaster the schoolhouse and have the babies . . ."

She slammed their plates together and strode off to the kitchen, fuming about the loss, a week before, of Ingeborg, who was honeymooning in Mexico City, forever lost to domestic service, enjoying intercultural harmony with Officer Macauliffe.

"I have a very touchy niece," the Governor said. "And she looked so sweet in her Communion dress."

Lupe brought the pie and coffee. "Damned fat-assed, ungrateful Swede," she said. "I wish her repetitive pregnancies and painful deliveries."

"Can we trust this *tejano* here?" the Governor asked when Lupe had retired to wash the dishes. "He looks like a red-neck Anglo racist to me."

"Hell, yes," Cruz said. "I pay him two seventy-five a month and all the frijoles he can eat. He's loyal down to his toes."

"I take the King's *peso*," David said, "and I fight the King's war."

Manny pushed his pie around on his plate, drank some coffee, lit a cigar and stared up at the *vigas*.

"Well, Christ," he said. "I have to trust somebody."

"I'm your brother," Cruz said.

"So is Carlos."

"You got a point there."

"Tell me again about Luis."

"I don't know, Manny. It's just a feeling. He's always

been waiting for me to die, always telling me how he's gonna screw up the ranch once I'm out of the way. Now I think he's stopped waiting. He hasn't really said anything, but he has that look in his eye. Whenever I say something about the ranch, or about the Upper Grant, he just smiles likes he's got more important things on his mind. He doesn't even curse the hands any more."

"He's taken an interest in my end of things," David said. "I moved a table into Cruz's little office there. Luis comes in sometimes, when Cruz isn't around, and asks me questions. I was flattered at first. I thought he'd finally forgiven me for tearing his comic book."

"What kind of questions?"

"Oh, we talk about the taxes a rancher has to worry about, and about the fluctuations in prices, and how to get bids on equipment and that kind of thing. He was taking a real interest."

"What do you think, Cruz?" the Governor asked. "Is Luis buying himself a ranch someplace?"

"No. I don't think so. I don't see how. He hasn't got enough money. Nobody would lend him money, either."

"I think you're right. I think he's trying to steal himself a ranch."

"Oh, come on, Manny. Luis? Who says so?"

"Tony Lujan says so. You remember Tony?"

"Well, sure," Cruz said. "He was one of my best people. He got sore when I made Perez *capataz*, and he quit. What about him?"

"He's *capataz* for D. D. Snow. Snow's been hit twice, now, the second time just last week. This time they busted everything in his house. I mean everything. His TV, his dishwasher, his goddamn coffee cups, his beds, everything. Tony came to my office yesterday—made an appointment with my secretary, like a real proper citizen. He was nervous as hell, but he said he was sure. Luis was with them, he said."

"I hear they all wear bandannas or something," Cruz said.

"Yeah, they all put something over their faces. But Luis was wearing María's old concho belt, you know? Tony said he could tell that thing from a mile off."

Cruz was silent for a minute. "Jesus Christ!" he said, finally. "That would be Luis. He's dumb enough to wear a badge like that." He turned to David. "My wife had some Navajo jewelry, you know? Squash blossoms and bracelets and stuff. A good collection. When she died, Lupe got it, but Luis had to have that goddamn belt. It had conchos on it big as saucers. A beautiful thing. Luis yelled and cried and pouted and got to be such a pain in the ass, Lupe finally gave it to him to shut him up."

"Tony didn't want to tell you, Cruz," Manny said. "He thought you might get sore at him or call him a liar."

"But Luis doesn't give a damn about politics, Manny."

"I know that, Cruz. But he sure is drooling for a ranch of his own."

"Well, what does he think? Does he think Snow's gonna give him his ranch just because his TV was busted?"

"I swear, Cruz, I don't know what the hell Luis thinks. He's not my favorite nephew, if you have to know, and I'm not sure he thinks much at all. But . . . look, man. Something like forty ranches have been raided now. No one's got killed yet, but there's been damage up in the hundreds of thousands. A lot of those people are scared. There've been a dozen or more quick sales, and there's a dozen more places going on the block. I mean, hell, the Upper Grant's a quick sale too. As far as I know, you're the only New Mexican buying. The rest are all Texans."

"Goddamn Texans," Cruz said.

"Any particular Texans?" David asked.

"I don't know," the Governor said. "They all look alike to me. Like Chinese."

The Governor asked Lupe about Primitivo Rael when she came in from the kitchen.

"No," she said. "Absolutely not. Primo simply could not be behind those raids. He doesn't think like that."

"I don't know," Manny said. "Every time he speaks up in El Gallo or Los Ritos or someplace there's always a raid in the next few days."

"Manny, he's a sweet man. He doesn't have any more guile than a kitten. Honest to God, I worked with that man for a year. He didn't have any political sophistication. The only revolutionary he'd ever heard of was Benito Juarez, and he wasn't quite sure who Juarez was. Really, Primo's a little bit like Moses. He's simple and good and innocent and a little stupid, and maybe more than a little crazy. There's no harm in him."

"Lupe, how'd you like to work for him again? Write him a few more speeches?"

"You want me to fink for you? Go screw yourself."

"I want to know where their money's coming from."

"There's no secret about that, Manny. It comes a dollar or two at a time. They take up collections at the speeches and the barbecues. It comes in the mail. I suppose I've given a couple of hundred dollars myself in the last year or so, and that probably makes me their biggest patron."

"I'd really appreciate it, Lupe. I could have their

headquarters busted and confiscate their files, but I have politics to think of. I like being Governor. I'm trying to walk the line. The police can't catch the raiders. Those country boys come in at night on horses or in pickups. They don't stay long, and by the time the cops have stopped tripping over their nightsticks and having their coffee breaks, they've scattered."

"No."

"Please, Lupe. I'm not trying to hang Primo or anybody else. I just want to find out. Jesus, don't *you* care?"

"You remember that dead bull up there, *chica*," Cruz told her. "Never mind the politics; they're criminals."

"I'm telling you, it's not Primo. He wouldn't do that. He wouldn't lie to me."

"Lupe, I keep telling the papers that I'm going to look into it. Don't make a liar out of your uncle Manny. Okay? Help me look into it."

Chapter 19

IGNORING MIGUELITO, who was trying to build a snowman out of the dry, feathery material that skiers call Aspen powder, Luis crunched through the littered yard, opened his front door, and found Marta in bed, her ankles locked behind the back of a tattooed gorilla from Villa Rica. The gorilla outweighed Luis by eighty pounds, so he went outside again and kicked his tires until the visitor left. He went back in to beat Marta up, but she pulled a kitchen knife on him.

"Where's our ranch?" she asked, holding the knife low, point up, as she'd been taught by her brothers in Vado Ancho.

"I'll get a ranch," he said. "Who was he?"

"Somebody."

"He looks like a monkey."

"He screws like a man. Get the ranch."

Luis spat at her, and missed. With her free hand she threw him a finger.

While watching Marta carefully, for she seemed to have serious plans for the kitchen knife, Luis collected his bedroll, his .30-30 carbine, a laundry bag full of canned food and his concho belt, which he buckled around his waist.

"I'm going," he told her. "I'll be back."

"Chinga tu madre," she said, in the neighborly fashion of Vado Ancho.

"Y tu madre," he said, by way of formal farewell.

He drove his wrinkled Mustang to the big house and parked it in the snow of the circular driveway, wondering whether or not it would be useful to tell his father that he had left Marta. He waited in the car for half an hour, and began to freeze because his heater didn't work any more. No one came out of the house to welcome him, or to chase him away, or to inquire about his health, so he drove skidding out of the driveway, punching his horn ring with fury, to let Cruz know that he'd been there. The horn didn't work either.

Two hours later, his Mustang collapsed in a snowdrift. Luis had tried to kill himself by crashing into a cottonwood, but had been unable to reach the necessary speed on the snowy roads. The impact had snapped his radiator hose. His right front tire was flat, and his muffler had worked loose, allowing engine exhaust to percolate upward. The carbon monoxide would have killed him, had it not been for ventilation through the broken windows. Luis emerged coughing, staggered in small circles for a few minutes, and threw up. He removed the bedroll, the food, and his rifle and struck out toward the *colina*. He had remembered that death by freezing was a comfortable way to go.

His toes began to sting after a hundred yards, particularly his recently broken toe. Soon they began to ache. After another hundred yards, he realized he couldn't feel them at all inside his boots. He stopped and set down the bedroll and the sack of cans. He unslung his carbine, worked the lever, and discovered he had no ammunition, so that he could neither signal for help nor shoot himself.

Echeagaray, who was walking in the deep snow for exercise and pleasure, found Luis trying to open a tin of candied yams by hammering on it with the butt of his carbine. The young man seemed hysterical, Echeagaray thought, because of too close contact with human beings. He helped Luis walk the half mile to the dome, his new residence, which he shared with several aged and fragrant sheep. Luis warmed himself at the cooking fire and felt his toes return painfully to life. He ate a bowl of Echeagaray's stew—a nourishing mixture of garlic and coyote broth—and went to sleep in his bedroll, curled up like a lamb.

Anita Pacheco tended to overcook eggs and undercook bacon, but she had a confident hand with *salsa*. When old Abundio's widow, Gloria, had died two years before, Anita had petitioned Lupe for the undemanding duty of cook in the big house. Lupe had subjected her to an incomprehensible lecture about dignity and pride, leaving Anita with the thought that the preparation of food for pay was similar to prostitution. Anita withdrew her petition and returned, bewildered, to her house in Pozo Verde. She loved to cook, but she hated cooking for herself alone. Her late husband had been extraordinarily appreciative of her skills and had died, suddenly and happily, with a compliment on his lips, while eating a third *empanadita*. Anita resented the employment of Ingeborg, the strange *gringa* who spoke such elegant Spanish, and was relieved when she married the enormous policeman and vanished.

And now, finally, at the personal, desperate request of Señor Tafoya himself, she had the position she had sought for so long. Lupe had gone to Santa Fe for a while, and the two men in the big house had given up after soiling all the plates and pans and skillets and casseroles in the kitchen, and singeing themselves while trying to extinguish a grease fire in the broiler.

She was making tortillas at six in the morning—not patting them flat between her hands, but fashioning them in a wonderful patented device called a tortilla press— when the unfamiliar pickup stopped in the driveway. Marta climbed down from the passenger's side and walked, in an unsure manner, to the kitchen door. She was wearing high-heeled, open-toed shoes, a skirt which showed forbidden areas above the knee, and a short fur coat. Anita sniffed as Marta handed her a sealed envelope and sniffed again as Marta tottered back to the waiting truck in the impractical shoes, to be driven off by the strange man at the wheel.

At seven, Cruz and David were drinking their first cups of coffee, both of them staring out at the inner court, where the naked Greeks stood in negligent postures, their heads and shoulders piled with snow.

They had talked and argued late the night before; Cruz wanted the hands to pile baled hay at regular intervals along the pasture fences, while David thought the hay should be unbaled and pitched loosely from the pickups, in rows. They did agree that hay would be necessary, as the natural forage was too deeply covered by snow, and they decided eventually to leave the details to Perez, who was seldom wrong about anything that had to do with cows.

"And my new ranch," Cruz had said. "I want to shake somebody's hand on it, or sign something. I got my million dollars burning a hole in the safe." David had explained that Rosenthal seemed to be holding things up, or putting things off, and had left the country to make a movie.

Now Cruz poured more coffee and went on complaining.

"Where is he again? Making that movie?"

"Rosenthal? He's in Yugoslavia. He said he was going to Yugoslavia to scout locations for a Western."

"You see? The son of a bitch is crazy. I'm trying to pay him a whole million dollars for his lousy ranch, and he's lost interest and gone to Yugoslavia."

"He said his representative would call us and then fly out. You remember. We'll meet him in the directors' room at the bank. I promise you, Cruz; we'll sign more papers than you ever saw before."

Anita carried their breakfast in, set it down and propped the note against the coffeepot. "From Marta Tafoya," she said, sniffing. "At six she came in a truck. She also left in a truck."

"Thank you, Anita. David, what the hell does he want to make a Western in Yugoslavia for? What's the matter with Arizona or someplace?"

"He gets to rent the whole Yugoslav Army for a few dollars a day. They'll be Indians and the U. S. Seventh Cavalry—he provides the uniforms and costumes, and the Army supplies the horses."

"Jesus," Cruz said. "The people I get tied up with." He opened the envelope and read the message in Marta's large, spiky hand: *"Que saques Miguel.* Marta."

"What the hell does this mean?" he asked, handing the note to David.

"It means 'Get Miguel' or maybe 'Remove Miguel.'"

"I know what it says, *cuate.* I mean what does it mean?"

"You have me there," David said. "Didn't Anita say something about a truck?"

Anita told them that no, Marta didn't have the little boy with her, but there was a gentleman driving the truck whom she didn't recognize, but she thought he had a tattoo on his hand.

Cruz and David drove the Nash pickup to Luis's house. Miguelito was sitting in his crib, talking to a stuffed rabbit. Cruz held him and hugged him and stormed around the untidy little house, cursing his son and his daughter-in-law, while David collected baby clothes and feeding bottles.

"I don't have the pediatrician's eye," Cruz said, "but he looks okay. Goddamnit, where the hell *are* they?"

Lupe returned that evening, pyrotechnic with anger, to take charge of her nephew. "What have you been feeding him? Steak, I suppose. Oh, *posole.* Well, that's just wonderful food for a baby. Just terrific. What's the matter with you, Papa? You never heard of diarrhea? Who put this goddamn diaper on, King Kong? Look at those fingernails. What if he scratches himself and gets septicemia? Did you boil those bottles first or just stick 'em in his mouth? Look at that nipple, David! It's plugged. He might as well be sucking on a knuckle. This is a baby, you know. Not a sheepdog. Does either of you know whether that stupid bitch had a regular baby doctor for him? I mean a real doctor, Papa, not like certain quacks I could mention. Christ, has he had any shots? You don't suppose this little rash down there is smallpox, do you? Well, *tell* me. Even *you* ought to be able to diagnose smallpox. All your ancestors had it, they gave it to the Indians. David, please tell Anita to *boil* those bottles, not just run warm water over them. *No, no, no, Miguelito chico, ésta es sopa. Es para comer.* Miguelito, don't throw the damned soup. Eat the damned soup or I'll pop you one on your little *trasero*. That's a boy. David, put that cradle in *my* room, and don't forget the rubber mat. Well, *find* a rubber mat. If I get my hands on Marta Elena Tafoya de Romero, I'm going to cut her nose off. Does anybody have *any* idea where that *puta* went? What do you mean, a tattoo? Jesus, she probably ran off with a sailor. Leave it to Marta to find the only sailor in New Mexico and run off with him. Where's Luis? Do you know where the hell Luis is? My God, just leaving a little boy like this!"

"It's really something to watch, eh, *cuate*? Just think what she'd be like with one of her own. You suppose it's instinct, or do they teach it at college?"

"He says he wants his *conejo*. Either of you know what he means? Has he got a rabbit? Well, you just get in that truck and go pick up his rabbit! He's already lost his parents today. Do you want him to lose his rabbit and *really* get wiped out? Move it!"

Lupe began to calm down only when Miguelito was asleep, with his little *trasero* sticking up in the air and his arm around his *conejo*.

"I'm glad you called me," she said. "I was through up there anyway."

"Did you write Primo a nice speech?" Cruz asked her. "Was he glad to see you?"

"Oh, man. Primo. He's twice as holy as he ever was,

and about four times as confused. At some point this year he woke up and realized he was famous. And important. God speaks in one ear, and Carlos speaks in the other. God tells him what's right, then Carlos tells him what's legal. Sometimes he gets it confused and thinks God is his legal advisor. Yes, I wrote him a few good speeches, and he's grateful. He's also grateful I didn't ask to be paid. Carlos is on full salary now. He's dropped his regular legal practice entirely."

She took a folded copy of *La Lucha* from her purse. "Page one. 'Primo Relates Movement's History.' That's one of mine. Primo's officially one of the immortals, along with Simón Bolívar, José Martí, Bernardo O'Higgins, Che Guevara and Ho Chi Minh. You didn't know Uncle Ho was a great Chicano hero, did you? Well, you boys just ain't up on your revolutionary rhetoric. He fought right alongside Pancho Villa, under the name of Martinez."

"I always knew you were a genius, *chica*."

"Where *does* the money come from, by the way?" David asked her.

"Oh, ho. Manny was right. Right in the files, along with those little crumpled dollar bills that come in from the faithful, they have some friendly business letters on corporate letterheads. With a five grand here, and a three grand there, here a grand, there a grand . . . I didn't even have to spook to find them. Carlos was so proud of them he pulled them out and waved them at me. 'Look,' he said. 'The Compañía is an intercultural movement. We got *Anglos* making contributions.'"

"Which corporate letterheads?"

"I don't remember, David. Most of them were Texas companies. I just put them through the old Xerox machine when Carlos was out and dropped the copies off at

Uncle Manny's little round office. I swear, I don't know how the revolutionaries hacked it in the old days without Xerox machines. Or the spies, either."

"You're a fine spy, Lupe. I hope your conscience doesn't hurt you."

"It does, a little bit, Papa. But if anybody's going to be in trouble, it'll be Carlos. Poor old Primo's just lost in that tangle."

When Lupe went into her bedroom to check on the health and sound sleep of Miguelito, Cruz poured another Scotch into her glass. "I have to dope her up a little," he explained. "She's gonna mother that kid to death."

"You know, it's odd that any Texas business would put money into the Compañía. They don't usually support anything more radical than the Petroleum Institute or the Dallas Cowboys."

"I don't give a damn for politics," Cruz said. "I stopped voting when Bob Taft lost the nomination. All I want is my few little cows and a chance to treat the clap once in a while."

Lupe came back and said, "Papa. I forgot. I was so sore about Miguelito I just forgot. Did you hear from Rosenthal?"

"No, not since he went off to Finland or wherever the hell it was."

"He sold the Grant."

"Sure he sold it. He sold it to me."

Lupe sat down across from him. "No, Papa. In the Santa Fe paper. He sold it to some land company. I'm sorry, I didn't remember to cut the clipping."

"I don't know what you read, Lupe, but Cruz is buying it."

"David, I'm not fooling. The Len-Jar-Rose, it said.

Part of the original Juan Tafoya Grant. What was it? Three hundred and something sections? Really, it was in the paper. Something called the, oh, I don't know, the Rancho Grande something, bought it."

"Lupe, you're just sleepy," Cruz said. "Go to bed, why don't you?"

"Look, I don't care whether you believe me or not. I'm telling you I read it." She drank her Scotch in a long swallow and stood up. "I'm going to bed and you *machos* can wrestle it out between you."

"Can they really do that?" Cruz asked after a while. "Can somebody really come in there and buy that land out from under me?"

"No, they can't," David said, "unless Rosenthal is a low-life son of a bitch with no professional ethics. It doesn't matter *how* much money he was offered, and it was probably a lot. If you've made a bargain you keep it, or you're dead in the business. Cruz, maybe Lupe's wrong. Let me call that business manager on the Coast right now. There *must* be some kind of mistake."

"I don't know, *cuate*. I got a feeling in my old Mexican bones there's no mistake. Anyway, don't bother. We can find out for sure tomorrow. Don't feel bad. It's not your fault."

Cruz sat in his big leather armchair and looked at the ceiling. "I got too ambitious. I'm not gonna be a *gachupín* after all. Hell, David, what does Rosenthal care? He's not in the land business or the cattle business. He's in the Yugoslavian Western business. Maybe they got their own set of principles out there in Hollywood."

"That's true," David admitted. "But it's dirty and it makes me mad."

"It doesn't bother old Cruz, though. No, sir. Win a

few, lose a few." Cruz wiped his wet eyes with his bandanna. "Goddamn, I'm just too old to do this. It's embarrassing. Don't tell Lupe, hey, *cuate?*"

Luis spent his second night in the dome. All that day he and Echeagaray had walked and hunted coyotes and hawks together, while the old Basque told him about sheep. Luis thought he made sheep sound almost lovable.

Chapter 20

EDITORIAL in the Albuquerque *Standard:*

Chicano leader Primitivo Rael, whose organizatoin claims porpietary rihgts to etaoin shrdluzzzxxxx clams proprietary rights to millions of acres in New Mexico, has announced that he and his followers plan to "taek over" or "occupy" the Cumbre National Monument on Schristmas Day.

Claiming the Momunent belongs "to all the people," Raels organization is disputing the Fedreal Government's pwnership of the land, and it's right to charge a camping fee.

We agree the land belongs to "all the poeple," but we challenge Mr. Rael's position on the basis that his grup represents only wore a floor-length empire gown of ivory embroidered faille accented with pearl trim. a minority of the citizens.

We hope New Mecixo's law-enforement agencies will act vigorously to prevnet this illegal "occupatoin."

Chapter 21

DAVID DROVE Cruz's Nash pickup across the river and north on the State Highway to the Len-Jar-Rose. Under snow there was little to see, but enough to confirm that almost four hundred square miles, no matter what the topography, has a certain feeling of limitlessness about it that makes it seem an unlikely parcel to be *owned* by anyone. The cowboys, herdsmen, cooks, smiths, and mechanics, and their families, were gone. All the stock, cows and calves too, had been sold; the buildings were stripped and hollow.

Sam Applewhite drove David in a Jeep on a crisscross route through the Upper Grant; friendly enough, but depressed and in a hurry to leave the great ranch for good, for quits, as soon as he could. David made notes as often as his cold, stiff fingers allowed. He examined the incomplete water maps the State Engineer's Office had sent him, all of them based on careful, intelligent guesses, but guesses for all that.

"Don't know what the hell those people want," Sam said. "This is cattle country, not house country. Too far from the cities to be a suburb. Maybe want to build a whole new city here."

"I don't know, Sam. It might be a retirement place, old people. Maybe they want to get away from their own towns."

"Yeah, but why here? This isn't a good place for old people. Too cold. Hell, it's too cold for me these days, and I've wintered some bad ones. Damn fool place to pick."

"Think the ranch could hold a lot of people?"

"Mr. Reed, this ranch could *hold* all the people in the world, if they didn't mind standing up all the time."

"What about water?"

"Oh, we never had any water problems. Streams and rivers run about eight months out of the year, wells are good. Artesian water. Tastes all right to drink. A little foxy, maybe, but it won't hurt you."

"How many people? I mean, there's water for how many people?"

"People? Hell, I couldn't say. We ran maybe six thousand head of cattle. They drink out of the streams or the stock tanks. Never heard one of them complain. Up to two hundred people, on top of that, spread around, when we're busy. Always water for them, too. We *got* eighteen wells. All of 'em have gas-generated pumps now. We unhooked the last windmill a couple of years ago. I had 'em leave it standing, though. Pretty. I love to watch a windmill turn."

David explained the water problem at dinner. Cruz didn't understand it. David said it another way. He spoke of aquifers and recovery time. He illustrated with three glasses of water, pouring measured amounts from the first to the second, the second to the third.

"You mean that if that development builds too many houses on the Upper Grant, and drill too many water wells, they'll all go dry?"

"Yes, that's partly it."

"I don't care if their damned wells go dry. The hell with them. I'll sell water to them myself, at ten dollars a bucket."

"No, I don't think so, Cruz. If they overuse their water, they'll go dry eventually. Their water table will sink and they'll have to drill deeper and deeper holes. But Cruz, your wells will go dry sooner. Years sooner. The Upper Grant, well, call it upstream from you on the aquifer. You share the same underground water system."

Cruz put his food down and thought about it. "No," he said finally. "They can't do that. It's against the law to steal water. People used to get killed for that out here. Hunh. They still get killed for it. You buy your water rights on a ditch. Somebody upstream diverts it. You ride up there and tell him to stop it. If he doesn't, you ride up there again and shoot him."

"I don't know your law very well, but the underground water is different. You can see a stream, but the location and capacity of water-bearing rock five hundred or a thousand feet underground isn't so easy to find and measure. It's all engineers' estimates."

"I'm not worried, *cuate*. They got the Upper Grant, but if they try to steal my water, I'll go see my lawyer. You worry too much; you're going to develop a gastric ulcer. You know what a Sippy regimen is? Don't even think about it."

David tried not to worry, but he worried anyway. He didn't know the water situation, he admitted that to himself, having only rough maps and imprecise knowledge of the drainage and water tables. But he knew the men who had yanked Cruz's dream from under him. He'd seen the same piano-box scatter in Texas, the houses packed together like dominoes, the sad, flat, treeless streets, the sandy golf courses set unwisely into each development, the flaking "country clubs."

"Cruz, I feel bad about this whole business. I take it personally."

"Me too," said Cruz, "but that's business. I shouldn't have tried to play with the big boys. There's nothing we can do about it. We're just gonna have lots of new neighbors."

On the wall of the Governor's outer office were photographs or etchings of every chief executive since the American occupation, from the earliest military governors, with their tight cheekbones and paranoid eyes, to the modern politicians, whose expressions indicated both malice and bonhomie. Warschauer, the Governor's press assistant, whose job it was to know the precise weight of power and leverage behind each visitor, couldn't place David A. Reed at all, but he had an appointment, and Warschauer found it wise to assume the existence of clout until it was proved absent.

"Mr. Reed," the Governor said. "I hope you're not bringing me more trouble. I already have a handful."

"I hope not too."

"You know I can't do anything about that land sale. Cruz told me it was dirty, but it's not illegal. A man can sell his land to anyone he wants, most of the time."

"If I may, let me tell you something about the buyers."

"The buyer's a man named Cotton," the Governor said. "He wants to develop the property. It's too bad Cruz lost out, but those Texans have all the cash. What did it sell for?"

"Two million, sir. It's worth three, easily, and Cruz only had one. I couldn't reach Rosenthal, the owner—he's in Europe—but his business manager told me when Dumas called and offered double our offer, he couldn't let Rosenthal turn it down. Cruz hadn't signed anything yet, and..."

"Dumas? Who's Dumas?"

"Well, he's a vice-president of the development company—Ranchito Grandes Mansions."

The Governor winced. "That's ungrammatical and it doesn't make sense. Big Plural Little Ranch Singular." He hunted among the papers on his desk and found a typed list. "Is that Philip Dumas of Fort Worth? Executive Vice-President of the Maravilloso Trailer Sales?"

"Yes," David said. "The same man. He administers several of Mr. Cotton's businesses for him. He's a weasel, but that's beside the point."

"You know these people?"

"Yes, I worked for C. C. Cotton once."

"I see. Now, what's this about water?"

"First of all, Ranchito Grandes builds junk. Their mansions run between eighteen and twenty-four thousand. Pressed Kleenex walls on cardboard studs. Rooms about the size of a horse's stall. You can punch a hole through the doors with your elbow. Each house comes with a big, big, full one-sixth-acre lot. Thirty-year mortgages. They cram houses into their land without regard for topography or green space or water availability."

"So it's not a class operation. Few developments are."

The telephone on Manny's desk buzzed. He said, "Have him come in," into it, and when a tall, skinny man entered he said, "Charlie, this is Mr. Reed, David Reed,

Charlie Dentan, the State Engineer, knows all about water. Sometimes I think he's got water on the brain. I thought Charlie had better listen to what you had to say, Mr. Reed, because to be honest, I don't know anything about that problem."

David spoke for ten minutes, compressing all he knew and all he could guess into his exposition. He used the water-resources map for reference. He described, with warm feeling, the crowded ugliness of Ranchito Grandes Mansions, and the sublime space of the Upper Grant as it stood.

"I can see," Manny said, "that Cruz wouldn't want a city for a neighbor, but that's progress, Mr. Reed. Many people are moving into our state; we're delighted to have them. Think of the boon to our economy. New money, lots of work for the construction industry. Arizona's been getting all that, up until now. We have much to offer."

"I'm not speaking for Cruz, Governor. He doesn't even know I'm here. I'm saying that Cruz's ranch is going to go dry—it's very likely to go dry, anyway—if they build that development the way they build their others. Governor, I admit that I'm not an engineer, but I've seen it happen in Texas, too. And that's not a desert state."

"Neither is New Mexico," the Governor said. "The tourist literature we put out stresses that."

"Maybe so," Dentan said, "but it's wrong. This is a desert state. We're a desert by every yardstick I can think of, except we don't have Arabs and camels."

"Charlie, is there any basis for Mr. Reed's worry?"

"Yes, sir. He may not be an engineer, but he knows what he's talking about. Our water estimates aren't gospel, but New Mexico can't handle many more people than it has now, unless somebody comes up with a substitute for water, or they find a way of piping the Mississippi uphill for a thousand miles."

"Governor," David said, "the developers have room for seventy-five or a hundred thousand houses on that land. They're a bulldozer operation; they flatten all the natural contours, lay out a square grid and start scraping."

"As far as I know, they haven't filed a plat with the county yet," Dentan said. "I haven't seen one. This kind of problem's never come up. We've adjudicated some little water hassles, but we've never stopped a whole city. I don't think there's machinery for anybody to do it. But, Lord, Governor, a couple of hundred thousand people in that basin will dry up the whole valley in three or four years."

"I'm not going to be the first Governor of New Mexico to stop the march of progress," Manny said. "The Legislature's growth-minded. They want the tax base to keep spreading. They like payrolls. Mr. Reed, this is a poor state."

"Mr. Dentan, how would you stop them, if you had to? How would you limit them?"

"I don't know," Dentan said. "Under the Fair Use statute, maybe. As I say, it's never come up. We'd have to do a resources survey, a good one, and then testify against their experts."

"Governor," said David. "I'm not a resident of this state, though I plan to be. I've always liked New Mexico because it didn't seem to have the . . . well, the diseases that Texas has. Through isolation or poverty, or lack of initiative, or maybe the simple fact that no one group dominates the whole state, New Mexico has been slow to catch up with the rest of the country. I know that's bad in some ways, but in another way it's an advantage. You've all had a chance to see what doesn't work. It's something like being able to see into the future. New Mexico may live in the past, but the future is all around you, and you can learn from it. I'd say New Mexico has an opportunity to profit by the mistakes of other states. And believe me, Ranchito Grandes Mansions is a mistake."

" 'Ranchito Grandes,' " the Governor mused. "I wish those Texans wouldn't mutilate our language, no offense intended."

"Governor, you should see them mutilate a landscape."

"Thank you for coming in, Mr. Reed. Charlie, here, isn't under my despotic sway, unfortunately. He's a professional and he's under the Personnel Act. Charlie can't be fired as long as he does his job. Now, I'm a prudent man, Mr. Reed. If I went before the Legislature, or on television, and said I wanted to discourage a reputable Texas business firm, to create barriers to its successful operation in New Mexico, I would have my Mexican hide nailed to the church door like Martin Luther's ninety-five theses. You see that, don't you?"

"Yes, sir, I can see that."

"But if I were to order Charlie Dentan, here, to do his job, why, nobody could criticize me for that, could they? So, I'll do that instead. Charlie, I want you to be sure to do your job."

"Do you mean you want me to . . ."

"I don't see why I should go into details. After all, I'm not a professional engineer. I can't quote the language, but I know the State Engineer is charged with studying water resources and making recommendations for water use, and that sort of technical thing. I always try to listen to my experts, Charlie."

"I'll put some people on it," Dentan said, standing up. "Good-bye, Mr. Reed. There'll probably be some of my boys out at Mr. Tafoya's place in a week or two, testing well pressure and volume and recovery time. We never have done a really good survey out in that area." He glanced at the Governor. "Kind of a stingy legislature. They don't appropriate our office hardly enough to buy a dipstick and a Mason jar. You ever try to hire a good ground-water geologist for four hundred and twenty dollars a month?"

"You're bitching at the wrong man, Charlie," Manny said. "I can cut appropriations, but I can't raise them."

When Dentan left, David collected his notes and maps and shook hands with Manny.

"I appreciate it, Governor. Thank you."

"I'm glad to help if I can. Ah, Mr. Reed, when you were speaking of this company, I got the impression you knew them very well."

"I do. I worked for several years for C. C. Cotton of Houston. I wasn't in the real estate development end of things, but I know a lot of the people."

Manny's eyebrows went up, briefly. "I'm impressed. A very well-known man. The fourth or fifth richest man in America, I believe."

"Something like that," David said.

"Yes. Yes, I see. Mr. Reed, you can do something for me, I think. My State Land Office and Bureau of Revenue—I don't know why I call them mine, actually; delusions of grandeur—are preparing a list for me. Meanwhile, I have *this* list." He took a sheet of paper from his desk. "Lupe got this for me."

"I remember," David said.

"Would you, as a favor, look it over for me? I don't know any of these people, but you might. Write me a note, or come in yourself. I'd appreciate your help."

"Happily. Thank you for your help, too. I . . . well, hell, Governor. I like your brother. He's been wonderful to me, and I feel I've let him down."

"Good-bye, Mr. Reed. Merry Christmas."

"Merry Christmas."

"Oh, I plan to have a splendid Christmas," the Governor said.

Chapter 22

STATE OF NEW MEXICO

Office of the Governor

Mr. David A. Reed
c/o Juan de la Cruz Tafoya y Evans
Tafoya Ranch
Pozo Verde, New Mexico

Dear Mr. Reed:

It was very pleasant to see you at my office yesterday and to learn your views of the proposed Ranchito Grandes Mansions housing development. I am unable to say at the present time what the state's official stance will be on this question, but I can assure you that Mr. Dentan is looking into it very carefully. In addition, I have asked the Attorney General to prepare an informal opinion concerning the various possibilities.

As you will recall, I asked you to peruse a list of names. I now enclose another list, prepared by the

214

Bureau of Revenue. These names represent the purchasers of record of various parcels of private land transferred in the last year. You will notice that both lists contain many of the same names. What I would like you to do is tell me, informally and privately, who they are and what they do.

I doubt that you will know all of them, but as you are a Texan and, so it seems, a Texan who functioned at a high level of business and industry, I imagine that you might be familiar with some of them.

Unfortunately, I cannot as yet tell you why I require this information. However, if you can't guess, I shall be disappointed.

Sincerely,

(s) Manuel Tafoya

Appendix attached

APPENDIX

Orin Crookshanks, San Antonio
Richard Gauvey, Lubbock
Harry Fuselle, Amarillo
Philip Dumas, Ft. Worth
Guy C. MacKay, Wichita Falls
W. D. Windom, Dallas
Thornton Baker, Dallas
Burke Spencer, Houston
Everett Purdy, Houston
Orville Post, Tulsa, Okla.
Dwayne Edington, Oklahoma City, Okla.

Tafoya Ranch
Pozo Verde, N.M.

The Honorable Manuel Tafoya
Governor of New Mexico
State Capitol
Santa Fe, New Mexico

Dear Governor Tafoya:

Thank you for your letter, and for hearing me out on what is very probably more of an emotional issue than a legal or administrative one.

With respect to the lists of names, I am able to report that I know all of them excepting Messrs. Gauvey and Post.

Philip Dumas, of course, is a former coworker of mine in the employ of C. C. Cotton. He was Mr. Cotton's agent in the purchase of the Len-Jar-Rose, or Upper Grant.

Orin Crookshanks is an executive of Sinclair Land & Cattle Company, owned by Chester Pope Enterprises, Inc., of Dallas. Harry Fuselle is an officer of the same company.

Guy MacKay, who was a classmate of mine at Rice, is a petroleum geologist, a vice-president at Pindell Oil Company, owned by Leroy Pindell, a successful independent operator.

W. D. Windom is, or was, a marketing representative of Tex-Ark-La, Inc., a land development subsidiary of the Shoreline South Corporation. The chairman and major stockholder of Shoreline is a somewhat mysterious gentleman named Warner Loehr, who has often denied that he is the richest man in America.

Thornton Baker is confidential secretary to Virgil S. Cole, a rancher, cattle-raiser, oil operator, frozen-food executive, and a dozen other things.

Burke Spencer is employed by C. C. Cotton. In fact, Spencer was one of my assistants. He may have my old job now, which carried no title, but which was domestic troubleshooter and general flunky.

Everett Purdy is the editor of the conservative newsletter *Clarion Call,* published by the aforementioned Shoreline South Corporation and distributed privately. Mr. Purdy has suggested several times that Adolf Hitler was soft on communism.

Dwayne Edington, whom I have met only once, and under hilarious circumstances (a convention in Oklahoma City during which everybody, 300 businessmen and their wives, got diarrhea from tainted mayonnaise at the formal banquet), is a Certified Life Underwriter for Plains-Osage Mutual Insurance Company. Chairman of the board is Walton Orendorff.

You insist upon mystery, but I will nevertheless assume that you seek a pattern. The men whose names you sent me are fairly diverse. Their only similarity is that they work, at the second or third level of responsibility, for extremely successful and wealthy men. I assume also that, as purchasers of record, and as contributors to Mr. Rael's organization, they were acting not for themselves but for their employers.

The employers—Cotton, Chester Pope, Leroy Pindell, Warner Loehr, Virgil Cole, and Walton Orendorff—belong to an informal but exclusive group. They are mutual acquaintances; they meet frequently; they play poker together (except Loehr, who believes that cards are sinful); they seldom compete directly with each other; they often gang up, corporately speaking, to intimidate and vanquish the less resourceful. They are all tougher than hell.

Sincerely,

(s) David Reed

Chapter 23

WHILE BETTY ARBUCKLE sat in the Park Service cabin and nursed her baby, Fletcher had scrounged for lumber and hammered together a sturdy but unsightly platform for the dignitaries he expected on Christmas. He cleared snow, tons of it, from the empty parking area, knowing that he would watch it fill again with snow just before the meeting, or the confrontation, or whatever it was, on the twenty-fifth, and take a perverse pleasure when it did.

The Monument was officially closed, but when the District Supervisor said to open the son of a bitch up, he opened the son of a bitch up. He didn't mind the work. He liked to work, Christmas or not. He didn't like the cold, but he'd bought some wonderful gloves, skier's gloves, with part of the magical $2,500 that Santa Claus or the Good Fairy had sent him.

He'd bought new uniform trousers, too, and a diaper service for the baby, and a washing machine, and subscriptions to a dozen magazines for Betty, who learned from reading one of them that her life was cruelly circumscribed by a feminine role, that she had never been allowed to realize her potential as a complete human being, that she was an exploited sexual object, and that Fletcher was himself both victim and victimizer, but mainly the latter. Just this morning he had offered, with the best will in the world, to suckle the baby while Betty slogged out in the snow to build a platform and set up the microphone and speakers. The suggestion, for some reason, had made her furious.

Fletcher didn't really believe that anyone would come to Cumbre in the middle of a snowstorm, but he set things up anyway. He said, "Testing, one, two," into the microphone and got a feedback squeal which must have terrified every hibernating bear in the canyon. He lowered the gain and sang "Jingle Bells."

The state and Federal cars arrived before the pickups, full of the "dignitaries" whom Fletcher always found to be such a pain during the summer, when they demanded and got specially conducted tours and asked foolish questions.

The District Supervisor came. He said, without much conviction, that Fletcher had done a good job, considering. The Governor arrived, with four State Policemen and the Chief himself. Fletcher was introduced to them, and to the state Attorney General, the U. S. Attorney from Albuquerque, the Director of the New Mexico Human Rights Commission, a Federal marshal with a genuine G-man badge, and a group of cold-looking reporters and photographers.

There wasn't room on the platform for everyone, and there was some jockeying and rank-pulling and protocol-quoting in the biting cold, but it ceased when the pickups drove in.

Fletcher had been told to expect as many as a thousand trucks, for which there wasn't nearly enough parking space. There were only eighty or ninety, crammed with people in bulky clothes. Seven hundred people, Fletcher estimated, of both sexes and all ages. They filled the open space before the platform, breathing mist and stamping their feet.

A small, dark-skinned man separated himself from the crowd and walked to the group near the Governor. They shook hands, and the Governor introduced him to the others. It all seemed very cordial. Another man, looking plump and out of breath, came half running, half walking down the snow-packed entrance road and pushed through the crowd toward the platform. Fletcher heard him gasping something about a flat tire. The man looked familiar, but Fletcher couldn't place him.

There didn't seem to be any organized agenda or order of speakers. The plump man spoke first, in Spanish. It was brief; Fletcher understood most of it.

"This place belongs to us. We are taking it back. We are occupying it. We will live on it. It is ours. No one can move us."

The crowd applauded, a hollow patting of thickly gloved hands. A few men whooped.

The District Supervisor spoke next, in English. "As a representative of the National Park Service, I welcome you to Cumbre National Monument."

No one applauded. The Supervisor looked confused. The Governor walked to the microphone and translated. There was scattered clapping.

The plump man didn't seem happy, for some reason. He spoke again. "This land belongs to us."

Again the District Supervisor spoke in English. "This land belongs to all Americans." Again the Governor translated.

The small man and the plump man stepped off the platform together and began to argue in whispers. The small man shrugged, and the plump one mounted the platform. Now it became a bilingual duel between him and the Governor, who frequently conferred, before answering, with the U. S. Attorney or the state Attorney General.

"We are here illegally. The Monument is closed," said the plump man.

"No," said the Governor. "The Monument has been opened."

"We have no permits. We refuse to buy permits."

"The District Supervisor has waived the necessity for permits. You are all welcome."

"We are trespassing. We are forcibly trespassing on Federal land."

"On whose land?"

"On . . . on our land. It is our land!"

"Then you are not trespassing."

"We will stay forever!"

"We hope you will be comfortable."

"We are breaking the law!"

"I have just talked to the United States Attorney, to the New Mexico Attorney General and to the Chief of the New Mexico State Police. They are all trained and skilled in questions of law. They have seen no lawbreaking."

"He's trying to trick you," the plump man said. "You know you're not really welcome here. As soon as these reporters leave, the police are going to start shooting. They're going to use tear gas on you. They're going to try to push you off the land. They're going to let you get comfortable, set up your tents and get your fires going,

222

then they're going to move in. And if they can't do it, the Governor will bring in Army tanks and soldiers."

The snow was blowing sideways, almost horizontally. The men near the platform and the crowd of people were taking on the pale coloration of the elements. Everyone stamped and waved arms and blew into cupped hands. The plump man at the microphone became aware that most of his audience were concentrating on keeping warm and paying him scant attention. He relinquished the microphone and said something to the Governor which Fletcher couldn't hear, but which, from the furious expression on the man's face, he could imagine.

The Governor took over the microphone and spoke in Spanish.

"There are policemen here. That is true. There are four of them, and hundreds of you. They are as cold as you. They are as unlikely to cause violence as you. Mr. Rael has assured me that you are here with peaceful and honest intentions, and all of us accept and respect that. You know me. Many of you voted for me. I am a *politico*, and your lives and the lives of your fathers have been made hell by all *politicos*, in Spain and in Mexico, and here when this was Mexico, and always."

The wind began to die and the snow fell more softly. The cold remained. The U. S. Attorney was doing what looked like a clog dance on the platform to restore life to his toes.

"I don't ask you to trust me," the Governor went on. "Trust only what a *politico* does, and does consistently. Be very careful about whom you believe. Many of you have given money, small amounts, to support the work of La Compañía de Tierra y Libertad. As you know, as I

223

have said, I do not agree with many of the principles of the Compañía, but that is unimportant. You agree with it, and you confirm your belief with money. That is the right thing to do.

"But . . . look at you, you're all freezing your *nalgas* off in the snow, on Christmas Day. If you really want to sleep out here in the woods from now on, you're welcome. I admire your tenacity, but just now I don't admire your sense.

"I'll try to help you when you make sense, because my name is Tafoya. But if you're not making sense, I'll try to show you where sense exists, because my name is also Evans. So I'm a half-breed *coyote*, and I can't listen to my blood, because it tells me two different things. I listen to my mind instead. And right now I'm freezing to death. Good luck and Merry Christmas."

The small dark man approached the microphone and tried to speak through it, but found it too high. Fletcher loosened the nut on the microphone stand, lowered it for him, and went back to his place beside the platform.

"I am forty-three years old," Primo Rael told them, "and like a child. I don't know anything. You are following a fool.

"But listen a short while longer, and then get into your pickups and go home, and wait until spring.

"You are not the only ones who support the Compañía. Your treasury is larger than you think. Our organization has two treasuries: the small one, to which you contribute your dollars, and a larger one of which you know nothing. Into this one has gone nearly one hundred thousand dollars. With this money, some of your members, mostly young men, have purchased rifles, pistols, ammunition, dangerous explosives, military grenades, and such devices for killing and destroying.

"I knew nothing of this treasury, believe me."

Everyone in the crowd was listening now. Even the children, too numb with cold to play, were listening.

"In the last year, many ranches and farms here in the north valleys have been plundered and burned, their owners frightened and injured. Some of the victims were Anglos, some were Hispanos, but all were frightened and many of them sold their lands as quickly as they could and left New Mexico. It has been a long time since there was violence of that kind here, and these people did not know how to protect themselves.

"The lands were bought quickly, for little money, by men from Texas who seemed almost able to read the minds of these ranchers and farmers. Sometimes they offered money before anyone knew these lands were for sale."

The plump man, Fletcher saw, had stopped moving his feet and arms and was staring at Primo, his head slowly shaking from side to side. He seemed to be in a dream.

"The men who bought these lands were the same men who poured money into the treasury, the secret treasury, of our Compañía. First they created a panic and a terror in honest people, and then they profited by it.

"I don't know what can be done about the damage already accomplished. We have all been victims of these people. Yet I doubt that they will ever go to jail, or be tried in a court, or pay a fine, or suffer on this earth for what they have done. I believe strongly that they will serve an eternity in hell, but that is a decision Someone Else must make.

"My trusted counselor arranged for all of this. Never

mind his name. I don't know why he did it. Perhaps the money. He helped the men from Texas. He arranged to buy weapons with their money. He recruited young men from within and without the Compañía, to raid the farms and ranches. He promised them payment in land, private payment. This is what I suppose, because I have no proof, but it can be nothing else."

Two of the State Policemen were watching Carlos apprehensively. The Governor had warned them that he might do something quick and stupid, but so far he seemed drugged.

"Thank you for listening to me. You may stay here all winter if you really want to. No one will bother you. I think it will be cold and uncomfortable. I do not believe the Government will ever return this place to us, but I will help you try to convince them. Thank you."

The people in the parking lot moved toward their trucks, while the big shots on the platform shook hands and smiled. Fletcher tried to disconnect the microphone, but the plump man shouldered him aside. Despite the cold, his face was sweating.

"I don't know what Señor Rael was talking about," Carlos yelled. "It's just a mistake. Don't worry. Now I am wondering about you. I have concern for you. It is so cold here that we will need a fire. You men with axes—chop down some of the trees, your own trees, and we'll make some fires and cook some coffee and *cabrito*. How about that?"

Carlos waited for half a minute and, when no one responded, he said, "I'll show you how. Don't be afraid of these *chotas*." He stepped heavily off the platform and walked through the crowd. *"Dame una hacha,"* he yelled to one of the men and, armed with a logging ax, he approached a ponderosa pine sapling at the edge of the snowy parking area. He spat on his gloves and waggled his shoulders in a cruel parody of an outdoorsman. He missed the tree entirely on the first swing and nearly fell. Soon he got into an uneven rhythm, puffing and gasping in the thin, cold air, and the little tree went down.

"Illegal logging," the U. S. Attorney said. "No permit."

"Destroying Government property," said the Chief of Police.

"Also conspiring to commit both offenses," said the District Supervisor, who'd been reading the newspapers.

"It's your jurisdiction here," Manny said to the U. S. Attorney, "but if I were you I'd lock his ass up."

The U. S. Attorney nodded to the Federal marshal. "Lock his ass up," he said.

A half mile past the entrance to the Monument, the Governor told his driver to pull into a logging road. Five hundred yards into the pine forest, in a clearing, was what appeared to be a Panzer division—parked half-tracks, troop carriers and four obsolete light tanks, all with their motors running. Two companies of soldiers, huddled in a loose formation, were stamping their feet and blowing on their fingers.

The Adjutant General of the New Mexico National Guard climbed out of his staff car and saluted Manny.

"All present and accounted for, sir. When do we move?"

"Oh, for Christ's sake, George," the Governor said. "I meant a platoon, or a squad, or something. How much is all this going to cost?"

"G-three will prepare cost analysis, sir. I've planned an armored spearhead down the main Monument road, and two infantry flank pincers. Nothing like armor to take the steam out of insurrection. Look at the Russians in Prague."

"Maybe you'd better let these kids go home," Manny said. "Just call this winter maneuvers or something. The insurrection fell apart."

"Yes, sir," the Adjutant General said. "I'll disperse the formation. Perhaps if the Governor would speak to the men. They've been in position since oh five hundred hours."

Manny slogged through the snow to a ragged line of Guardsmen and singled out a frostbitten corporal who was holding his hands under his armpits for warmth.

"Where're you from, son?" he asked, in the manner of Eisenhower on the eve of D-Day.

"Who the fuck wants to know?" the corporal asked.

Manny raised his voice. "Merry Christmas, men. We're proud of you."

Chapter 24

"I'M FIFTY-NINE years old," Cruz said, "and my stomach hurts all the time. I'm too old to be a *gachupín.*"..

"Oh, be quiet, Papa."

"I just want to ..."

"... run your few cows and cure the clap. I know."

Cruz looked out the *sala* window toward due north. Through the late-January mist he could barely see the *colina.*

"What's he gonna do to that good land?"

"Nothing, Papa. Tell him, David."

"She's right, Cruz. We're going to nibble old Cotton to death."

"No, we're not. He's got too much money. He's got more money than God. He's gonna suck up all the water. He's gonna use my ranch for his cesspool."

"Papa, don't be so gloomy. They're not going to dig a well or build a house up there. We're not going to let them."

Charlie Dentan and several other interested state officials had been assaulting Ranchito Grandes Mansions with a barrage of injunctions, estoppals, show-causes, and naked threats. They were inundated by unsolicited support in the form of sign carriers, ecology freaks, romantics, and an overwhelming number of citizens who, for one reason or another, held emotional grudges against Texans.

The developers dispatched platoons of lobbyists to Santa Fe, bribing and bullying and wheedling, but they were jammed in on so many fronts that their organization shattered. The winter provided a jolly round of open hearings. The Texans would wriggle through a day or two of ground-water inquisition, plugging breaches forced by state experts with the living bodies of rebuttal experts, in much the same way that defense and prosecution psychiatrists debate whether the defendant is a potential Secretary of State or a barely controlled child rapist.

When the water talk ended, Cotton's troops would hustle over to another chamber for smog talk, land-use talk, or just general abuse. A team of languid architects spent one corrosive afternoon discussing the Mansions' four basic home designs. Words like "lean-to," "duck blind," and "privy" were tossed about.

"I mean it, Cruz," David said. "Cotton gets bored fast when too many little things go wrong. Anyway, home-building's just a sideline with him. He won't waste too much time on it."

"A man should be able to do what he wants with his own land."

"Well, don't feel sorry for him, Cruz. He'll get out before he loses too much money. He'll sell it or give it to the Boy Scouts and take the loss off his taxes."

"I never saw you so gloomy, Papa. What's wrong?"

"Ahh, I don't know. I wanted to leave something to my children. You know, I thought Luis might . . . forget it. I'm tired. If Luis wants to live with the sheep, let him. Excuse me, I'm gonna lie down. My stomach hurts."

"I've never seen him like that; I worry about him, David."

"I think he'll brighten up when we finally get C. C. Cotton, Sr., off the Grant. It makes me a little nervous, too. He's a standard kind of son of a bitch, but that doesn't make him any more attractive."

"David, dear David, what did he *do* to you?"

"To me? Paid me very well, gave me lots of invaluable experience, taught me some tricks."

"What did you do to him?"

"Doesn't matter."

"Please tell me. Please, dear David. Tell me what happened."

"Not important."

"You're a standard kind of rat bastard," she said.

David was asleep when Lupe tiptoed into his room wearing men's pajamas and lay down beside him. She kissed him on a closed eye.

"Tell me."

"Hmmm?"

"*Tell* me."

"Lupe! For God's sake, Lupe."

"Okay. Tell me later. First let me say it's an honor to welcome such a fine gentleman into our house."

"Much later," David told her.

He had spent three weeks in Colorado, alone, learning all there was to know about sugar beets. They were, he discovered quickly, an extraordinarily ugly vegetable, edible only if you were very hungry, but when put through a smelly refining process they produced white sugar indistinguishable from cane squeezings. C. C. Cotton already owned cane plantations in Texas and Louisiana and a profitable refinery. Now he wanted to branch out, to get a full nelson on cane *and* beets. He wanted to be a Sugar King and bothered once to explain why. "Ah got me a sweet tooth, boy," he told David. It was reason enough.

David sent three written reports to Houston, telephoned every third night, and kept Cotton current on the Colorado sugar deal. Cotton had other young men, none with David's seniority, strewn about the world arranging for other investments and sales. Cotton liked to keep the pot stirred up. He always had a variety of objects spinning in the air. He enjoyed the exercise of skill, he enjoyed the profits. He knew, too, that fast hands and a quick mix kept the F.T.C. people confused and uncertain. When the Feds focused on Cotton's spinning plates and began to get their wits together, he would dispose of the plates and start to juggle lemons. He and his lawyers had a wide-eyed, country-boy way of answering those Federal inquiries: "Ain' nothin' wrong with jugglin' lemons, is theah?"

David eventually located and studied three big beet farms, two of them in potential trouble because of archaic equipment, and another that was sound but underpriced. He also examined a beet refinery, a recent conglomerate acquisition that wasn't paying off at a rate the stockholders admired. Cotton had his eyes on the refinery, too. He would even like, he admitted to David, to buy a nice little railroad and set his own freight rates, but John Rockefeller had tried that once and got his fingers mashed.

Cotton flew in on a Thursday. He and David sat up until past midnight in his Brown Palace suite, talking figures. The next morning David drove him to the beet farms so that he could "walk" them. So long as the entities Cotton purchased were tangible, not simply pieces of paper, he insisted on seeing them with his own pale blue eyes, walking over land, striding through the corridors of office buildings, touching the crude oil, or grains, or cattle, or sugar beets he was going to own. They drove next to the sugar-beet refinery, which Cotton pronounced solid but ripe-smelling.

Back in Denver, Cotton signed the letters David had readied for him. The preparations were sound and well organized, the offers were both reasonable and attractive. Neither David nor his employer had little doubt they would be accepted, as indeed they were.

Now Cotton felt buoyant and springy. He'd just offered to spend nearly four million dollars—a lot to support a sweet tooth—and had immediately lost interest in sugar beets, now that they were his. He and David drank bourbon until late, while Cotton regaled him with tales of his own country-boy shrewdness, the helpless fatuity of Easterners in any business deal, and the appalling leftward drift of all American institutions, including the Southern Baptist Convention and the Buffalo Bayou Country Club.

In Cotton's small but garishly appointed corporate jet plane, they flew south next morning toward an Albuquerque refueling stop. David, just a touch hung over, could concentrate on nothing more cerebral than *Business Week*. Cotton, however, traveled as always with maps draped over his knees, aligned with the plane's route, watching from the window as the land itself folded and

233

reared and flattened, checking the paper-and-ink representation of the terrain on his lap. It was one of his pleasures to read maps. It was a hobby to which he was faithful, and it paid off, too. He'd found the Fillmore Three oil field that way, in a part of Kansas that was supposed to produce nothing but hogs.

David had just gone to sleep, with *Business Week* draped tentlike over his face, when the plane's wheels bumped and squealed on the runway. Glancing out the window, he saw that they were not in Albuquerque, but in Trinidad, Colorado, just north of the New Mexico line.

"Ah want you to go talk to a fella," Cotton said.

"Okay," David said. "Who is he?"

"Well, now. Ah don' *know* who he is, boy. Ah don' even know exactly *wheah* he is. But first off we gone fahnd him, and then you gone *talk* to him. Whoevah he is, he's probably jus' a pore ol' boy, and we gone he'p him out."

Avarice and appreciation of his own cunning always thickened Cotton's rustic way of speaking, David reflected, and the bankruptcy-court dockets were choked with the names of people Cotton had, over the years, he'ped out.

They rented a car. Cotton gave directions and navigated while David drove.

"Be about sixteen, seventeen mahls," Cotton said. "Keep a lookout."

"I'm afraid I don't know what I'm keeping a lookout for," David admitted.

"You keep on like that, boy, an' Ah'm gone get *grumpy*. When we were up theah in that airplane, Ah was keepin' mah *ahs* open. You were lookin' at that ol' magazine." He made it sound as if he'd caught David shuffling slowly through a deck of erotic playing cards.

"You know wheah we are, boy? We're on the edge of the Trinidad Structure. Ah'm sure you studied up on that little numbah back at Rice, didn't you, boy?"

"Yes, sir."

"Yes, sir, you did indeed. It's a very promisin' little structure, and there's been a few ol' boys did good for themselves diggin' aroun' in it, and leasin' and all like that. But it isn't what you'd call saturated yet, on account of production hasn't lived up to promise. An' that's why Sinclair and Standard and Gulf and those others aren't out here gettin' theah elbows in each other's ribs. It just isn't worth theah tahm."

David shrugged. "It probably isn't worth ours, either."

"Now, that's why you probly always gone be drahvin' used Volkswagens and eatin' gristly steak, boy. Heah Ah am trying to make a few nickels for mah little family, so mah wife can weah somethin' beside Pansy flour sacks and mah boy can buy himself a little professional football team like all his friends have, and you're tellin' me it ain't worth my tahm. Turn left, theah, boy."

David opened a sagging wood-and-wire gate and drove into an arid farm. At Cotton's direction, he parked under a cottonwood, just leafing out in the late spring. Together they walked between rows of dry crops.

"Right heah, boy, there's a hole. A gap. Ah don' know if somebody missed it, or if somebody jus' figured it was a waste of tahm. There's natural-gas production on all *sahds* of this little spread. Ah bet the man owns this has even got a line easement right through his property.

"And with all that gas production, they're still hurtin', 'cause the reserves are way smaller than they thought. You know Ah got magic feet, boy. You know Ah kin feel thangs with mah feet cain't nobody else find with instruments. Cain't you feel that gas pressure way under your feet?"

"No, sir. Sorry."

"Well, you a good map reader, and you can talk geology like a left-wing professor, but you got bad feet and a bad nose. What you suppose the man's got planted heah?"

"This is probably a squash field," David said. "About ten acres in squash here. The field back by the car is fallow, but there were chilies growing there last year."

"Yeah," Cotton said. "Yeah, boy. There's a Meskin owns this place. Let's he'p that ol' boy out and get him off this poor land. He's gone bust his ass tryin' to grow chili peppers on this little patch."

County records showed that the 400-acre farm belonged to Elefterio Ortiz, that he paid his taxes—which increased slightly every three years—and that the title, while not questionable, had not been brought up to date in a generation.

"Ah know that little bitty farm's worth, Ah say *worth*, maybe fifty thousand," Cotton said in the Trinidad hotel room. "But it's not worth a nickel over twenty to me. You know how to buy from a greaseball; Ah've tol' you before. Just keep slappin' bills at him, and smilin', and tellin' him all about his own troubles. You can go twenty, and that's all. If the Mex holds out, just break it off and we'll get on back to Houston. Ah'd like to have that little piece theah; Ah don't own no gas in Colorado, and that's a shame, but it's not important. Ah'm really just doin' this to wind myself down from those damn sugar beets. Ah mean, it's the game. No reason Ah should break mah neck for a game."

"Twenty thousand, top," David said. "All right."

"You agree there's gas there, don't you?"

"There might be. The whole formation's good. But I'd like to have a survey. It's a gamble."

"Damn, boy, it's not no gamble. If Ah was a gambler Ah'd be out in the hot sun right now pickin' strawberries for fifteen cents a bucket. Ah *know* what's there. Now you go goose the goat and buy it for me. For some reason, every time a Mex sees mah purty face he freezes up. Ah'll never know why. All Ah want to do is he'p those people."

David drove back to the farm, bumped the car over the deeply rutted road through the poor acres. The house was adobe, frame and cinder-block, put together over fifty or sixty years, ramshackle and exhausted. Thin chickens pecked bugs among bedsprings and exploded tire cases in the yard.

David tried his Spanish on Elefterio Ortiz. Ortiz, middle-aged but looking eighty, smiled and answered in slow, careful English. He invited David inside and offered him coffee or Kool-Aid.

Despite the 400 acres of growing land, there was an overwhelming flavor of despairing poverty about the house. The furniture was sprung and dusty. Nothing seemed new but the television set, before which, on a gritty floor, six children sat, sharing a picnic-sized bag of potato chips. They seemed plump but unhealthy, a kind of potato-bloated apathy replacing what should have been vigor. Without comprehending it, they watched an afternoon soap opera, in which Anglos of fabulous wealth and ease nattered about impossible problems.

"My son," Ortiz said. The young man in the wheelchair only nodded when David offered his hand. All his limbs were still and shrunken. His eyes were dark, in-turning.

The woman at the foot-powered machine was young, too, and thin, with a tired bitterness in her face. "This is Mr. Reed, Pancha. Pancha is my son's wife."

"How do you do?" David said.

"Hello," she said, and turned back to her work.

In the kitchen, with the door closed on the hopelessness of the parlor, David sipped his Kool-Aid and talked slowly, with implacable reason, to Mr. Ortiz. "I'd like very much to buy your ranch, sir," he said, and smiled.

"It's a farm," Ortiz said. "It's dry. I got no water rights any more. Very bad rain."

"That's true," David said, "but I believe that with enough money invested we, I, could make it produce better. It's no one's fault that the weather is dry."

"It's a good farm," Ortiz said. "I made six thousand dollars in 1952."

Ortiz talked about 1952, the wonderful year of dreams and illusions, when everything went so well, his watershed year, while David smiled stiffly and nodded and glanced about the kitchen. A rusted wood stove. Religious prints on the walls. A 100-pound sack of pinto beans. A dozen potatoes, all sprouting, on a window sill. A pan of thin pork chops, marinating in chili sauce for *carne adovada,* the pot roast of poverty. And everywhere the glittering, too-expensive supermarket foods advertised on television, the foods that give you starch and grease in a glossy package—potato chips, cheese chips, corn chips, canned French fries, chocolate cookies, white, tasteless bread fashioned from amazing chemicals, cans of root beer and cream soda. A television-learned fantasy of the middle-class diet. A new and costly way to starve to death.

"I can't work it too good any more," Ortiz said. "I

try, but I'm getting too old. My knees, here in my arms. In the winter, I get all stiff. My boy, he was a good worker. He was strong, work all day, dance all night."

"What happened, can I ask you?"

"A piece of iron, from the war. A bomb . . . a shell blew up. A piece of iron in the back of his neck. Cut all the strings inside. Now his body doesn't work any more. He can talk, but he doesn't talk much. He can't help me. I . . . well . . . you know. It was a good farm. It was my father's farm. He bought it himself, with his own money."

David nodded, and reached into his jacket for his billfold. "I'm prepared to offer you a fair price, a good price, for your ranch, Mr. Ortiz." The lie gave him a brief pang. He laid a five-hundred-dollar bill on the kitchen table. Then another, and another, and another. As he deliberately put each new bill on the table he kept talking and watched Ortiz's eyes. The old man would have been a good poker player. His expression seemed frozen, as though each Federal Reserve note added a new layer of impassive dignity to his face. But he couldn't control his eyes. His pupils enlarged, the whites glistened. Ortiz kept his mouth straight and closed, but his eyes were screaming.

David had laid twenty bills on the table; ten thousand dollars. Now, watching the man's eyes, he laid down a thousand-dollar bill. The old, savvy political eyes of Grover Cleveland looked right at Ortiz. The farmer opened his mouth, but could only croak. David put down another bill. Twelve thousand. Then he waited.

From the parlor David could hear the brief, raucous song that sold a brand of dishwashing liquid. He could hear the rhythmic *thump-thump* of the sewing machine's treadle. He watched Ortiz for any sign of acceptance or rejection, but Ortiz seemed as paralyzed as his son.

David pulled a bill from the other side of his bill-fold and set it in place, neatly, on the stack. It was a hundred. Ortiz blinked, and glanced away from the money to look at David. David had already set his expression on "impatience."

The five-hundreds were gone; the one-thousands were finished. The switch to a bill of a lower denomination meant that the bulk of the offer had already been presented. The look of impatience indicated that David would nickel-and-dime for only a brief period before collecting his stack of bills, shaking hands and walking out.

Cotton had said twenty thousand, top, for the little farm. David could have laid down the twenty thousand dollars and said, "Take it or leave it."

But the cash game worked, worked beautifully, on certain kinds of people. Where there was real poverty, the sight of crisp money could change depression into a kind of manic insanity within seconds, for the money represented an object, the one object which, all alone, would change one's whole condition. "If we only had . . ." What? A car. An operation. A tractor. Ten bushels of seed. New boots. Paint on the barn. Eyeglasses. Asthma medicine. A new pump for the well. It didn't matter. There was always one thing which could fix everything else by its very presence.

Where there was not just the lack of money, but true despair, the money—shining and new-smelling on the table—meant something more: a move, a change, an escape from the hopelessness that could infest the timbers of a house like rot. "You can go, now," the money said, "and leave despair behind."

Cotton had taught David the rudiments of the cash game, but David himself had perfected it over the years. He'd made mistakes. He'd brought green cash into the open in front of the wrong people, and felt their cold sense of shock at his crudeness. But he had learned; he had developed, for professional purposes, a subtle sense of class snobbery. He knew what would insult one man, overwhelm another, and develop in another a lustful greed.

When Cotton decided to play the cash game, which he did only when he was feeling mischievous and arbitrary, he set his private bid very low and relied on David to make it lower through the brutal psychology of money on the table. Only twice had David been forced to lay down every bill in his possession during the process. Once, after he had worked down to twenty-dollar bills and offered his last one, on a thirty-thousand-dollar deal, the seller had reached across the table, picked up the pile, and said, "I can tell you're out of money, Mr. Reed, so I'll take what you offer. It's a poor price, but I'm in a crack." For months after this David worked on perfecting his poker face, knowing that some tiny sign had convinced the seller that David's offer could go no higher.

The second time it happened, both he and Cotton had misjudged their man sadly. He looked broke, but it was eccentricity and not poverty that caused him to dress in patched bib overalls. He talked like a dirt farmer, but only to hide the fact of his degree from Texas A. & M., to mention which, he felt, would have been foppish and sissified. Erroneously sniffing desperation, Cotton tried to get the man's soybean farm for forty thousand under fair value. When David had laid the last of the money down, the farmer had smiled a great, shark's smile and said, "You're about forty thousand below the market, sonny. You know it and I know it. Now why don't you just put it away, and we can have a glass of Jameson's Irish whiskey for friendship's sake. And then I'll give you about ten minutes to get your crooked wheeler-dealer ass out of my soybeans."

But Ortiz was no holdout. Ortiz, whose farm was worth at least fifty thousand dollars, even in its battered condition, but who had no idea of the proper way to sell it; Ortiz, who grew *chile* and squashes and pinto beans, the ancestral and traditional vegetables, on land that should have been in mixed rotated crops; Ortiz, who read Spanish and English with enormous difficulty, who had never heard of the Department of Agriculture, who had never been inside a bank, who was not exactly sure of the name of the President of the United States; Ortiz, who had a peasant's terror of wolves but was unable to recognize one in a dark blue suit—Ortiz saw over twelve thousand dollars lying on his kitchen table, between two glasses of Kool-Aid. He remembered 1952, the best year since the creation of the world, and thought that by picking up the money now he could make 1952 happen twice again.

"He was about to reach for it," David told Lupe as they lay beside each other. "His hand was quivering and actually moving toward that lousy stack of money. I don't know, I *still* don't know what the hell happened to me. It was as if something ruptured in my head. Everything looked white and bleached. I could see only outlines of things. I was on my feet yelling, yelling at that poor son of a bitch, cursing him, calling him a stupid *pendejo* ragged-assed blind Mexican fool. I kept saying, 'No! No! Don't touch it!'

"I shoved the money into my pocket; I found it there later, anyway, all crumpled up, thousands and hundreds and five-hundreds. I screamed at him. I can remember him, and his daughter-in-law—God knows when she came in— and a couple of the older kids all in the kitchen, backed against the old wooden pump-handle sink, looking at me with the damnedest . . . *terror* in their eyes. I must have looked absolutely crazy. Must have *been* crazy. The old man was too shocked to move. The woman got her wits back and began to scream back at me. 'Don't you hurt him. Don't you hurt my children. Don't you hurt my husband. My husband's a cripple. My husband's got a Bronze Star. Don't you hurt us.'

"Jesus! Hurt them! I was saying things like: 'Fifty thousand dollars. This place is worth fifty thousand dollars. For Christ's sake get off your dumb Mexican asses and sell it for fifty grand!' Oh, I don't know what the hell I said. I can remember running through that smelly little parlor, with the son sitting there in the wheelchair, looking at me. No terror in *his* eyes. If he could have moved one arm he'd have sliced me into five hundred pieces of Anglo and fed his chickens with me."

David shivered at the memory in the crisp predawn air. Lupe put her arms around his waist, pressed her head against his chest and squeezed him.

"I'm cold," she said. "Let's get back under the covers."

He lay with his arm under her shoulders, looking upward at the *vigas*, the old pine beams supporting the ceiling.

243

"I told Cotton the old boy wouldn't go for it, that he was a holdout. Cotton just shrugged and forgot about it until last summer. I was afraid he'd find out. I was scared to death he'd find out how I screwed it up for him. I thought I'd gone crazy that day in Colorado, and I was afraid I might go crazy again. I even felt bad about what I'd done to old Elefterio Ortiz. Hell, I could have dropped the twenty thousand on his table and left him richer. Cotton would have been happy. Ortiz would have been happy—for a while.

"I still don't know exactly how he found out. Someone probably began to kid him during a poker game, about how his bright boy from Rice University balled up the fattest deal in southern Colorado. Because Cotton was right. He *could* feel the pressure of natural gas under that squash patch. Encantado Transmission Corporation came in there—not buying land, but optioning leases. They sank a well on Elefterio's land and hit . . . God, I don't know how many billions of cubic feet they tapped into down there. Beautiful, high-pressure gas. People are always talking about crude oil, but gas is just as much fun and easier to handle. The company's first-year royalties will come to about four and a half million dollars, and there's reserves down there for a lot more than one year's production. I don't know what Ortiz is going to make from it. The usual deal is a sixteenth of royalties. He might have settled for a thirty-second; Encantado likes to haggle, too. But that old man's got an income somewhere between a hundred and forty and two hundred and eighty thousand dollars a year. All because I went crazy in his kitchen. I wish I knew what it meant."

Lupe kissed him gently on the ear. "It means you're

a good man. I sort of thought you were a good man, and now I know you are."

"Wrong," David said. "I wasn't working for Elefterio Ortiz. I was working for Clyde Clifton Cotton at sixty-five thousand dollars a year plus bonuses plus stock options, which I never bothered to pick up, plus spontaneous tips and gifts, plus a chance to walk around in his shadow which, believe it or not, had dollar signs all over it, like the capitalist's suit in a Mexican Revolutionary mural. Those royalties rightly belong to Cotton, not to Elefterio Ortiz. Anyway, luckily for Ortiz, the transmission company's agent doesn't like to play money games. 'We'd like to put down an exploratory well on your land, Mr. Ortiz. Here's our check for X thousand for the inconvenience. Is that enough? Fine. Now, there's a royalty contract. Be sure and have your attorney look it over before you sign it. What? You don't have an attorney? I suggest you go into Trinidad and retain one. Well, no, we can't be sure we'll find anything under your land, sir, but if we do, I'm sure you will want to be represented by counsel.' Hell, Lupe, that's the way to do business. That's the way Cotton himself does it, when he has to. When he's up against somebody as smart and mean and greedy as he it. But if he can swindle somebody he will. I helped him swindle and pressure and undercut and terrify more people than I can bear to think about."

This time Lupe nipped him with her teeth, not very gently, on the skin near his ribs. "Why don't you sneak into the kitchen right now and scrub some of the blood off your guilty hands with Ajax. Ah, bull, David. So you worked for a Texan with a lot of money. We've been having trouble with those bastards since 1846. We killed some of them and chased some of them away, but most of them got what they wanted because we were too dumb or too poor to stop them. The money-on-the-table trick Cotton taught you isn't something new. Primo Rael has been ranting for years about that, and with justification, but he's standing on a firm moral platform of quicksand. Sure, the Anglos are the sons of bitches today. A hundred and fifty years ago the Spaniards were the sons of bitches. Go ask the nearest Indian."

"Well, it's different. It's something I've been feeling sick about for years. I just didn't know how I felt until that hand grenade went off in my head."

"Listen to me, beautiful, wonderful man. I love you. I didn't come creeping in here tonight because I am an ordinary sex maniac. I love you. I would love you even if you'd left the twelve thousand dollars on Elefterio Ortiz's table and raped his daughter-in-law. I would love you if you had a Texas accent. I would love you if you were . . ."

She sat up. "You're not married, are you?"

"No."

"But you have a girl friend."

"I have one now," he said, and pulled her back down.

"You had one."

"Sure, I had a girl friend. Mary Agnes. She was one of the most thoughtful women in East Texas. She said she wouldn't dream of getting married until I had at least a million dollars of my own, because she didn't want to be a burden."

"Generous," Lupe said. "I don't think I care for Mary Agnes."

"It was a Thursday that I heard last from the beautiful Mary Agnes. Cotton plays poker on Wednesday nights. He's jolly on Thursday mornings if he won the night before, and he's all business if he lost. I got to work a few minutes before he did and was just unlocking my desk when he came to my door and began to stare at me. I said good morning, and he just stared at me. I'd almost forgotten about Elefterio Ortiz. I didn't recognize what was in his eyes. I started to fidget around. I spilled a cup of coffee all over a preliminary mineral report. He said, 'Come on in mah office, boy.'

"He fired me. Then he spent ten minutes telling me why. Then he spent a half hour explaining to me what kind of person I was. Then he began to list the names of the people and the companies he was going to inform about my personal dereliction. It isn't only kings, you know, who can banish a subject from the realm. Finally, he made threats, not one of which, so far as I can tell, was empty.

"When I was allowed to go back to my office, to clean the paper clips out of my desk, he had made it pretty clear that I was something he'd just scraped off his shoe.

"I left the building and wandered around in downtown Houston for a few hours, noticing what an unfriendly city it was. I went to my apartment and watched some kind of game show on television. I walked over to my bank—Cotton's bank, to be precise—and was surprised to find I still had an account there. I withdrew the princely sum of eighteen hundred dollars, leaving eleven dollars and change. Don't ask me what I'd done with my salary over the years. Ask Mary Agnes. The last thing I'd bought her was a six-hundred-dollar Irish wolfhound, the biggest model made in the dog factory, and a year's lease for the animal in the Presidential Suite at the Jacinto Kennels. Am I boring you?"

"You certainly are," Lupe said, and twined herself around him. "What happened then?"

"I drank some whiskey, at my place. About five I drove over to Mary Agnes's apartment, to tell her my troubles and to plan my next move with her. There was a pile of trash outside her door, I noticed. I knocked and rang, but she didn't answer, if she was there at all. I was about to leave when I looked at the pile of trash again. It wasn't trash, or rather, it was, but it was *my* trash. Little things of mine I'd left at her place over the years. Ties, handkerchiefs, toilet articles, some books, the . . . ah . . . bottom half of a pair of green pajamas."

"I love you," Lupe said, "because you have an eye for pornographic detail."

"I notice everything except the trains that hit me. When I picked up my pile of pitiful belongings I found a note from her. It was short, but it was crisp. I know a crew of stevedores at the port who don't talk that rough."

"That's the fourth saddest story I ever heard. Good night. Do you snore?"

"A little."

"Do you have nightmares?"

"Invariably."

Clyde Clifton Cotton thrust his hemispherical eyes above the soupy, green water of the swamp and swiveled them 360 degrees. They seemed not to be connected to his brain; they spun freely like marbles in jelly. He began to walk up the bank. The bank sloped gently, muddy and squishy. As his clawed feet touched the oozing earth, they released mephitic gases from below which bubbled up to the surface and puffed out foul odors.

The heavy, low-carried body dragged its enormous, muscled killing tail through the slime. Short, bowed legs, elbows out, claws extended, tore into the bank. Between his alligator jaws lay a great fish, a speckled trout, a gar, a bass, a tchoupique, a pompano, a croaker, a red snapper. The fish twisted and lurched, its lidless eyes stared and snapped, its tail jerked. The alligator tightened its snouty grip, grinned, drawing a leathery smile toward its earholes. The triangular teeth plunged through the snapping body. The fish's eyes made one last helpless pop toward heaven and dimmed beneath a death glaze. Its tail stiffened, snapped off and fell into the rank mud. The alligator chewed the body, allowed the fish's head to hang by a snippet of scaly skin from his jaws, crunched and chewed in pleasure, and let the head fall away.

"You not afraid of Minotaurs no mo', boy," the alligator said. "You learned how to live with hawns. But you ain't learned how to slush aroun' in the swamp, boy, an' Ah'm gone give you a lesson in jaws, boy. You cain't go to high ground, boy. Theah ain't no place you kin clahm to. Jus' turn aroun' and drop yo' draws, boy. Ah'm gone chew me some ass, you heah me?"

David flopped in the mud, tried to grow feet. The feet wouldn't grow; he had only fins, a flexible backbone, a mortal desperation, gills that sucked at the meager air.

The alligator was a thousand feet long, massive and ponderous as a blue whale. It stretched impossibly on its tiny, bent rear legs and rose towering above the swamp. Two scaled front limbs reached toward him, grasped his head, the talons biting in, turning to wool, to cotton, to velvet. The poisoned breath became air, flowers, perfume. "Hey," the alligator said. "Hey. David. Hey, now. Hey."

"No," David said.

"Why not?"

"Christ. Where? Lupe?"

"Yeah. Hey, now. Come on. Are you okay?"

"Lupe," David said.

Lupe pushed herself slowly against, above him, cool and firm against his sweating skin, and kissed his lips and his teeth and tongue. "It's me," she whispered. "It's me again. Still me. Who'd you think?"

"Lupe," David said, and snaked an arm beneath her.

"Who'd you think?" she asked again, after some more kissing and pushing, some feathery mouth-swooping on his chest, his ears, his eyes; her neck, her shoulders, her breasts, her lips, her nose. "Who?"

"I thought it was you. Nobody else. Just old Lupe."

"Not so old. Twenty-six. Just old enough to know where to look."

"*My* old Lupe. I don't mean old-old. I mean familiar-old. Hey, no, not around there! I am very sensitive around the belly button. Hee hee. No, please."

"I'm going to remember about that," Lupe said. "I'm going to keep that in the back of my mind, and some day when you're speaking to the Petroleum Fat Cats of America, I'm going to sneak up and unbutton the bottom button of your sober gray vest, unbutton two buttons of your shirt . . ."

"No, come on, Lupe . . ."

"Slow-o-owly pull up your T-shirt and put my tongue . . ."

"No, no, no . . ."

"This tickle?" she said.

"No. Not a bit. On the contrary. No."

"How about this?"

"Mmm. No. How about *this?*"

"Hoo. Yes and no. Try again. No. What's your middle name? A.?"

"Armand. What a time to ask."

Lupe moved a little. "I'm not going to think of you as Armand. I'm going to think of you as . . . this."

"There's more to me than that."

"Maybe so, but right now that's what I'm concentrating on."

"All right. How about if I concentrate on this?"

"It isn't necessary to ask. Let's just concentrate. Do you always do that when you sleep? Toss around, grit your teeth? Say, 'No, no'?"

"Probably when I dream. I was dreaming about an alligator. Thanks for waking me up. He almost had me."

Lupe traced the line of his backbone from neck to cleft. "You're supposed to sleep like a child with a sappy smile on your face. Did I give you the nightmare?"

"You know you didn't."

"It's daylight, darling. Let's kiss some more. I've never kissed you in the daylight."

Cruz chewed his way slowly through his breakfast, dismissing his depression in a few sentences, "Too damned old to start all over," talking about the long, slow winter, joking about the possibility of a new bull, darting quick glances at Lupe's silent, private smile and at the pouchy look of exhaustion under David's eyes. When Lupe kissed him on the forehead and left for school, Cruz took the paper off his cigar and rolled it under his nose.

"I'm gonna ask you a question. I never asked this question before. You ready?"

"Sure," David said, too sleepy to fathom implications.

"Okay. What are your intentions toward my daughter?"

David didn't know how his tired brain was able to invent and discard so many answers in so few seconds. He even savored briefly the idea of answering the question with another, the fruitless response of the ninth-grader who hasn't prepared his lesson: "Could you repeat the question, sir?"

Instead he made himself look steadily and sternly at Cruz, seeing the big nose inhaling the cigar's aroma, the brown face, the blue eyes, as he framed his reply.

"Carnal," he said. "Permanent." He sought the other word. "Dynastic."

Cruz said, "Well. All right, *cuate*. All right, then."

Chapter 25

LUIS DROVE his wrinkled Mustang to Santa Fe, nursing a cracked radiator. The sergeant behind the counter at the police station said visitors only at visitors' hours, but Luis insisted that he was a nephew and was able to prove it.

Carlos had been in his cell for nearly a month. He knew he could have been out on bond in a day, but he had other plans. He was waiting for the ground swell of angry emotion to develop among the Compañía members, who loved him. He knew his martyrdom would touch them, would make them proud of him and bitter at the injustice that kept him sleeping on a thin, questionable mattress. They would rise. They would storm the Santa Fe lockup, carrying the signs. Land and Liberty. Bread and Justice. Free Carlos. Primo would lead them in the chanting: Free our Counselor. It would embarrass the hell out of his smart-ass brother. The U. S. Attorney would have second thoughts about his silly goddamn charge. Free Carlos. Once more he considered a hunger strike. It was a hell of an idea. He'd tried it two days ago before, but after skipping breakfast and lunch, the hunger pangs got the best of him. Tomorrow he'd start. He'd start a real one.

He'd found nothing about a ground swell in the papers, but those Anglo papers never knew what was happening. It would be all over *La Lucha,* one long blistering editorial covering the whole issue. Damned stupid cops wouldn't bring him a copy of *La Lucha.*

The turnkey jangled over and unlocked the cell door. "In there," he said, pointing. "Guy to see you."

Luis was sitting on a bench in the depressing little visitors' room. A thin, knotty little man, sitting with his elbows on his knees, clenching and opening his hands.

"Luis," Carlos said in Spanish. "Are you going to the wedding?"

"What wedding?"

"Lupe's wedding. She's marrying that Anglo."

"I don't know nothing about a wedding. I want my ranch. Where is it? Where's my ranch? Where's my cheap ranch you talked about? Three times I went out with those guys. Broke my *chingao* toe. Worked my ass off."

"Now, Luis, it takes time."

Luis began to poke him in the shoulder with a finger. "What about the stuff Manny said? All that *cago* about the *tejanos* and the money? They got all the ranches, huh?"

"Luis, boy, there's no money. There are no Texans. Manny's making all that up. You'll get a nice little ranch, Luis. Very cheap. All the boys will get their land."

Luis poked him harder. "They gave you some money, huh? Those *tejanos?* You been out there polishing the *palo* with the gringo. You goddamn *chingao lambe* son of a bitch. I broke my toe!"

"Luis, never mind about that. Remember my promise,

okay. Now, what about the boys? All the members. What are they going to do? What do they say about me?"

"They don't say shit about you. They don't care what happens to you, as long as you die."

"What do you know about it, *estúpido?*"

"I want my ranch."

"There is no ranch, *tonto*. Not a horse. Not a chicken. Not a pig for you."

"I don't care about them. I want a ranch with sheep."

Luis took an eight-inch Buck hunting knife from his pocket and opened the blade.

"Put that away, *pendejo*. Go find out when Primo's coming with his people."

"When you get out of jail, I'm gonna stick this in you, someplace. You better stay in jail."

Cruz waved his good hand toward a window displaying, through frosted glass, two feet of snow upon a marble nude's head, sitting jauntily like a white stovepipe hat. The manure spreader was buried to its handles.

"Spring," he said. "No arguments about it. Spring is the time to get married. Clear all that crap out of the patio, find somebody to cut the weeds, have a *merienda* out there. Fiddlers. Eight hundred people. Two truckloads of Fritos. Guests getting drunk and horsing around in the hay. Maybe have a procession up from the church in Pozo Verde. A real old-time ethnic son of a bitch. Everybody can dance the varsoviana till they're on their knees. Nobody should get married in the winter. I don't want to hear any arguments."

Lupe was sitting on the floor near the fireplace, her knees drawn up, watching the piñon spark and snap, sipping boiling hot rum and apple cider.

"No, really, Lupe. Your novio's lying in there right now with the worst case of viral flu I ever saw. He'll never make it through a wedding. You know what that man's temperature is?"

"A hundred and two point four," Lupe said. "I just took it. He'll be all right in a few days. He didn't catch it because he's weak. He caught it in Albuquerque when we went in for the blood tests. You can catch anything in Albuquerque. Besides that, he's tired. He's been running your crazy ranch and making four or five speeches a week and writing letters and talking to all those state people. And worrying."

"He doesn't have to do it on my account. I told him I was through with my dreams of empire. Now, what's your hurry with marrying the gringo? You're not pregnant, are you?"

"Wouldn't you like to know."

"Spring weddings are beautiful. Your mother and I had one. I don't want to hear arguments."

"I'm not arguing, Papa. Either David joins the family immediately or I'll do the best I can to add to the family illegitimately. I'll start as soon as his temperature's down to ninety-nine." She smiled sweetly and sipped her rum.

"Why are you so coarse, Lupe?"

"I'm not coarse. I'm in love. I don't care if the snow's ass-deep to a camel. I don't care how cold it is. It'll be all the cozier in bed."

"Ahh!"

"Don't worry, Papa. I'll wear white. Even *Marta* wore white."

"Yaah! I really should have sent you to a convent school. Your mother went to a convent school."

"I know. She always had those little worry lines between her eyes."

Cruz stomped off to his workroom after looking in at David, who was asleep. He sat at his desk and shuffled papers around. He looked at the calendar and was displeased to see that it was still February. He put on his reading glasses, then took off his reading glasses and went back into the *sala*.

"You want Father Serex to perform the ceremony?"

"I don't care. I'd rather Uncle Pete did it, but I don't think he will. He thinks all the telegraph lines are down between him and God. He won't celebrate Mass any more."

"Well, since David's a Catholic . . . Lupe, are you sure David's a Catholic?"

"Sure. Would anybody lie about a thing like that?"

"Then you want a Catholic wedding? With a Mass?"

"Papa, I don't care. If it bothers you I'll try to round up the dome kids again. I think Kaminsky's ordained in seven or eight religions. David and I can pledge eternal groovy love and exchange gifts of organic honey. We just want to get married, and quick. Quick."

"Would about the first of March be all right, then? Jesus, you're in such a hurry!"

"Fine. I'm sure David will go along with it."

Cruz felt things moving far too fast, so he went into the kitchen to snap at Anita for some imaginary deficiency. When he returned he said, "He doesn't have a very good job. Two-seventy-five a month."

"Oh, for God's sake, Papa. Are you suggesting he's a bum?"

"No, of course not. I only pointed out . . ."

"Well, don't point out. If nothing else works, and you get bitten by a cow, he can take over the ranch for you permanently. Would you rather Luis took it over?"

Lupe helped David out of bed a few days later and sat him in the big leather chair, with an afghan over his knees. When she'd given him a mug of rum and apple cider, she kissed him on the neck. "Can I kiss you on the mouth? Or are you still catching?"

"I don't know," he said.

"Is he, Papa? Is he still contagious?"

"How the hell should I know? I can't see viruses with my naked eye."

"I'm for taking a chance," she said, and sat lightly in his lap to kiss him. "How you feel, *cuate?*"

"Okay. Dreamed a lot."

"Fever does that," Cruz said. "Once I saw an aircraft carrier steaming down the Pacheco River. All my cattle were penned on the deck."

Lupe whispered in David's ear: "How about alligators?"

"No," he said, "I dreamed about Mr. Cotton. He was just an old man in a wrinkled white linen suit."

Chapter 26

FROM the Albuquerque *Standard:*

Developers Call It Quits

Philip Dumas, vice-president of Rancheros Grande Mansoins, has announced his firm's intentions to halt development of residential housing on the former Juan Tofayo Grant.

"The action of the Interstate Commerce Commission, in bringnig and injunction against us, is the last stwar," Dumas said. (The Commission claims the firm failed to make porper disclorsure in it's advertising concerning water availablity, sewage treatment, mortgage interest payments, lot sizes and access to mupinilac seretaoinschrdluzzz and access to municipal services.)

"Mr. C. C. Cotton, Sr., owner of Ranchero Garneds, will make an announcement soon concerning dispostion of the property," body will lie in state at the Lopez Mortuary here this evening and Friday morning. Burial Dumas said.

Chapter 27

"PORFIRIO MARTINEZ," Lupe whispered.

"How do you do," David said.

"Rosina Martinez."

"Nice to meet you."

"Consuelo Baca."

"I'm glad you could come."

"Abedon Ortega."

"Hello. Thank you."

"Osmundo Serna."

"Nice to see you."

"Cruz Tafoya."

"How do you . . . oh, for God's sake."

"Aren't you gonna thank me for coming?" Cruz asked. "I paid for it."

"Thank you for coming. Is there any more champagne?"

"I'll have Anita bring you some more."

"See, Papa. I told you it wasn't too cold for a wedding."

Father Serex had said Mass, and Pete had performed

the ceremony. "Still enough magic left for that," he'd told them. "If a ship's captain can do it, so can I."

David and Lupe had walked from the little church to her little MG, preceded by two fiddlers who played "Tecolote" and "Enseñame a Amar." The car was covered with paper rosettes, and Lupe insisted on driving it up and down the single street in Pozo Verde, blowing the horn.

"Pretty tacky," David said.

"Never mind that, gringo. This is the way we do it around here."

They stood now in a loosely organized receiving line, while the fiddlers played "Peña de Cerro Alto" and "Me Gustan Todas" and "The Harlot of Jerusalem," which they'd learned recently from Perez, and "Las Coplas de Dennis Chavez," a bawdy folk song in heroic couplets about a former U. S. Senator. When the fiddlers stopped for Coors or cider, Echeagaray entertained with moody music on the Basque bagpipes.

"Hello, Mac, you *chota* son of a bitch."

"Now, Miss Lupe."

"Ingeborg, you look wonderful."

"Gracias, señora." She giggled. *"No diga nada a nadie, pero estoy embarazada."*

"What's she embarrassed about?" David asked.

"Not embarrassed, *estúpido.* Pregnant. . . . Uncle Pete," Lupe said. "I think you're drunk as a skunk."

"Drunk as a bishop. Happy as a skunk."

"Father."

"David, I would have sworn you were a black Presbyterian. How did you become a Catholic in that hotbed of nonconformism, as my late mother would have called it?"

"French. They were all Catholics. Reed used to be Roseau."

"Incredible."

"I had an uncle from Minou, Louisiana, named Bruiser Boudreau, the Battling Bougalee. A light heavy-weight."

"I wonder if there's any more of this delicious apple-jack."

"May I offer my congratulations again, Mr. Reed."

"Thank you, Governor. Please call me David."

"All right, but I must ask you to continue calling me Governor. I think I'm going to be out of a job soon, and I want to enjoy my last moments in office."

"That was a hell of a thing you did."

"I haven't done it yet," Manny said. "The Legislature still has to approve two and a half million in general obligation bonds. Anyway, it ought to keep Primo Rael quiet for a while. He says he'll put two hundred families on the Upper Grant, for a start, and prove the old way was the best. I personally think they'll all be back on Welfare in a year."

"You're a brave man, Uncle Manny. Maybe I'll vote for you next time. Imagine, my Tio Taco uncle push-ing a social experiment through the Statehouse."

"You can call it whatever you want, *chica*. The Legis-lature thinks it's blackmail. Anyway, it was your idea. My God, is that Luis?"

Luis was wearing a suit, cowboy boots, and his concho belt. He kissed Lupe and shook hands hesitantly with his new brother-in-law.

"Where's Papa?" he asked.

"I don't know. He's around somewhere."

"I got to talk to him."

Cruz lay on his bed, sipping champagne, while Luis talked earnestly to him. He had never been so bored in his life.

"So you see, Papa, I figured with the fine-wool breeds in your flock, for a start, I could make enough in maybe a year to pay on the Compañía lease *and* have enough to get some good mutton-type ewes, maybe Suffolks or Corriedales. I mean, you've been missing two thirds of the market, and even then your yield of clean content hasn't been high because of impurities and shrinkage. So with fine-wool and mutton-type—maybe I'll get Southdowns, instead, because of less separable fat on the carcass— I'll have a good market mix and access to the Denver slaughtering setup. Do you have any idea of the profit from the by-products? Not just edible by-products, but rendered tallow and casings and even tennis racket strings. So I thought I'd combine a pasture program, breed ewes in the fall, and instead of relying on single-roughage feed, I'd add supplemental grains and possibly try to get a feeder lamb operation going. That's for the Rambouillets, because the straight Delaine-bred are smaller framed and have less yield-to-weight . . ."

"Luis, what the hell are you talking about? Do you want me to give you all of my goddamn sheep?"

"Well, yes, sir."

"And you want to run 'em up on the Upper Grant?"

"Yes, sir. Mr. Rael's allocating me five thousand acres."

"Well, sure. Go ahead. I'm glad you found something to do."

"Echeagaray says he'd like to come with me. He has this idea about crossing the Merinos with mutton-type . . ."

"Please, don't tell me any more about it. Just go do it."

At three in the morning, Lupe brought out her bull-horn and hit the On button.

"ALL RIGHT! EVERYBODY LEAVE! IT'S TIME FOR MY HONEYMOON!"

Cruz was very drunk and very happy. He sat in the *sala* holding his daughter's hand.

"You gonna have a good time in Europe."

"I promise."

"I'm gonna give you Luis's house, if you want it."

"I know, Papa. You told me. Thank you. Thank you for the wedding, too."

"They drank forty cases of champagne. I'm a poor man."

"I still love you, Papa."

"Lupe. Lupe," Cruz said.

"Yes, Papa."

"Listen. Now I want you to listen very, very carefully, because what I'm going to tell you is very, very important."

"I'm listening, Papa."

"No. Really. Listen. This is very very very very important."

"Okay. Go ahead."

"You're listening?"

"Right."

"Good. Now. All that I used to always tell you about how you're homely and all that."

"Yes?"

"You 'member all of that stuff?"

"Oh, yes, Papa."

"Well, it's not true. Not a word of it was true. You are not homely. Lupe? You hear me? Not homely. Nossir."

"I hear you, Papa. Thank you."

"Lupe? You listenin'? You still listenin'?"

"Yes."

"Maybe you're just a little bit homely. Just . . . that much."

"I can live with that."

In the gray dawn, Lupe heard a whimper. She removed David's arm from her bare waist and sat up listening. Then she tiptoed into Miguelito's room, saw that he was curled up, deeply asleep, and heard the whimper again from farther off.

Cruz's light was on. He was sitting in his bed, his face a profound, inhuman violet. He was attempting with huge concentration to say something, his wide face stretched like the Mask of Comedy, his open hands pressed flat against his sternum, pushing it powerfully. Lupe turned back to the open door and screamed for David. Then she asked, "Oxygen?" and watched as her father nodded his head once.

"In the stable. A big green welding tank. Get it."

David floundered in his pajamas through the mushy snow, a hundred yards. The tank was heavy, sixty or seventy pounds. He didn't hear the horses nickering and stamping. He had lumbered into Cruz's bedroom when he noticed that his feet were bare.

Cruz wheezed and whispered something. "What?" He whispered again. "He says 'Three liters.'"

David turned a valve; the gas hissed. "I don't know how to measure three liters on this thing," he said. He snatched at a pocketknife on Cruz's dresser, to cut away the welding nozzle. "Cruz—can I just put this tube in your mouth, and the hell with three liters?" Another nod. Lupe stuck the hose in. Together they watched the terrible violet fade.

They waited for the ambulance from Albuquerque. Anita fed Miguelito, the boy laughing and dribbling food.

Cruz was talking, still wheezing, waiting for long breath pauses between phrases. "Seen them. Bad as they say. Worse. Jesus. Pain. Makes you a child."

David and Lupe spent two awful days in the clinic's antiseptic corridor, smoking packs of cigarettes, eating unidentifiable things from a basement vending machine. Cruz's doctor, Kelly Shaw, a young, gliding internist who seemed to skate over the waxed linoleum, said little about his patient except "Damned fool. Damned old fool. Not a checkup for five years. Now he's got me using every supportive gadget in the house for his rotten old pump."

Eventually, he said, "It's not the worst EKG I ever saw, Lupe. He's got plenty of muscle left in there. I'm going to take him out of Intensive and give him a nice room with Mickey Mouse decals on the ceiling. Leave him here for a few weeks, okay? Can you get a nurse? Private nurse? All our women are busy."

"I don't know," Lupe said. "I'll try to find somebody."

"I hear you're a fast man with a welding hose, David. He was oxygenated like a high-altitude miler."

David and Lupe spent two-day shifts: two with Cruz, two with Miguelito at the ranch. Cruz rested and ate, railing at the floor nurses. "I don't like these women," he said. "They treat me like a beef quarter. You can be my nurse."

"Sorry, Papa. The hell with that. You're going to have a big, fat R.N. who doesn't take the *cago*."

"No, I've worked with these nurses. Pigs. Prison wardens. You'll be my nurse."

"Let me try to find one," David told her.

In April, on the night before Cruz went home, Lupe told Kelly Shaw her news. "Can I tell him now, or wait?"

"Hell, tell him now. If he spikes at that I'll hang onto him another week."

"Papa," she said, sitting on his bed. She picked up the folds of the plastic tent. "Can you hear me in there with all the hissing?"

"Sure. What's the matter?"

"Nothing's the matter, Papa. I missed a period."

"That doesn't mean anything," Cruz said. "It might be newlywed nerves."

"Okay, Papa. You'll be counting backward anyway. I've missed two periods and seen the doctor."

"Goddamn," he said, smiling. "Goddamn. You're my sweet *chica*."

David and Miss Kovacks were waiting in Cruz's bedroom when Lupe and the attendants brought him in. The nurse arranged the oxygen equipment and accepted Kelly's envelope of records and instructions. Lupe bristled

267

to see the easy affection between David and the nurse, and when she heard the sharp West Texas speech. Miss Kovacks was busy, always moving, and Lupe felt misplaced and useless.

She was sarcastic when David told her he'd offered the nurse $250 a week and travel expenses from and back to Lamesa. He shrugged. "I'll send her back, then. Pay it myself if Cruz doesn't like her. I think she'll work out fine."

"She's a gringa bitch."

"Give her a chance."

Lupe held her pout for two days. Miss Kovacks, having breakfast in the kitchen, picked up Miguelito to give him a quick, warm hug. She saw Lupe's resentful expression immediately and set him down. "Cute kid," she said. "Someone's taking real good care of him." Thereafter she said only "Hi" to the boy.

The next evening, Lupe looked into Cruz's bedroom and saw the nurse, in stockinged feet, sitting beside the bed, gravely reading aloud an article from *Southwestern Stockman,* holding Cruz's hand. When he was asleep, she walked quietly into the *sala.* "Mrs. Reed," she said, "since I came here there's been something I've wanted to do. I forgot that first night because I was so busy. I want to look at Mr. Reed's head, his scar, but I won't do it if it disturbs either of you."

"Oh, look, for God's sake. Go ahead."

Miss Kovacks brushed back the hair from David's temple. "It looks real good," she said. "And I'll tell Dr. Cave when I get home, because he was wondering."

"Miss Kovacks, I'm very sorry," Lupe told her. "I

haven't been behaving well at all. I'm pregnant, but that's no excuse. You're a wonderful nurse. My father likes you and so does my husband. And I like you too. Now, sit down, please, and take a load off."

Chapter 28

NEW MEXICO'S SENIOR SENATOR died suddenly in May. The Statehouse pols waited for Manny to do the traditional little minuet: resign the governorship, and let the newly promoted ex-Lieutenant Governor appoint him to fill the unexpired term.

Manny said that he was too busy to go to Washington, which had the wrong kind of climate anyway. He appointed a bipartisan committee of state legislators to select three alternative candidates. Then Manny appointed the one he liked least.

The state of New Mexico bought the Upper Grant from C. C. Cotton, Sr., for two and a half million dollars and leased it to La Compañía de Tierra y Libertad for a dollar a year and the promise that the organization would try to pay some taxes on it. Nearly a thousand of the Compañía's members scattered themselves on the great ranch, built the beginnings of adobe houses, moved their stock onto the common pasture and began to cultivate beans, squash, and chili. The Albuquerque *Standard* pointed out, quite accurately, that the whole operation smacked of communism. *La Lucha* pointed out that the Pueblo Indians had been living that way for several thousand years, and no one had suggested that they go back to Russia, where they came from.

Carlos Tafoya paid a fine and discovered that he'd been disbarred. The Internal Revenue Service asked him about certain undeclared income, but he was able to prove that the *lambe, chingado, cochino puerco, jodido* people in Texas had never paid him his rake-off. He became Primo Rael's secretary and unofficial accountant. Whenever Carlos offered Primo any legal advice, Primo thought it over carefully and did the opposite.

By early summer, Cruz was up and stomping around, but gently. He had already upped Miss Kovacks to $275 a week, but she and he and everyone realized he had no further need for a private nurse, or even a paid companion.

Miss Kovacks was torn and bedeviled; she knew she had to get back to her pneumothoracic drainage people in Lamesa, and a leave of absence couldn't be extended forever.

The four were at dinner when Cruz asked the question. "Miss Kovacks, what would you do if I died? Just died on you?"

"I'd close your eyes and tie up your jaw with two-inch gauze bandage and call a doctor," she said, never missing a beat on her salad.

"There you are," Cruz said. "Practical. I don't plan to die, but if I do, there's the attendant I want. Let's go to Spain together, Miss Kovacks. Extremadura, where the Tafoyas come from. Strictly business. A vacation for both of us. Besides, these people need some privacy."

"Thank you, no. I'm going to Matador, Texas, pretty soon and see my mother."

"I'd go to Spain," David said. "I would sure as hell go. I've *seen* Matador."

"Are you seriously advising me to go tooting off to Europe with my own dear patient?"

"I am."

"Well. Let me think about it. All right."

In August, David watched Lupe grow heavier and ever more beautiful. They read inane postcards from Miss Kovacks, who compared Matador, Texas, to such objects as prawns and El Greco portraits and once to a *real* matador who was "much more attractive than the town of the same name."

One afternoon, they put Miguelito in the car and visited Luis on the Upper Grant. Though the young man smelled a bit muttony, he seemed to have lost his surliness. He greeted his son with friendly distraction.

"He's yours any time you want him back," Lupe said.

"He needs a mother," Luis told her, and turned to David. "Mr. Reed, what do you think about my idea for mixed-breed lambs? After shearing next year, I can buy an English Border Leicester ram—they're mutton-type *and* long-wool—and do a Rambouillet cross. That way I can probably get both high-grade fiber and carcass with good finish."

"It's certainly a thought," David admitted, wondering what he was talking about.

"I guess we'd better see about adopting this boy," Lupe said on their way back. "Luis isn't going to pay any attention to him unless he begins to grow wool."

That evening, after Miguelito's bath, Cruz called from Badajoz. "I met some Tafoyas over here, *cuate*. A terrible-looking bunch of people. I think the American branch improved the bloodlines a lot."

"When are you coming back, Papa? The cows miss you."

"Let the gringo take care of my cows. We're gonna toot around some more, spend the winter in Málaga or some place nice and warm."

Miss Kovacks got on the phone. "We've been talking about a clinic up on that big ranch next to yours," she said. "He said I could be head nurse. What do you think about that?"

"I like it," Lupe said. "I suppose Papa wants to be head doctor?"

"Well, he promised not to do any surgery. Hey, we'll see you-all, hear? This must be costing a bunch. *Hasta luego*. Did I say that all right?"